MW00964669

BYE-BYE, BADEN-BADEN

Bye-bye, Baden-Baden

Lucille de Saint-Andre

ECW PRESS

Copyright © Lucille de Saint-Andre, 1998

All rights reserved. No part of this publication may be reproduced, stored in a retrieval system, or transmitted in any form by any process — electronic, mechanical, photocopying, recording, or otherwise — without the prior written permission of ECW PRESS.

CANADIAN CATALOGUING IN PUBLICATION DATA

de Saint-Andre, Lucille
Bye-bye, Baden-Baden

ISBN 1-55022-320-8
1. Holocaust survivors — Fiction. I. Title.

PS8557.E675B93 1998   C813'.54   C98-930419-1
PR9199.3.D47B93 1998

Cover painting by Dominic Pirone.

Design and imaging by ECW Type & Art, Oakville, Ontario.
Printed by AGMV Marquis Imprimeur, Cap-Saint-Ignace, Québec.
Distributed in Canada by General Distribution Services,
30 Lesmill Road, Don Mills, Ontario M3B 2T6.

Published by ECW PRESS,
2120 Queen Street East, Suite 200,
Toronto, Ontario M4E 1E2.
www.ecw.ca/press

ECW PRESS *gratefully acknowledges the Canada Council for the Arts and the Ontario Arts Council for their support of our publishing program.*

To my husband, Robert Sandbo

ACKNOWLEDGEMENTS

I wish to thank Captain John Garrott, Robert Sandbo, Jack David, James Walsh, Leslie C. Smith, Professor Walter James Miller, Henry Myers, Dr. Ira Progoff, and Michael Holmes.

I would also like to acknowledge the valuable resources of *Menchen in Gurs* (Georg Heintz) by Hanna Schramm.

PART ONE

I

The freighter *Baleares* glistened in the sun. She had been a collier, a 5,000-tonner built between wars in Newcastle that could run up to eight knots. Newly painted, she lay moored at a dock in Seville, waiting for her human cargo. For more than two months she'd played peekaboo with her passengers and today was the day — their *rendezvous* by the brown-blue waters of the Guadalquivir.

To Uschi the ship looked larger than a soccer field. She stood in the customs queue small and plump with baby fat, her mousy hair streaked golden by the sun, her deep-set hazel eyes green with excitement. Uschi loved turmoil almost as much as she loved peace, sometimes more.

She squinted at the long lines of survivors shuffling forward, their shadows trailing over the cobblestones. Fear followed them. It descended like a cloud over the dock and seeped into the ship: its first passenger.

"Look at them," she said in disgust, not taking her eyes off all the white-knuckled fingers clutching their last possessions. Everyone trembled before a battery of robotic customs officers.

* * *

The Prince laughed his soft laugh. He was from Maia, one of the stars of Pleiades, some 350 light years from Earth.

How they cling to each other, he remarked.

"And in this heat," said Uschi.

Collective death, concluded the Prince.

"What d'you mean?"

Simply, my dear girl, that dying together seems easier than living alone. No options, no choices, no decisions.

"We must discuss this sometime," she said politely. He was at it again. Usually she loved his voice; it was a great comfort to her — but not right now. To get him off his orange crate, she quickly asked, "And where will we all sleep, with only 15 cabins?"

In the holds, most likely.

"What's the holds?"

Down below.

"In this heat? After paying all that money? And the trouble we had getting our dollars changed on the Black Market."

Her mother had threatened to drown herself in Marseilles Harbour if the black market man made off with their money. They'd been waiting all day in his apartment and when he did not return his wife, a fat, tightly girdled lady with a tall pompadour, said he'd been arrested. Uschi's mother said she was lying, but Uschi was willing to wait and see. She did not really believe her mother would jump into the harbour.

The man showed up next day with a pocketful of francs he'd bought with their dollars.

"Don't frown so, Liebchen, remember how well you did in camp."

"Ooff," said Uschi. She'd been looking forward to the voyage despite the present company, hoping the ocean breezes would blow off the stink of the old ladies squeezed together in the barracks, especially those dying in the typhoid ward.

The joke's on mankind, said the Prince, *wanting to cling together yet able to survive as individuals only.*

She could tell by his tiny chuckle that he was signing off. About time too. Must he always have the last word? He knows I can't concentrate with so much going on. She'd met the Prince under very painful circumstances and he had never left her. Not even when she became involved with the commandant.

Uschi nudged her little brother Michael, pointing at brown customs fingers rummaging through pink lace. The boy hopped up and down and clapped his hands in delight. Uschi smiled the smile of her superior 16 years and the customs officer looked at her, enraptured.

She never tired of her effect on men. Uschi felt herself churning with her own *élan vital*. It intoxicated her a hundred, a thousand times; made her drunk with her own exuberance, simultaneously liberating and imprisoning her. She never spoke of it, though, not even to the Prince: the knowing was in her eyes.

Customs waved Uschi's family through. The Spaniards smacked their lips, and cat-called *bonitas, bonitas, bonitas.* It was far from flattering, Uschi's mother said, and right away the rest of the men on the pier picked up the chant.

Her parents and Michael got sucked into the freighter's tumult. Turning to cast one last look at the city she'd come to love, Uschi thought of Lot's wife and involuntarily scrambled forward. Behind her, Seville, her sunny bastion of the Holy Grail, blinked its fond farewells.

Uschi's voice broke and her eyes filled with tears. "*Adios Sevilla, adios España*, I just know this is goodbye forever."

They made their way through the main deck, congested with luggage and perspiring passengers. Some tried to get off against the traffic while most were still trudging up the ship's gangway. To their horror they were directed down narrow rope ladders. Someone said halt. They were in the holds on F-deck.

By now the family was used to being separated. Father and son went to the men's section, while mother and daughter were sent to the women's. "All right, down the hatch," they said, smiling, waving short goodbyes to each other.

Uschi squinted through the half-light at rows and rows of

three-tiered bunks. "Gawd, it's hot in here." Carefully she deposited their banged-up luggage on one of the lower bunks, wiping her face with her arm. She watched her mother slowly count out her last Spanish coins to the porter who had followed them, knowing how she hated to part with her money. It was a habit that had become more pronounced over the last few years.

"You didn't forget anything?" Her mother anxiously eyed the abused leather suitcases and wailed, "Barracks and troopships, barracks and troopships. Has it come to this?"

"Aw, stop it, ma." Uschi felt she could never really comfort her. It seemed that her mother had filled that last year with enough wailing and whining to last a lifetime; it would overwhelm her if she didn't stop.

It's odd, Uschi thought, how camp had blown up people larger than life, made them more than what they were. It was as if a giant hand had placed them under a monster microscope, and when they went astray every little sin would show. She'd have to ask the Prince about it.

Uschi sighed. She had never mentioned the Prince to her best friend Bea. Bea knew all about Uschi's boyfriends but would have laughed at the thought of the Prince. It was an irritating little laugh, a laugh Uschi couldn't bear just now. Bea laughed alot. It wasn't that she was cruel — but the camp offered easy targets. She liked camp, and boys. Unfortunately for Bea, boys didn't like to be laughed at.

Uschi worried about her friend, still at the Hotel Terminus in Marseilles. If she didn't get her visa by next month she'd have to return to camp when her six-month permit expired. There, anything could happen. She could be shipped east. Uschi thought of the old saying: *good things come out of the East.* For those who shared in her plight, it definitely was not true.

The dark secrets of the East were only starting to spread. People sat or stumbled around the station for hours, wondering where their trains would go. When they were forced to board they watched anxiously to see which way they would head. There was a collective sigh of relief when they headed west.

But when they headed east . . .

She thought of Helmut, still in camp, and her eyes filled with tears. Adorable Helmut, with his tousled blond hair and dimples, and torn, patched pants. What would happen to him now?

Deep in the gloom of the hold Uschi pressed close to her bunk and frowned at the mutilated Spanish assailing her. The former camp inmates, dressed in their remaining finery, had changed again into middle-class matrons, calling commands to the porters in the narrow aisles. She hated these drab, self-righteous women whose bourgeois veneer had flaked off like old nail polish during the seven days of transport. Before her astonished eyes a generation of her hometown matrons had reverted to Marseilles fishwives. Now she knew why she'd never really been able to trust these coiffed and lacquered provincial *Hausfraus*.

"They make me sick. Sick and tired," she told the Prince. "One little bang and kaboom! They bust open like pistachios in a nutcracker."

It wasn't such a little bang.

"Well . . ."

But she wasn't too sick or tired to enjoy this huge joke on the hometown folks, seeing the good burghers ripped from middle-class righteousness into the bright glare of guns at high noon.

"For once they had to spill their collective guts in broad daylight," she told the Prince. "Pardon me, intestines."

How cruel you are, he laughed.

"*Frau* Spiegel, the wife of Notary *Herr* Doctor Spiegel, slapped me when I returned her glass a day late so I slapped her right back. I was horrified. I'd never slapped anyone, let alone an older woman. Age before beauty, according to old *Fräulein* Schneider from boarding school. I'd borrowed the glass to eat with. Packing glasses to eat soup out of was not on our minds in the 20 minutes or so they gave us to pack."

It's all evolution, the Prince said soothingly.

"Packing glasses? Spoons too?"

The Prince laughed.

"I never spoke to her again. Too embarrassed to apologize. *Fräulein* Schneider never taught us how to borrow glasses, or how to return them properly in a camp-type situation."

A well-placed slap now and then can't do any harm.

2

Uschi's father was a gentleman and a warrior who had fought in the Great War. He was a big man who loved his family, his jokes and his food. "They threw away the mold when they made him," said Ottilie, the maid. "You won't find nobody like him in a hurry."

He enjoyed good conversation, horse races, and a game of poker. Most of all, he liked a neat and orderly household. Disruptions were not tolerated. He needed peace and quiet to rest from his strenuous business trips. He was fond of attending nostalgic reunions with buddies from his regiment. There was singing and beer and lengthy auto excursions into the nearby Black Forest. His children liked these reunions; his wife didn't. Despite his virtues he had a temper — a spot of dirt on a spoon could make him hurl the offending object against the wall of the sunny breakfast room.

"I hate him when he's like that," Uschi confided to Ottilie, her closest childhood friend. Whenever possible, she tried to spend her Sundays with Ottilie rather than drive with her family to Baden-Baden for coffee at the *Café Gretl*. With Ottilie and her soldier boyfriend she could go to the October *Weinlesen*, the Christmas market or to the zoo.

"Oh, you're a lot like your father," said Ottilie, smiling wickedly.

"No, I'm not. And I don't throw spoons, not even clean ones."

"The day will come. Don't take it so hard, your father's worried."

"What's he so worried about?"

Ottilie looked at her strangely. "You'll find out soon enough, little mouse," she said, and gave her a little pat on the fanny.

Uschi loathed confrontations. Her father's rages frightened her, made her ill. But she pretended all was fine and put on her clown face. This later blossomed into a kind of village idiot act, her most favourite role. She could hide behind it without having to think, let her brain idle in neutral. It did not fool Ottilie. And her family? She wasn't so sure. But it fooled strangers. When she came out of her torpor again she could, to onlookers' amazement, propel herself into immediate action.

"Sometimes I surprise myself," she told Ottilie. "As you know, I'm not the least bit aggressive, but then I get into these rages . . ."

"Like your father?"

"Aw, I knew you'd say that."

"I love you anyway, little mouse."

"Well, one out of three isn't bad." She sighed. "Sometimes, I feel so heavy, so confused." It was true. Her normally sweet, outgoing nature tended to turn inward.

Yet she loved people, needed them.

People were men. Women she didn't trust.

Once during the transport the trains suddenly stopped. The fall sun shed benign rays as the people climbed out of the moving lavatories and stood enjoying the warm, open fields. Their captors had pushed them across the border like a cargo of over-ripe bananas.

Later, in Marseilles, Uschi watched, fascinated, as a shipload of bananas stood boiling in the harbour, the *Vieux Port*, and people queued up to buy bunch after bunch. The next day they were given away free. Two days later, sated and sick, people still queued up — out of greed.

Uschi remembered standing beside the silent train. The French guards filled her round arms with tins of food. Dazed and smiling, she agonized over the dead man in their compartment. He was covered with their beige camelhair blanket. It had black fringes. She hadn't eaten in four or five days, but wasn't hungry. She couldn't eat near the dead man. She hadn't touched him, she'd been standing out in the corridor, but she felt her hands had touched death, her mouth had tasted death: all the world's waters could not cleanse her again. She'd burn the blanket later.

Her fellow passengers had torn the tins from her . . . vultures, vultures. Should she get furious or escape into her inertia? The Prince said, *understand yourself.* Uschi was tired and the sun felt warm on her skin. She smiled benignly at them. Time enough to get angry. Later, after she understood herself. If they wanted to eat with unclean hands . . .

She had no need for food now, there'd be food when she was clean again. There'd always be food for Uschi.

*   *   *

"I'll take the lower, you take the middle, let's put the luggage on the upper and hope none of these wretched people will want our upper." Her mother's sharp glances warned Uschi she was getting ready to grab the thicker mattresses from the adjoining bunks before they were claimed. Was it the urge for perfection, the artist in her, Uschi wondered, that made her mother insist on changing tables, sometimes two, three times, in the much lamented restaurants and cafés of their hometown? Or was it plain, unadorned greed and the need to deny others the best?

"And start unpacking, lazy Miss."

Uschi climbed up and wiggled around her mattress. It was definitely superior to the strawsacks, the focal point of the barracks. Those sacks lay on frames fashioned from that lowly mother of campbeds, the orange crate, over which barbed wire had been strung by the resourceful Spaniards. Thoughtfully, the barbs had been pulled out like unwanted wisdom teeth. Heavy, homemade benches on each side of the precarious bed guarded the sleepers. From time to time the wires broke. Uschi and her mother would crash down, exciting harsh words from the surrounding sleepers.

Uschi would cringe in a corner while her mother, complaining bitterly, gathered herself back up to sleep despite her legendary insomnia. The next morning a smiling Spaniard would arrive for a thorough reconstruction job.

Shortly after their arrival in camp a shy young guard invited Uschi for a walk to the village. "You're very pretty, Mademoiselle," said the guard who took her hand as they strolled peacefully through the village, laughing in the rain. His name was André and he grew up on a farm near Saint-Lô in Normandy. He'd never been away before and she could see that he was homesick. She saw him every day. He always brought gifts: apples, eggs, thick meat sandwiches, once even roses.

Her French improved marvellously.

André treated her like a porcelain doll, demanding nothing but joyful greetings and happy smiles. When he told her he was being shipped out she clung to him and would not be comforted. She cried all night. She ran a little after the truck that took him away. She could see his broad peasant's hand waving to her. When he was gone from sight Uschi went back to her barracks, lay down on her cold strawsack and turned her back to the world.

3

Her mother was a great puzzle. Although she had managed to get their furniture packed into the overseas lift she didn't want to leave. She had heard horror stories about the new country and they terrified her. Uschi concluded that her mother was happiest when she was in bed eating truffles or strawberries dipped in chocolate, but she also liked to eat chicken crackling, mostly in the afternoons, which she'd hide from the family in the oddest places. It seemed to Uschi that her mother saw a bed as a haven. A safe place. When her children were sick she was always very solicitous. She'd never whine then, and would share her chocolates liberally — but not the chicken crackling.

Most of their good furniture had been shipped out. Uschi missed her piano, stepping gingerly around what few household items remained. Where the piano should have been there was an enormous empty space. It was odd, a little like living on a stage where one set had been stripped and nothing was ready for the next act.

They were all waiting for visas. The visa that would fix everything.

The new edicts ordered them to disconnect their phone, sell the cars, and dismiss the servants. Uschi missed the coffeehouses, the restaurants, the casino in Baden-Baden with it's gilded columns. But most of all she missed her beloved Ottilie.

She began to prepare what she called her going-away outfit. She wanted to be ready when they came. She'd take her low-heeled, navy suedes with the alligator insets. She loved the alligators. And her new navy frock with the red polka dot inset and matching bolero jacket. In the end she forgot to take many things, including her umbrella with the initialled silver handle, a gift from her favourite uncle. She'd never be able to buy another.

Finally, long hours of sleep and daylight dreaming blurred together. Only fantasy, her last indulgence, remained. She made furtive forays, anxious and hurried, across the pretty tree-lined plaza to her favourite cinema. During intermission, reality returned abruptly when the houselights came up and the brownshirts foraged the aisles with their collection boxes while Uschi tried to sink deep into her plush seat. Later, to beat the curfew, she'd race home through the twilight to an evening of brooding or squabbling with Michael. Uschi had been to her friends' "going-away parties." In the end there was no party for Uschi.

Uschi's father seldom spoke of their future now, going about his business as usual, walking carefully through the spacious and nearly empty rooms. He played poker with the other trapped men at the only hotel still accessible to them. Her father was like a man caught in a revolving door, unable to stop, a man between trains, with nothing but his watch and old timetable.

*   *   *

It had been one of those cold, gusty days in early March when Uschi was called from class. Her father sat in the headmaster's office, looking solemn. "Pack your things," he said, "we're going home."

"The war?" she whispered. He nodded and seemed preoccupied.

On the train he said little and told none of his jokes. They had not been able to get a first-class compartment and sat crowded in with brusque and frightened folk. Soldiers and men in brown shirts and matching pants — others in black uniforms — were everywhere. Some slept up in the luggage nets, some sat on the floors of the corridors and people climbed over them. The long train was slow. They lunched in the dining car.

A heavy snowstorm stopped their progress. By dinnertime the dining car had run out of food and was serving black coffee and carafes of wine. For a generous tip the waiter brought some fresh rolls with jam but no butter. Uschi stared into the falling snowflakes and thought of her friend, Edith. She was back at school, with the others. There'd been barely time to say goodbye.

Uschi breathed deeply. The train air seemed so tense that she feared her breath would start a conflagration. This marked the beginning of her guilt. She felt guilty about leaving her friends, about being alive, about taking up space on the planet, breathing, sleeping and eating. At home during that summer, doing nothing, a succession of psychiatrists, adherents of different disciplines, endeavoured to help her slough off the effects of the psychic baggage she was accumulating.

Her life had become stagnant. The transition from the Spartan life of school to one of lazy, aimless drifting was rapid: late sleeping, lingering in bed, daydreaming and waiting for something to happen; trips to the hated dressmaker, watching her father play poker with the other men, arguing with her mother and brother; riding her bicycle through the woods surrounding the city; talking to the trees as if they were her friends. Sometimes she thought of Goethe's Erl König poem, where the Tree King kills the child. This, she believed, in no way applied to her. Uschi's trees loved her. It was people she feared.

The day they came and made them pack their things, and drove them off to the station, 7,200 across the province, was like a birthday.

* * *

Uschi sat squinting through the light filtering down into F-deck. She sat stock-still and her breath became shallow.

22

The heat seemed to squeeze every ounce of thought from her so that she felt swamped; it closed in and filled her with the overpowering urge to get up and run somewhere, anywhere. But where can you run to on a small ship? All of this added to her sense of helplessness. And guilt. It made her feel evil and she heard a metallic voice say, "unclean, unclean, unclean."

"Oh, shut up," she said aloud.

"You're not talking to me, I hope," said her mother.

"No, to myself. And not even money in the bank."

Her mother shrugged and continued unpacking, hanging up things on nails.

Uschi thought of the movie house across the tree-lined plaza, its deep red plush seats and golden carpet and silken walls. There she'd watched Dragan Vukovich, the Serbian movie star, on the steppes of Kirghiz, assault burly Teutonics like Hans Albers, and win. And he didn't even wear a brown shirt. He, of the high cheekbones, was always victorious, and the end of the movie saw him an even better man. It inspired her and made her want to be an actress, a movie star. She wanted to inspire others to be strong, too. But as soon as Dragan's magic wore off she had to face her old horrible and terrifying world again.

"And start unpacking, you lazy girl! Every single one of the girls in camp would give her right arm to be here in your place. Not to mention your friend, Bea, in Marseilles."

Uschi sighed. Poor Bea. Still trading cigarettes at the *Vieux Port* and the *Canebière*.

"Still running around with those Arabs, I presume."

"Oh, mother. You were happy enough to let them cook those meals for us."

"If she doesn't get out of there she'll soon enough be back in camp — and you know what that means."

"Yes, mother."

"It means being shipped east to the work camps, and worse, God knows. And where, may I ask, are you going now on this misbegotten ship? Oh, Lord, why did you give me such a daughter?"

"See you later, I'm suffocating down here," and she ran toward the exit. Uschi had to get away from the impotent, enraged whine that reverberated through the barracks. Her legendary escapes from her mother, chronicled in camp, scouting expeditions ranging from a few hours to entire days, tickled the gossip mills of *îlot* K. It boggled the imagination. Where could anyone disappear to within the three kilometres of tidily laid out rows of sixteen *îlots*, without tree or bush, and neatly fenced in barbed wire surrounding the totally visible, muddy camp paths?

The camp was located high in the Pyrénées mountains in a moist valley on loamy soil which downpours made slippery despite the deep trenches the Spaniards had cut around the barracks.

The young Spaniards, the pilots especially in their brown leather jackets, became the freelance repair men and maintenance workers of the camp. With pliers, a spool of wire, and a smile they could fix anything. Their buoyant manner charmed all the women, old as well as young.

The Spaniards, as the builders and original inmates, as well as the latrine engineers on the outhouse railway, enjoyed a certain freedom of movement, and the arrival of pretty young girls was highly welcome.

In camp, the most romantic place was the latrine, especially around 11 in the morning when the Spaniards arrived on wagons affectionately baptized *Das Scheisshausbähnchen, les petits chiottes roulantes* — in less poetic English, the little shithouse railroad — to collect the buckets and flirt with the girls. The latrine was the incubator of many a passionate romance.

The women usually began to arrive about half an hour early. They would stand about gossiping, with a special sparkle.

When the smiling Spaniards arrived pushing their little rail-carts it was almost like the scene from *Carmen* with the cigarette girls. The Spaniards seemed to have divided their work. Some did the dirty work and others were foremen. They rotated the tasks on a daily basis. The work would drag more slowly if an especially promising flirtation was in progress. As they filled their carts and moved on it was not unknown for a foreman or two to be left behind at some of the stops. Some days there were as many foremen as workers, all in love.

Uschi was the target of much speculation. Rumours circulated quickly to *îlots* L and M, where the good bourgeois women professed to be too deeply shocked to repeat her evil doings. Their shock, however, was not permanent. It did not outlast the ovens they were sent to, not long after Uschi and her family were safely aboard the *Baleares*.

4

Scouting for *Lebensraum*, Uschi climbed over luggage and noisy people on the main deck, inching toward the poop deck which seemed to offer a little space. Hugging the rail with her damaged fingers, she toyed with the idea of jumping ship. She'd leave a note: "Have gone AWOL. *Adios*." Better yet, "*Adios, muchachos*."

Her mother would wail. Her father would suffer. And Michael? He didn't care, she thought. The Prince wouldn't like it. He was sort of stuffy about her escapades in camp. He wouldn't say it, he didn't have to. People of a higher morality never say much. She'd have to think about it when there was time. She was only 16 now and she'd give herself till she was 20 to make up her mind about these confusing things. By 20 she expected to have it all settled.

She thought of her new friend Irma, the one her mother insisted on calling a prostitute, who seemed to know what she was doing. But then Irma was from Seville and it seemed to her that these people were a very self-assured lot. Irma had explained it. Maybe it was the sun. The sun covered a whole range of holes. Was Irma a prostitute? It did not matter to Uschi. She'd whiled away many pleasant hours with *La Tigresse* and her mec, and François and the other mecs, pimps, at the Hotel Terminus near the *Vieux Port* in Marseilles. Her mother, a thorough bourgeoisie, was no judge of people. Her life had generally moved in the middle lane.

"François, the nice Italian boy."

"Oh, Mother! He's a mec, a Corsican pimp."

"I really don't know what's become of you, my girl. Is that why we sent you to finishing school? Back home you never talked like that."

"You gotta move with the times, Mother." Uschi giggled in fond recollection at her mother's admiration of François, the tall, young Corsican with his black shirt, pants, and soft black hat. A sack of black market potatoes on his elegant, bony shoulders, near the gold cross; kissing her mother's hand he'd squire them from the hotel to the *Canebière* for their afternoon *apéritifs*, carefully depositing the potatoes under the table.

"*L'addition, garçon,*" her mother said, graciously letting him pay the bill with his black market potato money. Or was it pimp money from his stable of four girls, two working out of town?

"But why do they do it, François?"

"They love me."

"I may be simple, but isn't it just as easy to love a man without sending him money orders?" She stared at him, hazel-eyed, and François laughed.

"My girls don't want me to work. They say, 'François, rest yourself. Take a little siesta.'"

"You look pretty rested to me."

"One day maybe you and I take a siesta, *non?*"

"Then I'd make you work for me, yes?" she said sweetly to the handsome young Corsican.

"Le cul de ma tante," he laughed with his even, white teeth, then gave her a little pat on her round fanny.

"You be careful of him, *La Poupée,*" counselled Emile the barkeep. "He's after one thing only."

Uschi smiled her sweet smile and Emile looked at her, enraptured. Even the prostitutes were charmed and protective. Especially the prostitutes. Virginity seemed a highly prized quantity in these parts of the *Vieux Port.* Uschi hated to dispel their illusions; it seemed too cruel. She'd have liked to tell *Onkel* Fritz about it. How he'd have laughed. She missed *Onkel* Fritz.

The Terminus was located in the Red Light District. There was no lounge and the guests shared the bar area with the local prostitutes and pimps. Uschi met *La Tigresse* in the morning over breakfast *brioches* and *café au lait* and the handsome, black-haired woman became a friend and a mother figure, fiercely loyal and protective.

La Tigresse did not like François so Uschi paid little attention to him when she was around. She let her friend's affections wash over her like warm ocean waves and told her nothing, certainly not of her great secret love for the camp commandant. Love, in *La Tigresse*'s eyes, had little to do with men, and it didn't matter whether they were straight or pimps.

The camp women could stay at the Terminus hotel in Marseilles for six months to try to get their visas from the American consulate. Those who were successful were allowed to leave the country; the others had to return to camp. The Vichy government had arranged their lodging; European plan, four to a room without bath, with meals of chickpeas and *topinambours,* a sort of Jerusalem artichoke. Uschi swore she'd never eat another chickpea in her life, and both gave her a royal pain in the ass. She was generally proud of the purity of her language, but in this case, *oh merde.*

The men were in camp in nearby Aix-en-Provence, the hometown of Paul Cézanne and Emile Zola. They were given passes to get into Marseilles, but no one was supposed to leave town and disappear into the countryside without a permit. As far as anyone knew, no one wanted to frolic on the Corniche — all hands were anxious to escape Europe to new worlds. Each man was to report back to the camp by nightfall. But in Marseilles the hotel *concièrge* was far more lenient with the ladies, letting them drift back in at midnight. Sometimes a kindly night porter would open the portals even later.

Uschi developed a lovely routine. Coffee with *La Tigresse*, then to the consulate where the queue started at six in the morning. People brought food and campstools. She never had to queue up. Soon the guards knew her and her friend Bea, and invited them to the movies. Sometimes she'd grab an old lady, offering to interpret for her, and the guards would let her through. She had a thing for languages: it was like she picked them up by osmosis.

It didn't do much good. They had no chance of getting visas. Their affidavits of support had been lost in transit, they were told on their first appointment. Uschi was deeply disappointed but felt it her duty to visit the consulate once a day. "I like to stick around," she told François, "you never know." During long sunny afternoons they'd sit in the open-air café across from the consulate, drinking campari, making jokes, and monitoring the queues.

All action at the consulate was important. Uschi knew the guards would tell her of incoming quota numbers. She hoped for a miracle. Miracles did happen, according to François, who seemed to be working on one of his own. "Tell me again, why do you need a quota?"

"You need them to get in. So many apples, so many oranges."

"With a visa?" Uschi asked.

"Especially with a visa."

"Hmmm. And where'd you get the ship?"

"Here in Marseilles."

"They go to Oran, to Casablanca. But to go west, where'd you have to go?"

"Spain?" François smiled. Uschi thought: how handsome he is.

The scandal at the hotel surpassed even the one in camp that began the day Uschi and Bea started to date the tall Arabs from Oran. The matrons looked down from their windows in shock when the Arabs came serenading. In no time at all they invited the two girls and Uschi's mother — sister, they said to flatter — to home-cooked meals à l'Oranaise. Her mother devoured the food lustily.

"What lovely babushkas," her mother said. "Just look at those embroideries."

"Burnouses, mother."

"Have it your way," she said and Uschi smiled.

"What a pretty mother," one tall, stately Arab said. "Sister," said the other.

Her mother preened. Uschi scowled.

But a meal was a meal, and a welcome break from *garbanzos* and *topinambours*. The hotel cook's struggles with the chickpeas were legendary but the jolly Marseillaise's good humour never flagged.

Uschi loved cooks. Everyone loves cooks.

*   *   *

The camp cooks were volunteers, jokesters working in open-air kitchens from dawn to dusk with cinder-filled eyes and charcoal-smeared faces to produce kettles of thin, watery soup where tiny cubes of suet would sometimes rendezvous with a sliver of meat.

By late afternoon the cast-iron kettles were dragged to the barracks. The cooks slithered across and sometimes fell into the mud, spilling some of the soup that rapidly lost its heat. In the barracks it was ladled into cups and saucers and whatever else was available. The suet was treated like Russian caviar, and Uschi saw women shove, push and cuff each other over these little cubes. Her mother was above it, of course; she'd rather bribe a Spaniard for some eggs. But Fannie's mother was right in there, fighting for every hard bit of fat for her scrawny daughter. Mrs. Shtrowise was pretty scrawny herself but she diverted every extra bite to her daughter, managing to scrounge together an assortment of tiny morsels.

"The baby needs nourishment every hour," Uschi's mother said derisively.

"A young girl has to keep her strength up. My Fannie needs food," said Mrs. Shtrowise.

"The baby's just the right side of 30," Uschi's mother whispered, ignored by Mrs. Shtrowise.

But her mother almost got into trouble with Mrs. Polanski, the lion-maned mother of Norma, with whom she fought over a strawsack. Uschi's mother snatched one of the newly arrived sacks to which Mrs P. claimed first rights.

"Pushy Pollacks," stage-whispered Uschi's mother.

"You wanna make something of it?" Mrs. Polanski put up her fists.

"No thank you," she replied retreating, rolling her blue eyes heavenward. People who had lived in houses with an *Obergeheimrat* did not bow to a pushy Polanski.

"Chicory water again?" said Uschi.

"Today it's only black water," said Norma. "I'm saving my marmalade for the tea." The evening tea, which the îlot overseer liked to call high tea, tasted of nothing at all. With it they ate some of their four inches of white bread, saved from the morning rations.

At the *cantine*, they would queue up to buy apples and chestnuts, to be cooked with a little scooped up virgin Pyrénées mountain snow. "It's filling," said Norma.

"But your nails fall out just the same," said Uschi.

"Oh, don't be so fussy, they grow in again."

"We need vitamin C," said Uschi, who liked Norma.

"Go get it."

"Ooff."

But after she met her commandant she hardly ever ate snow. He sat her on his knees and fed her. He was worse than Fannie's mother. She didn't really care that much for the food but she liked his attention. Since the transport she'd developed a supreme indifference to food. After their arrival in camp they were allowed out to the main road to search for their luggage, which had been dumped there. It was nice to get out of their *îlot* and chat with the men from *îlots* G and H, who leaned against the barbed wire in the fall sunshine.

Everyone was hungry for information from the outside and Uschi told them all about the transport. She felt a little light-headed, very happy, not in the least hungry. She had the sensation of still rolling in the train, the earth beneath her slightly heaving. It was not unpleasant. To be in this fascinating camp high in the mountains, in a foreign country on a sunny fall day, out of the horrible old place she'd called her home country, to breathe in the pure air. To have been sent west, instead of east. God, she'd hate these people forever and ever, the way they'd made her father tremble when they asked for her pocketbook. He tore it away from her to give it to them. When she got it back she took out her lipstick and slowly painted her mouth. She did this instead of spitting at them, taking her time and gazing carefully into her pocket mirror. Then, when her family had to pass the row of tall, young, blond, uniformed youths she looked straight at them, vowing that one day she would return and make them pay for what they were doing to other human beings. As long as I live, I will never forget it, she vowed.

She remembered the whole train — all the people — breathing sighs of relief when they started west.

"God, I don't know how long it's been since I've eaten," Uschi said to a nice blond, blue-eyed man. She did not mean anything by it. She just liked his smile.

"Don't go away," said the man, who left her standing there. He came back with a small, shrivelled apple that he handed to her as if it were the Hope Diamond.

"Thank you," she said before she ate it. "Thank you very much." And they both felt magnificently generous.

In Marseilles people spent a lot of time in queues. Everyone queued up for everything. As soon as a line formed people got in it. Later, they'd find out what it was for . . . sardines, horsemeat, freshly slaughtered chickens, wooden shoes. Horse salami was faintly sweet but tasty, and was not rationed. They had ration cards, but not nearly enough.

Once in a café her mother talked a man into letting them have some of his coupons. Uschi was very embarrassed. Her mother's old whine had been converted into almost cheerful and helpless sounds for the occasion, and Uschi was keenly aware that she was being used as bait as her mother pushed and shoved at her and whispered, "Smile, you silly girl." Had she accused her mother of pandering, her porcelain-blue eyes would have grown wide in hurt puzzlement. Imagine a daughter so devoid of feeling as to read gross indecency into her poor mother's every harmless little ploy.

Food. Uschi remembered her chicken-cooking friend. The man who had an apartment at the Corniche, the road that runs along the Mediterranean from Marseilles to Nice. He would take her to the nearby horse races. Even his memory made her shudder. Thank God he'd been unable to get on this boat, and good riddance. He was one of those suave old men — and it seemed to her they got smoother with age — a libertine, a lecher, a louse, a gourmet who'd turned into a perfect old idiot, a sad old sack. At times he was a nice old louse, and he'd bought her the only dinners she ate those days — in black market restaurants where they didn't ask for ration cards. He looked after her in a way her father couldn't any longer. He was in camp with her father but had an apartment in town. While her father needed passes to leave, this man moved around freely and only reported back to camp at night. He protected and fed her the way her commandant had, blessed be His memory: but the difference was she would love that handsome, towering man to her grave.

All Uschi had to do for old suavy, and she did not do it graciously, was to lie there until it was over. More than anything she detested him kissing her down there; she would not let him near her afterward, at least not until he'd rinsed out his mouth with gobs of Odol. And the stuff was concentrated, too. It was then that she took the first of her long flights up to Maia to talk to the Prince. She did this rarely, because he generally was around when she needed him.

On the poop deck, scratching *Baleares*'s rail with her ruined fingernails, she frowned and tried to forget the old man. One of the boys from the camp she'd had a brief fling with told her about a barracks rumour: talk of the old man smacking his lips in his sleep, muttering her name.

"I don't believe it, you're making it up."

"Scout's honour. The whole barracks knows what he's doing to you."

"Aw cut it out."

Uschi shuddered, as if to shake off the hotel fleas, and longingly looked at Seville where only yesterday she'd danced in the park on the waterfront for half the night. She'd danced with the slim girls and boys till she was out of breath. Even now, closing her eyes on the shimmering hot river, she could see delicate white gardenias in black hair, drink in scented mystery, hear the clickety-clack of the *castañuelas*. She climbed down to the main deck and stood near the cargo booms, watching the cargo being loaded.

Black hair flying, black eyes flashing, white teeth gleaming between moist lips, heads tossed in joyous rhythms: Uschi's nostrils flared in remembrance, and her mouth opened with the aftertaste of river and night. River, night, air, moon and music. How could she leave it for a land of skyscrapers and neon lights?

A shadow fell across her dream dance and Uschi sighed into the glare of the white sun. He was one of those desiccated old men from camp. Probably a nice old man, not a gourmet pussy eater like her former benefactor.

Both of these characters made her sick, the nice and the greedy. Uschi shuddered again in the heat. But even the nice were greedy, or had become so, their greed fallow ground before camp. They were greedy for life but too cowardly to take it. If these people were her own kind she certainly wanted no part of them. And if she ever got off this ship, please God, she'd run away from them as fast and far as possible. This collection of old flesh, filled with the putrefaction of a thousand meals, had been made more greedy by a year or two of starvation; old fear rotted in this flesh, festering and giving off a stench all the scents in the world could not overcome.

There's no end to man's stupidity, the Prince had said, *or to the goodness of God.* But where did God come in? Uschi wasn't sure who God was. The God of her childhood seemed so far, gone with the comfort of her former life. Somehow He must have slipped in among the rubble, lost between pillows and pianos and pinafores, things to which she could never return.

Stupidity, anger, and greed were the hallmarks of the age. Oh, but how greedy they were. Greedy, greedy, grasping at life's greenness with black arthritic fingers, separated from death but by a threshold. She blinked at the old man by the rail as if she could blink him away — off into space — but he stood there solid, so solid. For comfort she hugged herself with her own round arms. From far her mother's querulous voice crept into her ear: "You'll work. By God, how you will work." Uschi knew she was referring to the new country.

She also knew work was the only form of punishment her mother feared. Her mother would rave for hours about how they pressed people into slave labour and called it democracy. Uschi by now feared the new shores more than she had feared camp. She scratched her head reflectively. She really hadn't feared camp at all.

What she feared was her mother. All her running away could not shut out the voice that seemed to haunt her wherever she went. Cutting through the barbed wire did not help her escape it. They cut through the wire with a pair of scissors Bea had stolen from the infirmary to make their nocturnal escapades possible. The round-cheeked young guards from their own *îlot* looked the other way, especially when they were on duty at the F-barrier. The guards made it clear they wanted them to get out of camp. God knew they'd left the exits unguarded on Christmas and on New Year's Eve during a major camp outpouring of good will. It was one of the few times Uschi had not felt lonely: she was happily connected with kindred spirits, with the other prisoners, mostly male, and the nice guards who'd slip them food whenever they could.

The *îlot* K girls would talk to their guards for hours while they were on duty at the tiny guardhouse and greet them warmly whenever they passed the F-barrier.

A girl needed a Spaniard for romance, a guard for connections and a prisoner for money. Unlike the others, a Spaniard tolerated no rivals and one had to be careful about him and his knife. But most of the prisoners had money and probably were the most civilized. They may not have been as handsome as the Spaniards, especially the ones she met later in Spain, but they were adorable and handsome in their own way. Uschi liked them all. Uschi liked men. She smiled. Once she'd made love with a Spaniard in camp who held the much coveted job of orderly in the infirmary and ate regular meals. After they made love he invited her to a delicious omelette. Uschi believed she would be able to taste it forever. Fearing Spaniards and their knives, she was glad enough the orderly lost interest in her after their lovemaking. Anyway, shortly afterward she met the commandant.

Uschi sighed. Safely on the ship, she felt less secure than she had in camp. It now seemed a haven of friendly people — except the women, of course.

People were still embarking at a steady pace. Uschi stood at the rail taking in the drama unfolding on the dock. There was considerable competition for porters and much counting and recounting of suitcases. Now and then there was a cry of relief when a precious bag was located. She watched a tall, chic creature with red hair tied up in a green bandanna emerge from a taxi. One of her green high-heeled sandals caught in the door and was extricated with the help of the driver. She smiled and thanked him in fluent Spanish and seemed to give him a large tip because the driver turned himself into a thankful pretzel. Oversized sunglasses hid most of her face but from what Uschi could see she was beautiful. To get a better view of this princess Uschi climbed up on the rail and dangled a pair of shapely and deeply tanned legs overboard. She noted that the porters took very respectful charge of the many Louis Vuitton suitcases.

The tall beauty hesitated at the sight of the *Baleares* and Uschi remembered her own hesitation. She threw her an encouraging smile. It was pleasant to have a front row seat to this elegant person's dilemma, and she hoped fervently that they would meet on board.

5

Tamara Adler, tall, sleek, 24, with smooth red hair and green eyes, squinted at the freighter *Baleares*. Another adventure, she thought, shifting her blue-lensed sunglasses up to her forehead. More fodder for a girl's diary.

She smoothed down the green Quennel chiffon dress that billowed in the breeze and bent to tighten the strap of her matching high-heeled sandal. She'd been in such a hurry that she left Xav's yellow silk scarf at the hotel. Not that it mattered. There seemed to be no one around to appreciate her outfit, she thought, oblivious to the stares from the pier.

She should have been suspicious of the tall Corsican with the persuasive voice but by then despair had taken over. "No more ships, cara señorita. For mucho tiempo."

"I speak perfect French," Tamara said, refusing his Gauloise. "You can talk to me in French." She'd been referred to a man selling ship cabins in this waterfront bar.

"Much, much time," he said in French, and inhaled deeply. With his long, sensitive fingers he seemed to stretch time's passage like a string of spaghetti. "You go, *señorita*." He looked out over the docks and the Guadalquivir and then, quickly, with an apologetic smile, back to Tamara.

"There'll be no more ships for the duration of the war." Definitely, his French was better than his Spanish.

He fixed her with his luminous black eyes. "I can only encourage you to go. I myself would go but I must return to Marseilles for now, to my girls."

"Your children?"

"Not exactly."

"And what'd you mean, *for now*. You just told me the *Baleares* was the last ship."

"The last ship for you, señorita. As for François . . ."
He raised his hands and shrugged.

"Some people like to take chances, some don't," she smiled
at him. "Perhaps I fit into the latter category, hmmm?"

"But you're a lady."

"Aha! Here we go again."

He looked at her speculatively. "Of course. But I don't
think you'd want to join my girls, hmmm? . . . No, of course
not."

"Give me that ticket," she said furiously, and handed him
the packet. The last of her money.

He tricked me, she thought, the impertinent Corsican. I
shouldn't have listened to him. Shouldn't have bought the
ticket, shouldn't have. Her thoughts scurried round her
head like squirrels in a cage until she saw the young girl
sitting atop the rail, tan legs dangling, smiling. Regret
welled up at the sight of this wholesome teenager, dressed
in a stylish white bathing suit and matching shorts, so sure
and so carefree among the refugees. Suddenly Tamara felt
old. Only this morning she'd have resented this plump
junior miss's friendly stares as intrusive, but now she drank
them in greedily. She smiled at the girl.

Tamara Adler never admitted to being lonely. From behind
her mask of costly unguents, and clothes from Rue St.
Honoré, she preferred to address the world in neutral terms
with a gracious frown, a pretty wrinkling of her patrician
nose. Since leaving camp she'd managed to distance herself
another notch or two from most of the inhabitants of this
deplorable planet, with corresponding isolation. Strangely,
despite her Pierre Balmains, Mainbochers, and Courrèges,
and favourite perfume, *Nuits d'amour*, she continued to
feel neither cleaner, nor, hell, more beautiful, than any of
the ragged women from the barracks.

"Chickening out?"

Tamara flinched, whirled round and flashed the speaker
her ivory smile. Hirsch was hooked. A director at UFA, the

MGM of Berlin, he adored artificiality. Alexander Hirsch, a master of simulation, could tell a phony from a mile away.

"No boarding fever? No desire to get in line, join the crowd? *Sans blague?*" She couldn't tell if his smile was good-humoured or malicious.

"I'm still mulling it over. Fortunately this thing isn't scheduled to sail till tomorrow. In the meantime, I am going back to my hotel." She was surprised to hear herself say it.

"Sailing tomorrow, across the Seven Seas, where perhaps my sweetheart is waiting for me," sang Hirsch.

"Off-key," called Uschi from her perch on the rail and Tamara automatically uttered *"quizás."*

Hirsch scribbled something in his notebook and tore out the page. *"Chère señorita,* should you decide to honour us with your presence aboard, here's my card. Cabin C." He bowed, gravely handed it to her, and clicked the heels of his black and white correspondent's shoes, producing little sound.

"Thank you," said Tamara, stuffing it into her elegant Hermès handbag. Uschi, following the scene from her perch, giggled in anticipation.

"Would you believe I've a new batch of cards in my luggage?" Cards had been a top priority for Alex Hirsch after what he called his parole from camp. Also monogrammed Sulka shirts, the Optimo panama hat and a new gold Dunhill cigarette lighter. He still had his Patek Philippe watch, "a souvenir tschotchke," as he liked to say, "from my *Gestapo* wife."

His unsound origin, the fault of a pair of non-Aryan ancestors (who'd much to answer for), would always rankle.

"We'd be neighbours," said Tamara absently. "I'm cabin B."

"Cabin B? Wonderful." Tamara shrugged.

"Merde! Chère Goddess, why don't we rush aboard and start a little pre-celebration. I happen to have a few bottles of the Veuve with me, 1926. We'll toast bon voyage and all that." His glasses glistened enthusiastically under the panama, making Tamara smile.

"I hope the bottles are not too close to the cards? And ice? What about ice?"

"Leave everything to Lex Hirsch, Goddess, but ice or no ice, I gather there are only 15 cabins in toto. Somebody's made a killing." He whistled through his teeth and shook his right hand energetically.

Tamara thought of the Corsican but could not help using her old standby, "Oh, really?"

"So you'd better show, Goddess, or these kiddies won't lose any sleep reselling your cabin B. Or was it C?"

"I've got my receipt. And . . . and I could sue." She gnawed on her lower lip and for the first time seemed to become aware of the stares from the people waiting in the queues. "And where will they stuff them all, I wonder?" The memory of the barracks made her wrinkle her nose. The smells, and the sounds. By God, what smells.

"And thereby hangs the donkey's tail. Search me, chère señorita, *cherchez-moi*." Hirsch lit another Gitane and she let him light one for her, unaware that she found a Berliner's Gitane more appealing than a Corsican's Gauloise.

His French is atrocious, she thought; learned a little in school, probably lived only a short time in Paris before being shipped off to camp. But there was something — almost — endearing about the man. It was like she felt sorry for him and his bottles of Veuve Clicquot.

Tamara stood there, uncertain. She looked up at Uschi, who gave her a wide smile. Then she said to Hirsch, "I suppose you're right: they won't refund."

"*Sans blague*, you're not kidding."

Tamara bit her lip. If she stayed she'd have to cable Xav for more money. And this time he wasn't around to help with the visa: if she couldn't pay off the local gendarmes they'd put her in jail. This time there'd be no handy consul to bail her out.

"So your visa's up?" asked Hirsch who'd been watching her closely.

"How do you know?"

"The eye of experience, Goddess."

Tamara tossed her head back and the red hair sprang from it's green bandanna. Hirsch gallantly bent to retrieve the cloth but a tall, elegant bony figure picked it up and handed it to Tamara with a flourish.

From above on the rail Uschi let out a shriek. "François, what are you doing here?"

"Psst," said François, and put his finger to his mouth.

Tamara looked at Hirsch and François, shrugged in exasperation, and hailed a cab discharging passengers. As the cab made a U-turn on the cobblestones she gave a dismissive wave — as if she wanted to escape the whole bothersome situation.

Hirsch called, "*Adios*, Goddess," and threw her a kiss. Tamara returned it.

"She'll be back," Uschi predicted from her observation post, calling to François, "and you, *mon petit*, what are you doing here?"

"Not so loud," said François, gesticulating mysteriously, "meet me at the waterfront café later."

Hirsch squinted at Uschi and at the jostling hysterical crowd trying to come onboard. To no one in particular, he said: "Like in camp, they shit with fear. They'll never change. They'll be doing it aboard and forever after, wherever they go. They'll contaminate the whole fucking planet."

"Who's gonna stop them?" He pushed back his Optimo panama: "Extermination? But, hell, what else? I hear that's what's in the cards. The survivors, bah. Look at them, shaking, pushing and shoving." He frowned at the queues. "Yeah, decidedly, we're not getting any better. What we need is an Einstein in people management." He looked up at Uschi and broke into a wide grin. "Well, who knows, perhaps there's still hope. Perhaps, I say."

Hirsch blew smoke rings, barely visible in the hot air, and strolled over to the customs officers. Using his best director's voice, once the terror of the UFA studios, "And just how many are we in this floating enterprise?"

"One thousand, *señor, mas o menos.*"

"More or less? More, I rather think, my good man. The question is, how many more. And what are the statistics on survival? Lifeboat data? Submarines? And how does all this affect the stock market? Frankfurt, Zürich, London, New York? Maybe one can make a little survival side bet." He looked at the queues, as if searching for a taker. He didn't seem encouraged. "War writes strange scripts," he noted. "The thing is to be a star in the lifeboat."

Hirsch was always the star. In camp he had practically lived down in the main infirmary tent. Chow, champagne, girls, cabaret shows, concerts, little dinners. It's not what you'd want in real life, but people with unsound ethnic origins had to suffer. At least in this part of the world. But once Hirsch hit the West he fully intended to make up for lost time and, who knew, maybe one day come back and make the bastards pay. And then — see who had the last laugh. He distributed tips lavishly and the Spaniards grinned and escorted him and his luggage on board.

"*Adios España,*" he called and entered the turmoil aboard with a springy step. He collided with *Herrn* Stanislaus Steinheil, who bullied his way up the gangway followed by his anxious *Frau* and their two pudgy offspring. Barrel-chested, with a handsome and roving eye, *Herr* Steinheil gave Hirsch a dirty look and Hirsch said, "Sorry, *mein Herr,*" disliking him on sight.

Engaged in boarding his mini department store, Steinheil merely grunted.

"Fuck you too, buddy," Hirsch muttered under his breath. He knew his stock types and experience had taught him to stay clear of the Steinheils of this world. And despite his outburst about the fear of his fellow survivors, he was afraid too. "*Merde,* let's go, *muchachos,*" he told the Spaniards, and they made their way toward his cabin. It turned out to be a tiny room aft on the cabin deck.

For his part, Steinheil had survived camp unscarred, unseeing, unhearing. Even before the ordeal he had never felt much of anything. Porters and cabbies never dared grumble at his tips; waiters sprang at the snap of his thick powerful fingers. *Herr* S. was wont to measure his well-nourished body against those of his emaciated camp fellows and pronounce himself God.

His luggage was unscuffed. From the military commandant down to the lowliest civilian auxiliary no one would have been brave enough to risk retribution from his gorilla hamhocks. His wife and children never lacked for food, drink, medicine, recreation. They even had luxuries: large cookie-type *Nürnburger Lebkuchen* at Hannukah and Easter bunnies at Passover. The family shamelessly luxuriated, and *Herrn* Steinheil felt himself irresistible to man, woman or child: not above a little strategic pinch of any woman — any age. Yet beneath his apparent lack of feeling lurked real fear too, and he was ready to spring to the attack, especially when trapped.

"Hoopla," said Steinheil now, colliding with a husky youth. Uschi, who'd wandered over, watched with interest.

Accustomed to grief, *Frau* Steinheil held her breath. Life with Steinheil had taught her never to interfere. The youth glared at Steinheil, saw Uschi, smiled, and moved on. *Frau* Steinheil exhaled. Uschi laughed out loud. Only the Steinheil offspring seemed disappointed.

"Why didn't you fight him, Dad, why didn't you?" asked the bigger one.

"Aw, gee dad, you should have hit him, you should've," said the younger.

*   *   *

Uschi had managed to fight the traffic and gone ashore. At the waterfront bar she interrogated François. "What's going on and why are you here?"

"I'm selling cabins."

"So it's you who's making the killing? My, my, what unsuspected talents. You could have given us first pick."

"I didn't want to cheat your parents, *La Petite*."

"Aha! Friendship! What delicate sentiments, I'm touched." François lit his Gauloise and grinned.

"What's with your girls now that you're here. And have you seen Bea? I'm worried about her."

"No need to worry on her account. She's supervising my girls. And, as a matter of fact, I was going to tell you, she's gone to Casablanca to break in two new ones."

"Casablanca? I don't believe it."

"On the *Sidi Ben Afghan*."

"*Sans blague!* She must have gone with one of those Arab cooks she was always whispering with. And what d'you mean? Breaking in your girls? She knows as much about your business as I do. Maybe less."

"You'd be surprised," said François, sucking on his Gauloise.

*　*　*

When Tamara's cab pulled up at the hotel people were gathering in the lobby for a late Spanish lunch. Since she wasn't hungry she went straight upstairs to her suite. The maid was changing the linen and greeted her with a smile. Large tips always pay off, Tamara thought cynically. She was ashamed when the girl pointed to her best bottle of perfume on the dressing table.

"*Señorita* forget to pack."

Bet she's sorry now she didn't grab it, thought Tamara. Then she held the flacon out to her. "Here, you take it."

"*Muchas gracias, señorita*," said the girl, delighted. At $75 a bottle Tamara wondered when she'd be able to buy another. But what the hell.

"No lunch for you, *señorita*?"

"No, I'm not very hungry, I think I'll take a nap."

"It's nice to have you back, *señorita*."

"*Gracias*." Tamara was strangely reluctant to say this might be her last night.

The girl drew the heavy curtains for her and turned down the bed. Gathering her things, she said, "*Que le vaya bien*, be well, *señorita*," and gently closed the door.

Tamara fell into an uneasy slumber. She dreamt she was back in Germany, a small girl in a white ruffled dress with her hair in thick reddish pigtails that pranced down her back.

* ★ *

Uschi watched thin coins sucked into greedy palms. The people in line cringed before those greedy palms. They're so lost, so disgusting, even if their bodies are still whole. Too bad *Onkel* Fritz wasn't here. Uschi smiled, thinking of all the good burghers queueing up for *Onkel* Fritz's couch. Maybe he could innoculate them against neurosis and psychosis.

Ha, thought Uschi, here we have a shipload of fear not yet experienced in the history of migration. Remembering her physics, she considered it a fear so great that it threatened the atom, to freeze it instead of splitting it. Far better they died before they spread this fear to others. What would the Prince say about that? Slowly, past the little trestle tables, the long straggling queues shuffle forward on the cobbles, to the faint rhythm of rubber stamps. And in these queues the poison fermented and multiplied. It was eager to cross the rope barrier, pass up the waiting gangways, and spill down the hatchways to fill up the ship. But at the pier, the sun shined down in soundless white explosion, assaulting the broken and the unbroken, making all equal in perspiration.

* ★ *

Her two-time-zone Beaume Mercier watch showed ten o'clock and Tamara realized with a pang of guilt that she'd slept through the whole afternoon, hadn't unpacked or rearranged her luggage as she had intended. The suitcases were a mess. And she hadn't even eaten; hadn't, in fact, eaten since yesterday. She took a quick shower and wondered about a restaurant. Eating alone, without an escort, would not do. The hotel patio then, again. Hastily she slipped into a white lace dress which set off her red hair and smooth suntanned skin.

A flamenco guitarist played under the palm trees. The flame of the red candles reflected in the silver on the white tablecloths and the air was fragrant with gardenia blossoms. Laughter and conversation filled the patio. The *maître d'* led her to her favourite corner table, far enough from the music to hear herself think, yet near enough not to feel alone. So engrossed was she in her thoughts that she did not even notice the admiring glances coming from the bar.

A voice said, "Good evening, Goddess."

She gave a little start. Hirsch, the pest from the ship. No ivory smile for him; yet he came over, bowed and clicked his heels. "Maybe you like a little company, eh? It's not good to eat alone."

"And what brings you here, may one ask?"

"Frankly, my dear, I need a last night off from the extras. The thought had also crossed my mind I'd find you here."

"But why here?"

"That's easy. The best hotel in town. Nothing's too good for a goddess. Which reminds me. How come this goddess dines alone? Cigarette?" Out came the silver case with the monogrammed sticks. Tamara took one. "May I sit down? We're not sailing till *mañana*, you know. Possibly later."

"Much later?"

"Who knows?"

"I know," she said nervously.

"So let's have some laughs. What are you drinking?"

"White wine."

"Oh, we can do better than that. Lets order a little bubbly then."

"Why not?"

"Waiter, bring us a bottle of your best Piper-Heidsieck. Or would you prefer the Veuve?"

"Piper's fine."

"What are you eating? Looks intriguing. Waiter, I'll have the same as the young lady."

When the waiter served the food from a hot silver dish Hirsch tasted it and grimaced. "Rice with rainworms?"

Tamara laughed, "*Paella.*"

After the waiter left Hirsch said, "These Spaniards stick everything into their rice. In Switzerland, at least, you see what you get." He emptied his glass. "I'm glad I make you laugh, Goddess. Tell me about yourself."

Tamara immediately looked stern.

"Aw, come on. I make films. I can smell a good story a mile off."

"You're not going to write about me?"

"Now that you mention it . . ." He laughed.

It makes him look boyish, she thought.

"I could make you a star."

"Cut it out. What d'you want to know?" she asked guardedly.

"The usual. How come such a beautiful . . . young woman . . . is stranded here alone?"

Some of the humanity behind his glasses must have shown because she suddenly relaxed and met his glance. "Well, I'm Tamara Adler. We're from Dresden. Father is a lawyer, loves politics."

Hirsch wrinkled his forehead and leaned forward. "Adler?"

"Joshua Adler. Politics is his whole life. He is a Social Democrat, a patriot."

"Red Adler!" cried Hirsch.

47

Tamara took another sip and Hirsch quickly reached across the table and touched her hand.

She gave him her glass to refill. "Mother was a good Catholic and as things at home got more difficult she sent me off to Notre Dame des Oiseaux, her old convent school in Paris. I hated it." She laughed lightly, "I'm afraid I was a great nuisance to the good nuns. They did the best they could with me and after I got my bac. I applied to the *École des Beaux Arts.*"

"A painter. With money in her voice!"

"I was lucky. I was accepted and stayed there till . . ." she bit her lip.

"Montparnasse?"

"Boulevard Saint Germain. La Place Furstenberg."

"Café Le Flore, Les Deux Magots." Hirsch pursed his lips, lost in thought. Then he said, "An *artiste.* I like artists." He gave her a broad smile and Tamara wondered why he was smiling.

But Hirsch raised his glass, "A toast to artists, all noble survivors and death to the bastards of the world."

* * *

Tamara took a sip and thought, survivors indeed. She loved Paris and she loved to paint. She was happy with her life. Her parents sent her regular allowance and wrote of their busy social life, but between the lines she could read of their mounting unease. By the time the war started Tamara had turned into a Parisian. She worried about her family but didn't know what to do. Upon coming home from a party one night she found her parents in her apartment. The *concièrge* had given them the key. Her father looked dishevelled, his aggressive middle-aged demeanour gone. She got a glimpse of his old age.

"We made it out in the nick of time," her mother said. "We took all we could carry." She pointed to the pile of luggage scattered over the deep blue Chinese rug and her black sable and white ermine coats on the sofa.

"Where's your ring?" asked Tamara. Her mother scratched her head and said, "ERDE. Emerald, ruby, diamonds: EARTH." She laughed, and extracted the big green and red and white family heirloom, a ring made of emerald, ruby, and rose diamonds, from her tightly woven blond wig. She stuck it on her left ring finger. "The bastards didn't get it," she said triumphantly. Her father also laughed and said, "Behave yourself, Babette."

"I'll make us some coffee," said Tamara. "Have a cognac? I'm so glad to see you." She looked at them fondly.

Later she asked, "And the office?"

"Sold," said her mother.

"The villa?"

"Confiscated."

"The money, the cars?"

Her mother looked at her husband and put a finger to her lips. Tamara asked no more. Poor father. For days he sat around doing crosswords, playing Mahler, going for walks, and suddenly shaking himself like a dog that's just come out of water. But by spring he was talking of Colombia and Shanghai where some of his business friends had gone. "A man might get a second start," he said, carefully stuffing his Merschaum.

In May the "Phony War" ended when the Germans marched into Holland, Belgium and Luxembourg. The French newspapers carried notices ordering all German nationals to report to collection points from where they'd be routed to internment camps, paying for their own transportation.

"It's outrageous," raved Tamara. "First they kick us out of Germany, then they stick us into French camps. We're not even Germans any more."

"What are we?" asked her mother.

"Pariahs," said Josh Adler.

"Let's not report," said Tamara. "Let's go to Switzerland."

"Coffee? Desert?" The waiter rolled over a pastry and fruit trolley and Tamara stared at him.

"I prefer Swiss waiters," Hirsch said in German. "The soul of discretion." He was surveying the pastries, deciding against them. "These young *muchachos* are too . . . too . . ."

"Physical?"

"That's it. Cigarette? Waiter, I'll have a cappuccino and a cherry jubilée."

"Yes, sir."

"*Flambé*. What type of brandy d'you use?"

"Let me check, sir."

Tamara thought he was going too far. Clearly it was an act, a sort of gauntlet, thrown down to the world.

"And what will you have, my dear?"

"Switzerland," said Tamara, leaning on her elbows and staring at Hirsch. "We had the money there but when we didn't report they came and arrested us and sent us to camp." She laughed. "They didn't charge us for the transportation."

She was lying. Or at least she didn't tell the whole story. They were never arrested, at least not then, not at home at Boulevard Saint Germain. And they'd had ample time to try to get to Switzerland.

* * *

"The money, father, the money in the Crédit Suisse Union," lighting a cigarette with shaking hands.

"I was going to tell you," he coughed slightly, there's a complication."

"But why, father, why?"

"First of all there isn't all that much. We needed some for emergency loans. We had to get some people out of the country, to Shanghai as I told you. Now don't upset yourself, Tam, dear," he patted her arm, "we'll get it back."

"But when, when? We need it now!" screamed Tamara.

"There's another thing. I can't reach Wolfgang, you know, the man who deposited the money for me. He has to go get it out, it's his signature. Be patient, dear, it'll be alright, I promise you. A slight miscalculation in timing."

"Why didn't you leave earlier?" asked Tamara. "You were quick enough to get everyone else out. And why didn't you deposit the money yourself?"

"I couldn't at the time, I had to stay to help these people."

"Typical. Charity begins at home. Always help others, and perish."

"That's enough," said her mother.

"No, let her, Babette. She's upset. She'll come to see what we were doing. I think I'll go for a walk." He got up and put on his hat and coat.

"How could you talk to him like that," said her mother.

"I'm sorry, mother, but we've got to get a hold of that money if we're to save ourselves."

"We'll talk to him. I'm sure there's something we can do."

When her father returned the next morning he looked terrible. He must have walked all night. Tamara decided to let the matter drop. Soon afterward came the notice to report to camp.

"We won't linger there. We'll be in Shanghai soon."

"How, father, how?" Tamara felt like she couldn't breathe.

"It will be like a camping trip," said her mother. "So we rough it a little. How terrible can the camp be? It's got to be on the beach or in the mountains. A healthy atmosphere. After all, the French are honourable."

"Usually," said Josh Adler.

They sublet the flat and stored the furniture and heavy luggage. "Let's have no more fights then, said her father, our little family's sticking together."

That night they embraced and drank their last Moet & Chandon in a toast to Shanghai.

Next morning her father was gone. He left a note saying:

Will try to see Wolfgang and arrange for power-of-attorney so that we can get the Swiss money.

* * *

"A little more champagne, Goddess?" Hirsch poured. It was getting chilly and Tamara drew her wrap closer. "How late is it?"

"It's past the witching hour."

"That late? I hadn't noticed."

"It's the company."

She smiled and glanced round the patio. They were almost the only diners left. A weary waiter was leaning against a palm, smoking a cigarette.

"Ready for a nightcap?"

They rose and the bill appeared as if by magic. "Let's go up to your room."

"Want to seduce me?"

"But of course."

She looked at him speculatively. "How about friends for now?"

"You're sure?"

"I'm not sure of anything."

"Well, if you change your mind."

"Fair enough."

He smiled and guided her to the bar and ordered two brandies. "So, Goddess, you're sailing with us?"

"I have to, I guess, else my number's up. You see, I'm engaged to this Spanish diplomat who's waiting for me in Cuba. She wrinkled her patrician nose. "Don Xavier Garcilaso de Montalvo. So I'd better marry him before someone else grabs him."

"I see your point. Congratulations. Not much money left and the visa's about to expire? The jail here's full of people without visas."

"We haven't been able to get at our money in Switzerland.

So far." She bit her lip. "In truth, I don't know where my father is. He was in Switzerland, then he came back for us and they stuck him in the camp. But he escaped and I fear he's joined the Resistance."

"From what I've heard of the Red Adler he wouldn't stick around any camp long. Couldn't afford to. Don't look so sad, Tamara." For the first time he called her by her name. "And what about your mother?"

"She died in camp."

"I'm so sorry."

"Enough. Let's talk about you." She looked at him; her clear green eyes had lost some of their coldness. Perhaps it was the champagne.

Hirsch took his time, but she kept her gaze on him. Finally he said, "OK, my dear. The lady I was married to . . ."

"Your wife."

"My wife. And UFA's pride and joy, divorced me and married an S.S. *Obersturmbannführer*. All on account of the man with the club foot."

"An actress, then?"

"A star."

"So you got it from both sides?"

"You might say that. My career and my wife."

"I . . . I'm sorry." There was an awkward silence. She took his hand in hers. "Do you feel bitter?"

"You might say I don't feel at all. Feeling's a luxury. I made up my mind never to think about it again."

"It sounds so easy."

"One has to do it. What else is there?" He held on to her hand and looked at her searchingly. She disengaged. It would be so easy to sleep with him, and so comforting, but she had to be on her guard.

"And now, I must say good night. Tomorrow is my day of reckoning." She sighed.

"Well, if you must, you must." He lit a cigarette and for a moment looked as if he couldn't bear to return to the ship.

But then he said quickly, "Then let us rouse the porter to get a cab." He kissed her hand. "Good night, Goddess. Thank you for a great evening and don't forget, we expect you aboard."

She gave him a quick kiss but Hirsch turned round and waved to the night porter. He's withdrawn again, she thought sadly. A moment earlier he seemed so open, so close, that for a short while he'd made her feel less alone, less isolated. She went up to her room, locked the door, undressed and fell into a troubled sleep.

6

Herr Steinheil found no rest. He paced around the decks topside and discovered he deeply resented the presence of people sitting in deckchairs and breathing in fresh sea air for which they had not paid. They should be in steerage, he felt, with the rest of the riff-raff, especially those from Casablanca. But then he remembered, they were only to come aboard in Lisbon. A deckchair held high above his massive head, butting the air like a hornless bull, he charged with an enthusiastic thrust of his powerful shoulders and arms but rage did not guide him well. He missed his opponent, stumbled and nearly plunged overboard. His next thrust crashed wood on the rail but the third attempt connected wood to flesh and *Herr* Steinheil let out a Teutonic howl of victory. It was, however, shortlived. A puny, contemptible, rag-tag collection of enemies ganged up on the noble figure, and chased him in a headlong plunge behind the lifeboats. By now at least a dozen passengers were swinging chairs like sumo wrestlers and Steinheil, bleeding from a deep cut on his forehead, emerged cautiously, grabbing chairs with renewed fury and hurling them overboard. A crew party moved in and separated the combatants. Pressing a handkerchief to his wounds, Steinheil shuffled over to *Frau* Steinheil who beheld the defeat of her spouse in happy astonishment. Steinheil put on his contrite St. Bernard's mien and escorted his wife down to the women's section with abject humility. He'd been philosophical about their separation in camp and turned down one of the 15 choice cabins on the upper decks offered him by the pimp François. Papa Steinheil cherished as yet unformulated plans for a glorious bachelor sea voyage, especially after seeing the tall young redhead whose name seemed to be Tamara something.

"You keep the children, sweetheart, and I'll rough it in steerage with the menfolk." He gave his short, sharp laugh. "We will save the extra cabin money for our new life." He conveniently ignored the fact that she, with small children, was getting a raw deal. But he knew she wouldn't object. She never did. It wouldn't have done any good. Camp and the ship had exacerbated her insecure position. Steinheil was her cross to bear.

The night had deepened. People made their beds on deck, under the stars that seemed so near. The murmur and hustle gradually subsided and at last silence fell over the ship as the waves tumbled in softly. Ancient as the planet, they flowed smoothly, gurgling as if in subdued laughter at the fools and knaves on their backs.

* * *

Uschi lay on her bunk and gazed drowsily into the half-light of the steerage. Below, her mother tossed in her sleep. Uschi wiped sweat from her face. Normally she never perspired but now the heat covered her like an eiderdown. She thought of the beach at Cadiz with its cool breezes. They'd loitered there six weeks waiting for the *Baleares*. She'd been content to wait forever but her father began to worry about money. Then she saw herself in camp delivering the mail and acting out her favourite role as femme fatale, vamp to her adoring fans. Men. She never really thought about women, and only lately of her friend Bea, who was or wasn't in trouble, depending whether you believed François. She'd never been friendly with other girls, or at least not overly so, and certainly not with her mother. In camp, her male audience was captive; some were rather wealthy, and all were sympathetic.

Until she met the commandant Uschi had never felt moved to prolong her playful one-night or afternoon encounters. Her whole plump little person seemed to ignite men, making them dream of God knows what.

Because in a way, men did not interest her. Locked up and deprived of freedom, they lacked the authority she craved, the power to tell others what to do and where to go. She'd never thought of power until they were crammed into the transport with not as much as a "By your leave." What would *Fräulein* Schneider have said? She, who told them the Führer's hairs might be brown or black but were golden in the back of his neck. Of course it was only hearsay.

Power vibrated from the tall commandant, whose aphrodisiacal symbolism she recognized at once. The Prince had it too, but his was more spiritual. The commandant, shades of Freud, seemed to spread it around him like hay ready for mowing. For Uschi, whose life had been pulled out from under her, this sexy father spelled warmth and protection. She felt her life was no longer a gift but had to be defended, justified, earned. But the commandant, this marvellous man, gave her back her childhood. With him she was innocent, deserving of life.

She hated the women in the barracks; they always picked on her. Her own mother, at times, was the ringleader. Other moms fought for their daughters, shielding them against attacks. Not hers.

7

Bea was describing her new find. "He's gorgeous." She swallowed hard, searching for another adjective.

"He has a big round face," said Norma Polanski.

Uschi looked to Bea for confirmation.

"He's a high forehead and twinkly blue eyes," said Bea. "His name is Helmut and he doesn't notice me."

"He's real smart too," said Norma.

"But you said Michel was gorgeous."

"For a guard."

"Till he got transferred down to the men?"

Bea ignored that. "Wasn't I lucky to meet Helmut?"

"Who doesn't notice you."

Bea sighed. "That's where you come in."

"You also said Antonio was gorgeous," said Uschi.

"Did I? Antonio and his knife!"

"What's the knife got to do with his looks?"

Bea gazed at Uschi obliquely. "A lot."

"He hasn't been up here lately?"

Bea shrugged.

"Gorgeous no longer?"

"It's the knife. I'm cooped up here behind barbed wire and that madman thinks he owns me."

"They're all alike," said Norma.

"So why'd you carry on with him?"

Bea shrugged. "A dance, a laugh . . ."

"Purely platonic!"

"Well, perhaps not entirely purely."

"So the knife follows the hanky panky."

"That's how they are," said Norma.

"Enough of Antonio," said Bea. "You tell Helmut I adore

him, I'll get you a pass."

"Oh? Must I?"

Bea cuddled up to her. "Please, Usch, pretty please?"

Uschi loved being cuddled, could never get enough of it. "We'll see," she promised her friend.

They met behind the field kitchen of *îlot* K. The kitchen was a small open-air roofed-over area where volunteer cooks struggled from dawn to dusk with cinders in their eyes to keep the fires going under heavy iron kettles. By late afternoon they'd served the thin evening soup and the place was deserted.

Helmut was about 18. And gorgeous, Uschi had to concede. For once Bea had not exaggerated. Not as tough as a soccer player but compact, with a gamin face, cute nose and blue eyes. Uschi fully intended to proposition him for Bea. Darkness set in as the sky turned aflame with its magic Pyrénées sunset. Uschi gazed at it from the orange crate and Helmut squatted companionably on the kitchen floor. Both munched fistful of sticky brown sugar from the barrel, the only edibles around.

"D'you come here often?" he asked into the stillness.

"Off and on. It's my hide-out from the barracks. When it's dark and gloomy and I can't make them prop up the drop."

"Prop the drop? You're quite the poet, aren't you?"

"Slats. The drop slat windows. According to Bea I'm an intellectual."

"Who's Bea?"

Here was her chance, but she was anxious to explain to someone what bothered her in the barracks, why she had to escape when the slats were shut down. She'd never defined it to herself, but as she tried to tell him it became clear. "It's the fear, the smell of fear, God, how I hate it."

"Fear?"

"Have you noticed it? Isn't it in your barracks too?"

Helmut frowned. "You know, I never thought of it that way, but now since you mention it, I suppose it's true."

"It doesn't bother you?"

"Aw, I don't let things bother me that much," he slapped his knee. It stuck out of a hole in his pants that, Uschi decided, on him looked good.

"Maybe you're right," she said doubtfully, "but my dad's plenty bothered. He and that young lawyer friend of his have these long talks. Strategy sessions. Planning things."

"Well, we're here. I guess there's nothing much we can do about it," said Helmut, smiling through even white teeth.

"My dad says there's always something you can do. The Prince too."

"Who's he?"

Uschi smiled. "My *guru*, my friend."

"Ah. So why be afraid, then?"

"This fear's like a drippy faucet, I can't help it. I seem to be soaking it up like a sponge. If you squeeze me it'll stream out of me."

He gave her a good squeeze and she slapped his hand. "No kidding, sometimes I feel so pregnant with it that I think I need an abortion."

"Now that's serious."

"Also impossible. They don't do it here, no facilities. Believe me, I've asked. No matter. I only feel symbolically pregnant."

"But you feel other things too?" He moved in on her as they watched the sun sink orange-red behind the horizon.

Before she had time to ask him to clarify this remark she found herself on the damp ground, one sticky hand around his hard shoulder, the other still clutching the brown sugar, and Helmut lustily pumping away in her. When it was all over, she said, "This was so sudden. D'you do this often, I mean, your *mode d'opération*. If so, you gotta learn to approach a lady with sweet talk — the Spaniards call it romance and they do it very well. You could skip the knife routine, though. Ooff, I forgot to tell you, Bea adores you and wants to be your girl friend."

She got up from the ground and brushed off her skirt and he said, "Who's Bea?"

"My best friend here in camp."

"I adore *you*," he put his arm round her and ruffled her soft hair.

"Well, thanks. But what should I tell Bea?" She frowned. "Getting you two together was the purpose of our meeting here and now look what's happened."

"I told you, you worry too much, baby. It'll all come out in the wash. What time is it?"

They looked at the darkening sky and he said, "I must run. We'll discuss it next time, *ciao* for now." He kissed her tenderly and left her squatting on the orange crate, slowly munching sugar from her hand.

★ ★ ★

"You talked to him?"

"Who?"

"Helmut!"

"Sure." Uschi wished she'd never heard of him.

"Sooooooo?"

"He's not exactly an intellectual, you know."

"So who cares, what'd he say about me?"

"Ughugh, nothing memorable, I guess; really Bea, he's the guy who doesn't notice you."

"I know, and you're supposed to fix that." She held up her knitting: "Do you think he'll like it?" It was a multicoloured muffler, made out of bits of wool industriously collected from people in *îlots* G, H and I. With her bounty from *îlot* I, Bea figured there was enough wool not to bother to solicit *îlot* J.

"Well?"

"It's very nice. Somebody will like it."

"Helmut. It's for Helmut."

"Helmut will love it," said Uschi, "and he's better looking than most, any day."

"Now you made me drop a stitch," Bea frowned, "knit one, purl one . . . you needn't grin at me, you always let me down . . . purl one, knit one . . . I told some people you're a scholar . . ."

"Ah, the quantum theory again; a tenuous connection with my course in qualitative analysis."

"So you remember . . . six, five, four . . ."

"And that from a person who can't count backwards from ten. But do not worry, your Helmut's not stupid, haha, only sort of half smart."

"Half smart, quarter smart," counting stitches, "he's the most gorgeous thing. Go talk to him again, in his *îlot*, I'll see to the pass."

"I've my own pass."

"Oh? Since when, may one ask."

"Since I met the commandant."

"What commandant?"

"Ughugh, he's a chief . . . a sort of overseer . . . over the whole caboodle. The other civilian *îlot* chiefs," Uschi said cheerfully.

"Well, I'll be . . . purl two, knit one."

Uschi glowed as she thought of the pass the blond giant had given her, a *carte blanche* to all the *îlots*. With it, she could get past the formidable F-barrier to the main infirmary and its nightly cabaret, and even to the *îlots* of the Spaniards and the International Brigade. It was a small pass, easy to handle, and all she'd have to do was place her thumb firmly over his picture.

"Come visit me at my office," he'd said, "anytime. And don't worry, I've a spare pass." He had the same deep reassuring voice her father used to have before all these happenings, and was more available than the Prince who was often far off.

Uschi thanked him profusely. What luck. She'd met him on one of her strolls along main street, without a pass, as she confided to him breathlessly. He was in the company of her own *îlot* chief, a pleasant corpulent lady named Mrs. Wolf. He laughed and gave her the pass. Mrs. Wolf told her she didn't have to go see him but to Uschi he was so much more intriguing than all the silly boys, and she was flattered by his attention. She stuck out her lower lip and said nothing to Mrs. Wolf. But she knew damn well that she'd see him again.

She could feel no fear around her at that moment. Yet she knew it was there. It was there always, lurking around the camp like a monster, waiting to get it's fangs into her. No one could shield her from it. Certainly not her father, and probably not even the commandant. Yet she knew also, deep within her, beneath that fear, in another dimension, that she must survive and escape it, rid herself, divest herself of it before it consumed her.

She could hear the Prince: *Uschi has to survive whole.* What did he mean? She frowned and pulled at her nails. He did not even want her to be afraid, she thought. Fear was a cowardly thing.

Can one ever get rid of it? It makes me feel so guilty. Almost as guilty as my mother makes me feel. Without this fear life seemed easy. She was on top, people smiled at her and the camp red tape unravelled like a smooth yoyo. Food and passes appeared without effort, and there was lovely fall weather. At this point Uschi felt young and strong, healthy and unscarred.

It could not last. Nothing could, according to the Prince. Life was an endless flow. Up or down, depending on how you looked at it. Soon enough the demons showed their claws again. The women in the barracks hated her, were jealous, and the tiniest incident might set them off. The fear was everpresent, waiting in the wings.

Uschi fought bravely against it, a small warrior going into battle, winning and losing. Each day she waged a war between horror and happiness. "It's enough to make you seasick the way I go up and down," she told Bea.

"Well, at least you go up. Most people in this place only go to hell. It's what makes this place so boring."

Uschi smiled at Bea's ultra sophistication. "I don't find it the least bit boring here. I think it's very interesting. A social experiment. I'm happy. At least at times."

She liked to be happy. Little Miss Sunshine of the Pyrénées — a junior femme fatale. Her daily postmistress romps amused good-looking prisoners and guards alike. She hated ugly men. Women she ignored. When she was happy she didn't feel she was missing out, missing love. She hugged herself, full of delight. She was her own centre, her own love, growing, growing . . .

* * *

"I liked the wine," said Uschi.

"Yes, it was a lucky haul," he said. "We were able to get hold of a whole case." The commandant sat up in bed and looked at her with a slight grin. "What else did you like?"

"Oh," she said politely, "that wasn't bad, either." She really preferred the wine. She let out a luxurious burp. I'm stuffed. Everything was delicious."

"I'm glad. Too bad you don't get as much from it as I do, *Liebchen.*" He patted her fondly, "You miss a lot. You see, for me it's a great . . . an enormous explosion."

"And the earth shakes?"

He laughed. "It will come for you, too, all in good time. You'll tell me."

Obviously he expected a long stay in camp, she thought, wondering briefly how her father's sessions with the young attorney were going. "I'm only a beginner," she said modestly.

He laughed again. "Little doll. How you remind me of my wife."

"Wife! You're married, then. Where is she?"

"In Canada."

"Canada? How'd she get there?"

"It's a long story. I've some connections in Canada and I thought she'd safely sit out the war there, breathe the good air and eat the good food."

"Like the Dutch Queen. Will you join her?"

He lit a cigar and thoughtfully blew out the smoke. "Who knows."

"D'you miss her?"

"Not as much now that I have you." His blue eyes darkened as he pulled her close to him.

"Maybe I ought to go back to my barracks."

"Oh, stay and have breakfast with me, *Liebchen*. We'll heat water for your bath."

"Bath?" squealed Uschi, and then she drifted to sleep in his arms, snuggling contentedly against his broad chest.

* * *

Next morning saw a scene of untroubled domesticity in the partitioned off half of the rooms the commandant shared with the assistant commandant. A delighted Uschi wiggled in the primitive hot tub while the commandant hovered over her with a huge pink sponge.

"It sure beats washing at the wooden trough, in full sight of the populace."

"Don't tell me. You wash outside in this weather?"

"Only if I can't find a bucket to carry the water to the barracks," Uschi assured him, shivering at the thought of the eight spigots spilling their pure and icy Pyrénées water for the ablutions of the inmates.

"WATER HOURS FROM 10:00 TO 14:00, NO LOITERING." Except, she thought ruefully, from 11:00 to 13:00, or 10:00 to 11:00, or any other time the water stopped. She looked at him and grinned, "Sometimes I bring the ice in and let it melt on me. As a lesson to the smelly old dames. You should see their faces when it smokes."

"Why not wait for the Friday showers, you crazy girl, you'll catch your death of cold."

"How's a cold of the bladder for a start? But I can't wait till every second Friday, I'd smell as bad as them. It's heaps of trouble. Line up and wait for the guards, march out of the *îlot*, in pairs, line up again, get soaped, with the water sometimes so hot you can't rinse off, and march back in the cold air, soapy.

"You poor kid," rubbing her back vigorously. "It's better with me?"

"Yes!" Papa Commandant bathed his baby. "Ooff, you're tickling me." She sneezed. "It's thinking of the spigots. Makes me pee, too."

"Now?"

"I can wait. But sometimes I do. I laughed so hard at Michel the other day at the F-barrier I peed into my panties. Michel's the guard from our *îlot*. He comes from Caumont, in Normandy." She thought of André who'd been from Normandy, too. And now he was gone. She said quickly, "Michel was telling me this joke about poisoned mushrooms. As if anyone has seen mushrooms around here. He's so dense he didn't notice a thing." She smiled delightedly.

"You girls are sure friendly with the guards."

"D'you want to hear about the mushrooms? This man was killing off his four women, one wife and three girlfriends. Three died from poison mushrooms. Guess what the fourth died from?"

"I'm sure you'll tell me."

"A blow to her head when she didn't want to eat the mushrooms."

He laughed. "Come on, you wicked little miss, let's get you dried off and have our breakfast."

"It's so nice and warm, can I sit just a little longer? Please, please?"

"All right, little miss. You can stay till I count to ten. It's getting late."

She made a face.

"One, two, three . . ."

When he came to nine and a half she said, "Turn around."

"Oh?" But he turned obediently. She dressed and skipped around the room, admiring the furnishings. "I haven't seen so much space since we were kicked out." Her eyes misted. "We lived in a beautiful high-ceilinged apartment, opposite the zoo, on a street with linden trees."

"Many of us did. How do you like your eggs?"

"Scrambled, please. Sausages, too? And real coffee?"

"Another cup?"

"I haven't had any so long now. Even at home it was black water and here the water's sometimes not even black."

"And now you must go. I've work to do." He bundled her up. "Put on your shoes."

"It's too nice here." She looked sadly at her car tire clogs.

"I'll get you a pair of shoes."

"Oh, I've got a pair. I'm saving them for when we get out of here."

"Do you think you will?"

She looked at him out of her precocious hazel eyes. "Sure, why not?"

⋆   ⋆   ⋆

Uschi felt sick. Her period was going into its third week, but still every morning she waddled off to the typhoid barracks to help feed and wash the sick old ladies. She combed the strands of thin white or yellow hair. No more blue rinses for them, she thought with a mixture of amusement and horror. Uschi felt so weak this morning that her hand shook and she spilled the bowl of watery lukewarm soup on her charge. The woman shrieked with her last strength. The spoon clattered from Uschi's hand to the wooden floor and the commotion brought over a wrathful supervisor.

"Let's pay some attention to what we're doing here, Miss Daydream."

"Yes, Madame," said Uschi as she fainted.

She came to on her strawsack, her mother's tragic mien falling slowly into focus. "Ha! Just what I expected! O God, O God, what a fright you gave me when they brought you in. Didn't I tell you not to go near those poor old ladies. Do you see Mrs. Strohwise's Fanny going? O God, O God, what's going to happen next?"

"And how was I to get out of it, mother?"

"Fanny Strohwise did. Of course she's not running around camp playing postmistress, claiming to sleep over to watch the mail, making herself conspicuous with the men. You could have said no."

Uschi felt this was a dirty blow when she felt so sick, but in a way she had to agree with her mother because the word "no" seemed to have disappeared from her vocabulary. Her mother was of the old school where "discretion surpassed valour." But she knew for a fact her mother was also guilty of making googoo eyes, especially when no one was looking. Since no one had ever caught her mother, no one had to give her "the benefit of doubt." This was one of Uschi's chief grievances. Perhaps her mother didn't realize (was it possible?) that she was a flirt of the first order, never having enjoyed the efforts of *Onkel* Fritz, the Freudian, or Drs. Vogel, the Adlerian, and Heldenheim, the Teutonic Jungian, to whose offices Uschi had been tirelessly dragged.

"And don't you put on your know-it-all face, Miss, even after what *Onkel* Fritz told you." Her mother ran her fingers through her thick, wavy brown hair and circled the strawsack with mincing little steps.

"You're making me dizzy, mother."

But her mother went right on circling. The rhythm of her steps rivalled the dull drip of the rain on the barracks roof.

Since no one in the barracks paid the slightest attention, Uschi closed her eyes and hoped her mother would go away. Next time she woke up, she'd left. In the morning she felt a little better.

"Have you told Daddy?"

"Not yet."

"Oh please do. I need some laughs."

"There isn't anything to laugh about, Miss Postmistress. Besides, you know your father is pathologically unable to manage a pass. God knows, other men get passes."

"He hates lying to them. But now he doesn't have to lie as I'm really sick."

But her mother shook her head. "There's no use worrying him when we know he can't get a pass."

"Oh, mother!" Why was she so negative? Again she felt the old hurt — she'd never been able to cope with her mother's insensitivity. She needed her dad now. She could hear his quiet voice, "Be patient with her, it's her nerves." It sometimes seemed to Uschi that her mother's nerves encompassed quite a range: politics, that singled her out as chief victim; the camp; bad weather; the barracks women; a universe out of kilter, an absent God . . .

She never asked her father, who was very much in love with his wife, just why she should be patient with her. People praised her mother's classic profile, the Grecian nose, the finely wrought, often frowning, brow, the thick, wavy chestnut hair, the tiny waist, the big bosom. But how could that excuse anything? Her mother wasn't evil, or malicious, even if her sharp tongue sometimes made close encounters with her a little risky. It was just, well . . . Uschi had to face it, her mother was a frivolous person. Perhaps now was the time to point this out to her father.

Her stomach cramped, her head ached. She felt nauseous, and very guilty for becoming this great burden upon her mother's graceful shoulders. She sank into a stone-heavy sleep. Next morning she felt well enough to ask her mother to go in search of a doctor. "And cotton wool, please."

"It's no use," she said, sadly shaking the Grecian profile, "you know they're only coming for dying Nabobs."

"You can be very convincing, Mother. Very! What? No

Doc for female postmistresses? Only for male millionaires, rich political prisoners, famous artists, wise Nobel scientists? Come on. And that after my — not entirely voluntary — exertions in the senior typhoid barracks?"

"My poor child. I told you doing for them won't pay off."

"Mother! I'm not a cash register."

Damn. If the commandant were here, he'd help her. But she couldn't send for him and risk the scandal. Her mother'd never forgive her. If only this stupid menstrual flow would stop. She felt herself getting weaker but no one came, neither her dad nor the commandant. All she could hear was her mother's plaintive voice and she felt herself slipping into a place where such things did not matter anymore. I'm dying, she thought with wonder. It's not so bad. Then she heard the Prince's strong voice, *Get up, Liebchen, and go to the infirmary.* She went back to sleep, greatly comforted. Tomorrow she'd do it.

* * *

"My poor girl," said the nurse, "we've nothing to bring it on, no matter how desirable. And, unfortunately for you, nothing to make it stop. Consider yourself lucky it's not the other way round. Nature will take its course. Go get a good rest, I'll get you some cotton."

"I've been working in the typhoid barracks and I'm on my deathbed for days, weeks."

"Yes, that will do it. Wait, I'll write you a note to be excused from work."

"Hah," said Uschi.

The nurse disappeared into another booth and Uschi heard her say, "Now, just relax, dear, and let's have a look."

"She's too nervous." Uschi heard a familiar voice. "Do what the nurse says, treasure, she's on our side." Where had she heard that voice? It doesn't really matter, I'm too sick to care, she thought, but then it reminded her of her friend

Bea. Suddenly Uschi felt better. She got up to sneak a peak into the neighbouring booth from which little sobs trembled. The nurse's body was blocking out the weeping girl who said, "No one can help me now."

"Tell your mother it's Antonio," said Bea's clear voice. "The one with the curly hair and brown leather jacket who always fixes your bed. Your mother likes Antonio."

"I'm so afraid," sobbed Mrs. Strohwise's virtuous Fanny. Despite her exhaustion Uschi grinned with delight. Now Mrs. Strohwise would have to stop bragging about her Fanny and start hustling to feed another mouth.

8

Uschi loved Marseilles. The sun, the sea, the palm-lined Corniche snaking along the Mediterranean made her almost drunk with freedom. She loved to squeeze into the crowded tram and gaze out at the sun-woven water, humming softly under her breath and ignoring a pinch or two from one of the intrepid, misguided Arabs. She loved the city's good-natured, witty folk, so alien to her heavy, Teutonic roots. They fitted her as snugly as the custom-made gowns her mother forced on her.

The refugee women were housed in the Hotel Terminus, four to a room, and their movements were guided by a somewhat elastic and arbitrary code. Day trips into the nearby countryside were OK, so long as one returned to the hotel by midnight to be greeted by the night watchman's conspiratorial winks. He always made Uschi feel as if she'd just left someone's warm bed as he unlocked the heavy gate with much rattling of his keys.

One of Uschi's first excursions was a visit to the men's camp near Aix-en-Provence. Aix's 100 pretty fountains still spouted the fresh pure water the Roman General Marius, conqueror of the Teuton army, first brought into the city.

It was so pure and fresh that people loved to drink it during the hot summer months. For a while, she sat under the huge trees on the Cours Mirabeau, their crowns touching the façades of stately patrician houses.

Then Uschi walked to the Place des Quatre Dauphins and took a drink from its graceful fountain. Next she had some ice cream, *Ersatz* chocolate, and cautiously approached the camp. Her father was fine and immediately told her his latest collection of refugee jokes. He seemed a little distracted. Her brother was clearly envious. "The rotten apples get all the luck. Only us poor men are stuck in the mud here."

"I don't see any mud. It's lovely sunshine and no one's bothering you. Got enough to eat? Get rid of your lice?" Scrawny 13-year-old Michael looked more scrubbed than in the Pyrénées camp.

"You'll be out of here soon, you'll see," Uschi said, suddenly feeling guilty about being a girl, free to come and go as she pleased. She promised herself that she'd put extra energy in the pursuit of the elusive visa. Cheering them up became a priority.

"See you soon." She kissed her dad.

"Ciao, sis," said Michael, who ran out to play soccer.

*   *   *

Uschi and Bea's favourite haunt was the *Vieux Port* with its spectacular transport bridge and its exotic mix of people. The girls loved the dockside cafés, bars serving pastis, and restaurants with the famous local *bouillabaisse*. On a cliff 500 feet above the harbour towered the huge *Basilica de Notre-Dame-de-la-Garde*.

The two pretty girls strolling along the docks quickly became a familiar sight. Tall Moroccans and Algerians treated them to cigarettes; fishermen offered boat rides. Uschi got used to seeing Bea in animated conversation with Arab sailors, but was too busy with her daily schedule to pay much attention.

One fine Saturday Uschi and Bea set out in a heavy boat with two young fishermen eager to show them the harbour's famous sights. It was one of those clear days when life sparkles and makes one forget war, camps and visas. On top they saw the mighty Basilica guarding the harbour like a heavy messenger from God. Ahead was *Château d'If*, the grim 16th-century prison rock of Edmund Dantès and the Abbé Faria of Alexandre Dumas's *Count of Monte Cristo*.

"I love the *Count of Monte Cristo*; it's so romantic," said Bea.

Romance also seemed to be on the mind of their young hosts. And the voyage soon deteriorated into a game of wiggling from searching fingers and seeking hands.

"What are you, an octa . . . octopus?" asked Bea.

Their giggles subsided with the heavier swells of the sea, "Oh, I'm going to be sick."

"Me too." To take her mind off her queasy stomach, Uschi took the oars and rowed diligently, but after glancing at the beleaguered Bea she quickly gave her the other oar.

"Row, row, row the boat, gently down the stream," they croaked.

"Another of your lousy ideas."

"You could have said no — but then you never do."

"How do we get out of this, genius?"

"Leave it to Aunt Bea."

"Hurry, hurry, I think I'm going to throw up."

"Boys," said Bea, "we simply adore your wonderful company but my friend here is sick, so could we have a raincheck?"

"Next week, then? Saturday?"

"It's a date," cried Bea. And their hosts, after a brief consultation, turned the boat around and landed them safely. The girls rushed off along the *Canebière* and nursed their espressos in one of the spacious outdoor cafés, safely away from their suitors.

"Now you made me fall behind in my schedule again."

"Relax, kid, it's Saturday, Can't you take a day off?"

"Death takes no holiday. Damn, where is it?"

"It? What?'

"The list, my list, oh God, oh God, I hope I didn't drop it in that damned boat."

"You're starting to sound like your mother."

She's right, thought Uschi, furiously rummaging through her pockets and purse. Finally, she fished out a crumpled piece of paper, carefully smoothing it.

"Here, it's yours."

"No, no, you hang on to it."

"I know it by heart."

"Your Bible."

But Uschi saw that her friend did not want to dilute her fascinating Marseilles adventures with the daily routine of strenuous and odious errands in quest of a visa.

"I get dizzy looking at it." Bea handed the list back to Uschi.

"Wake up, stupid. We need an affidavit, visa, quota, passage."

"Hah! You haven't even got the first."

"I have, too. It's on the way."

"You told me it's lost in the mail."

"I'm working on it. Which is more than you're doing."

"I've time."

Uschi gave her friend a sharp glance. "You're fooling yourself, little one. Look around. Why are people rushing, shoving and pushing like crazy? You tell me."

"They're hysterical."

"Next thing you'll say it's human nature."

When Uschi said she was working on their affidavit it wasn't strictly true. Beyond writing to her aunt Millie to ask her to replace the lost document, the family had not done anything. The only one really busy was Uschi. The affidavit had, in fact, been sent years ago to the nearest consulate at home. Their names were on the waiting list, they were duly informed. In the meantime they'd been deported, sent to the infamous camp, and now that they'd managed to get out of there and to Marseilles the consulate informed them the precious document had vanished, lost in the mail between consulates.

"D'you think your aunt will send another?"

"No doubt," said Uschi in a firm voice.

"I'd hate to see all your organizing efforts wasted."

"No, no, no. Right action is never wasted," Uschi was quoting the Prince. "And you better get off your fanny. No time to lose."

"Something will work out. Got any cigarettes?"

"Not this time, Little Miss. Three of our six months are gone . . . three more and it's *adios, muchachos*, back to camp for you."

"Hold it. There's the Arabs. Did I mention the cook on the *Sidi Ben Afghan*?"

"So that's what all the whispering was about."

"No need to be so high and mighty, Madam, they've been offering to smuggle us out to Casablanca."

"Ahhh. The hell-hole of North Africa. Even the scum of Europe are trying to get out of there."

"I thought the scum of Europe were here. Who told you?"

"My father's friend, the young lawyer. The elite's here."

"You could have fooled me. But never fear, he'll get us out."

"Who?"

"The cook, the cook," said Bea impatiently.

"Remember our recent boat ride? Down in the harbour?"

"You don't think? The cook?"

"And his friends . . . why else would he risk it?"

"My, my, have we become cynical.

She might be cynical, but Uschi felt unfailingly, exhilaratingly in control of her life. "I'll be out of here," she said to Bea, "and when I'm out I'll send you a postcard."

9

From dawn to dusk people in the queue snaked around the consulate. They only scattered at nightfall.

Patiently they stood, sat on campstools, squatted on the sidewalk, gossiped and munched food scrounged from the hotel kitchen or the men's camp. Every morning they waited with fresh hope that today would be the day that brought the visa or quota number — a passport to life. Every evening they slunk off. They'd been waiting for years. First in their homes and later in camp, they'd waited to be one of the few fortunate enough to get into that queue — and now they had to wait some more.

"What's new?" said Uschi.

"The guards invited us to go to the movies Sunday. They're expecting new quota numbers," said Bea importantly.

"They always say that."

"They can get us into the consulate anytime," said Bea with a sage nod. "Without waiting in line."

"So we're in. But what about all the stuff we need." Uschi was trying not to mention the lost affidavit.

As if she didn't want to hurt her friend's feelings, Bea said quickly, "Look, there's the cook. From the ship I told you about."

"And his pals. Honestly, getting aboard that ship with him and his pals is not my idea of The Great Escape."

"Allah u Akbar, La Allah il Allah, che sarà, sarà."

"I see your time with the Arabs is paying off."

Still, they had drinks aboard the Moroccan-bound freighter with the cook and his friends and hatched an alternate escape plan. By Sunday they decided to accept the guards' invitation to a Sacha Guitry film, and they did some heavy handholding. On Monday they walked right ahead of the queues and into the consulate when their handsome dates winked them through the holy portals.

"You see, it paid off."

"So we're in. Now what?" They wandered around the consulate. No one talked to them and after a while they left.

But one sunny day around lunchtime Uschi's career as a volunteer interpreter took off when a thin old lady with a walking stick crossed the street from the consulate directly to Uschi and François's table at the café.

"Maybe one of you two lovely children know the English, *ja?*" she asked hopefully. "The consul he no speak Yiddish, and me, I no speak the English. French be all right, too, although not so good."

François invited the old lady to sit down and got up to pull over a chair. "You never do that for me," said Uschi, suspecting ulterior motives.

François shrugged and smiled. "A little cognac for Madame?"

"*Ja*, why not," said the lady gratefully.

"She can't be one of your girls."

"You see the rings, and the silver handle on the walking stick?" whispered François.

"I see."

"Money. That makes her a worthy person in my book."

"François, you don't read." But Uschi could see that this lady was a tough old bird. Like her mother, she'd sit and cry and wail and drive the consul crazy until he'd give her a visa just to get rid of her. Uschi agreed at once to provide her services. "Might as well," she told François, "since I have nothing better to do at the moment."

To the old lady she said, "I can speak anything if I make up my mind to it. Think in it, too. Just put a nickel into me, *Pfennig* or *franc*, and try to stop me. Swahili, Chinese, Mayan, Egyptian, Tibetan — give me a few weeks and out it comes. Let's go."

"*Merde, La Poupée,*" said François in admiration.

"Can't do any harm," Uschi said and gave him a peck on the cheek.

As word got round of Uschi's free interpretation service she quickly became a face inside the consulate. People greeted her. Suddenly she felt accepted, able to survive gossip about her friendship with the old man, the Arabs, Bea, the commandant, poor adorable Helmut and all her other adventures. She now had a ringside view of events in the consulate halls, daily rituals of live drama.

Uschi saw a tall dark woman spread out her jewels, big as hazelnuts, on the vice consul's desk. She was weeping. He shrugged and lifted up his arms, then shook his head, and she fell down and clutched at his knees. Then she collapsed into her husband's arms, shaking and screaming. The consul got his secretary to call for an ambulance.

She sure hasn't got the knack, thought Uschi heartlessly, despite her jewels. My mother could teach her a thing or two. She remembered the casinos at Baden-Baden and Monte Carlo where Uschi, because she was still too young, had to wait outside with Ottilie. There was the same gamble at the consulate, but deadlier.

"*Rouge ou noir,* red or black. *Mesdames, messieurs, faites vos jeux. Rien ne va plus.* Place your bets, ladies and gents. Winners live, losers die." Uschi scratched her head. She'd have to ask the Prince when she wasn't so busy. Just who was winning here, and who was losing? And why?

"We walk now, *ja,* little one," the old lady was nudging her, "we hold up the line."

"What's new at the visa front?" Bea had joined Uschi and *La Tigresse* at the Terminus hotel bar. The place served a double duty: dining room for the refugee guests, and hangout for the neighbourhood whores and pimps. "How's it coming," her mouth full of brioche.

"We have two and a half months left."

"Not good," said *La Tigresse*. "Have another. My treat." Pastry was relatively easy to get at the Terminus.

"Cigarette?" Bea offered *La Tigresse* one from a pack she'd talked off a Moroccan at the *Vieux Port*.

"It may not look too good but I'm hopeful." Uschi was furiously scratching her bare leg.

"You look sort of flushed," said Bea.

"You're not sick, *chérie*?" said *La Tigresse*.

"I'm fine. Leave me alone, both of you." Uschi knew better than to get sick now. "I'm off to the consulate. You coming?"

"No, thanks. I'm after some black market coffee."

"*Ciao*, then."

"*Ciao*."

It pained Uschi to see her friend so unconcerned, her life in Marseilles a new and fascinating toy, filled with charming Frenchmen and Arabs from the ships, refusing to admit to the sense of urgency that drove Uschi night and day.

10

Uschi adored the vice consul. He was tall and handsome, with his smooth dark hair and green eyes framed by long black lashes. He was very serious. Only the sight of the ugly secretary bustling in with another stack of files could make a little smile play across his face. She dressed badly, too, Uschi noted with glee. She could just hear her mother's comments, "Skirts and blouses, like a shop girl, pleated and frilly." What could he see in her, attired in his divine three-piece suit and lovely red silk tie?

Uschi smiled at him every time she happened to pass his office. Had he noticed her? She would have liked to wait for him at night when he left the consulate, like a stage door admirer, but it might make him angry. A person in her situation could not afford to anger a vice consul. Besides, what would she say to him? She'd better not mention the lost affidavit. That would make him feel exploited when, in fact, she adored the man himself. She could talk to him about quantum theory, something the ugly secretary couldn't, she was sure. She smiled.

She began to think of him as her friend, her lover, her companion, a prince in a three-piece suit. In the morning she could hardly wait to get to the consulate to catch a glimpse of him. Forgotten was the commandant, and even François, who patiently waited at the café. Her heart beat wildly the day he asked her, "And what are you doing here all the time, little Miss?"

He'd noticed her! "I am the interpreter," she said proudly.

"A very laudable function, young lady, but what about yourself? Don't you want to go to my country?"

No point mentioning the lost affidavit, Uschi thought sadly, and be told not to expect another appointment without it. "Sure, sir, I'd love to go."

"What's your name, young lady?" he asked, and sent for their file.

The rabbi with the long beard and skullcap and faded black coat had followed the scene. Trembling, he said, "My poor child, now you've done it." Then, quoting an old proverb, he said, "*Go not near the duke if you're not called.* Kaput." And he sank onto his seat, covering his yarmulka with his hands as if they were a prayer shawl, moaning softly.

Uschi frowned. The rabbi was rocking back and forth. How she hated people to carry on in public. It was so undignified. But here came the ugly secretary with their file. The vice consul leafed through it and wrote out an appointment slip for the following week.

Uschi couldn't believe her luck and stammered, "Thank you, sir. She gave him a shy smile and turned to leave, conscious of keeping her back straight. The rabbi threw her a disgusted look, the way she'd sometimes caught people gaze at *La Tigresse*.

She didn't see the vice consul again till two days later when she accompanied a friend of the old lady's. It had been raining all day and when they left the consulate people were waiting for the friend. It was coming down hard now and she did not have an umbrella. Uschi thought there was no point checking for François at the outdoor café so she stood at the door wondering what to do when the vice consul came down the stairs. Alone. The ugly secretary was nowhere in sight.

He smiled at her and asked, in English, "Need a ride?"

Unable to believe her good fortune, Uschi nodded, mute.

"You'll be drenched. Wait here till I get the car."

He drove up, opened the passenger door. "Jump in." They drove off. "Where's home?"

She swallowed hard and directed him down the *Canebière*, past the *Vieux Port* to the Red Light District and the Hotel Terminus. *La Tigresse* stood by the entrance smoking a cigarette. Uschi got quickly out of the car and shot a glance back at the consul. He seemed surprised.

"Thanks a million, sir," she mumbled.

"You're entirely welcome," he said, and drove off through the downpour.

"Ahhh, you're managing nicely, *La Petite*." *La Tigresse* pulled her into the hotel and out of the rain. "Who's the dreamboat?"

"The vice consul," whispered Uschi, and her friend smiled.

"God, I'm hungry. Wonder what's for supper?"

"Chickpeas," said *La Tigresse*.

11

When the time came for their appointment Uschi collected her family and took them to the vice consul's office. Dressed in a pale linen suit, pale pastel shirt and maroon silk tie, he looked up from the file on his desk and sternly eyed mother, father, brother until his eyes came to rest on Uschi, the interpreter.

There was a long pause. Michael fidgeted. Her mother clutched her purse, and her father forced a smile. Uschi stared straight ahead, oblivious to the street noises streaming through the open windows. The consul closed the file and seemed to come to a decision. He looked at Uschi and said, "Raise your right hand. Do you swear your affidavit's in the mail?"

Uschi gazed at him adoringly, raised her right hand and, willing to say anything he told her, repeated, "I swear it."

Down came the consular seal. "Congratulations," said the vice consul as he handed them their visas. They shook hands all around. Outside in the hall people embraced them ecstatically, like the backstage crowd after a successful opening. Uschi looked for the rabbi, but he was not present. Too bad.

"And we haven't even used up all our time. I must tell Bea." But first they crossed the plaza to the outdoor café to tell François.

"*Merde, La Poupée*, I take my *chapeau* off to you. A talented daughter."

"Yes," said Uschi's father.

"Sometimes," said her mother.

François ordered champagne and they toasted the brand-new visas. Then her father said they must catch the tram back to Aix. Her mother wept. When she dried her tears she sighed and whispered, "Make François buy us dinner first."

* * *

Now Uschi's troubles started in earnest. There was a bad scene at the refugee agency when they showed up with their visas.

"How dare you get them without booking passage?" screamed the man who was supposed to handle their file. His curly mop shook over his horn-rimmed glasses.

"I beg your pardon?" said her mother.

"You realize, dear lady, that I have people with passages booked waiting for the visas you've taken — almost under false pretences, I might say."

"And I say to you, how dare you talk to me like that, you monster?"

The agency man lit his pipe, puffed passionately, and pronounced: "But it won't help you, I promise you. Without the quota numbers, your visa's no damn good, and without the ship's passage you won't be able to get them."

This made Uschi very angry. "You want to bet?"

"Bet, my dear?" He laughed, belly and curls wobbling. "I'm not a betting man. But to show you my heart's in the right place, I'll take your bet."

"He hasn't got a heart," Uschi said to her mother, "but I bet you the best dinner on the black market I'll get those quotas."

"OK by me. You bring me those quotas, and you got your passages."

"Done," said Uschi, and they shook hands on it.

Out of the corner of her eye she glimpsed him suppressing

a tight smile and whispered to her mother, "He doesn't know us."

"Not yet," said her mother. "I've an idea. Let's go to that place on the *Canebière* and see if we can scrounge ration coupons from the man who likes you so much. The one who always wants to buy you a dress."

"Oh, Mother, don't you ever think of anything but food!"

"Not when I'm hungry."

Why did her mother always manage to make her feel like a prostitute, when *La Tigresse* treated her like a sweet young girl?

*   *   *

They spent July surveying the consulate for news of arriving quota numbers. Uschi's source was one of the handsome consulate guards. Still, after a month, nothing had happened.

"One and a half months to go yet," Uschi marked on her calendar. She hated reminding Bea.

In the afternoons they haunted shipping companies in quest of a letter, any letter, something on paper promising passage, should a ship be found. Ships were still running to Africa, Morocco, Martinique and such places. After much of her mother's hand-wringing and weeping, they attained this limited goal in the form of just such a document.

Then, one morning, one of her guard friends came rushing across the plaza to the café. "Good morning, *La Petite*. Quick, go get your family, a dozen quota numbers came in last night."

Uschi took the tram to Aix and persuaded camp headquarters to issue emergency passes to her father and Michael. The family met after lunch and rushed to the consulate, presenting visas and the required ship agent's letter . . . promising passage on the first ship out.

"These numbers must have had your names," smiled her vice consul. "Here are the last four."

83

Uschi kissed him. Her mother kissed him. They embraced each other and then her father and Michael caught the tram back to camp. Uschi and her mother went in triumph to the agency man who started howling.

"Now you've done it. You've jumped the line and taken four places away from people with visas. Visas which will expire."

"You know how long we've been waiting?" cried her mother.

"No difference to me. The whole world's waiting."

"Years," stressed her mother.

"You jumped the line," and he was not chuckling now.

"You promised us passages if we bring you the quotas," said Uschi, "and here they are. We made a bet, and you lost. But I'll be generous. We'll still buy you dinner in the black market restaurant."

"I also said it was impossible for you to get them. You must have done something you shouldn't. Hmmmm?"

"We got them," said Uschi, inspecting her infected fingernails.

"What did you want us to do?" cried her mother. "Lay down and die?"

* * *

The agency had hired a ship to sail from Spain. The *Baleares*. They paid their tickets with black market money and set out for the Spanish consulate. Different locale, same scenario. Getting through the door was easy enough, but a visa was . . . "how shall I put it," said the secretary, "out of the question." Spain's border was sealed "for the duration," whatever that meant, but Uschi's mother refused to take that sitting down. "I've not come so far to be stopped now. We need to travel to Spain to board this ship. That's the long and short of it. No use talking to me, I haven't heard a word you said. Certainly not 'NO!' " She repeated this all

84

afternoon. It was her mantra, making it clear to the consular staff that she was going to sit here till she had the visa or hell froze over, whichever came first. By the end of the third day they were faced with the choice of handing her a visa and going home or locking her up for the night and facing her again in the morning.

"I knew you'd do it," said Uschi during their simple dinner of chickpeas.

12

They almost missed their train. "My arms are going to break off any minute now," Uschi told her mother. Between them they dragged all their new possessions, bought with black market money left over from the purchase of their berths on the *Baleares*.

"Hurry," said her mother.

"Look, there's a cab."

"Don't talk, just hurry."

"What have you got against cabs, Mother?" asked Uschi, not daring to stop and wipe her damp forehead.

"We'll miss the train."

This made no sense to Uschi but she struggled on. It was getting late when she lumbered up the station steps. She decided to rest for a second to pull down the new blue-and-white-striped blouse which seemed glued to her back. It wouldn't be the first time she'd missed a train. Once, coming back from boarding school she'd been early enough at the station for a short visit to the nearby Museum of Fine Arts. But she lingered and missed two departures. The third was snowed in and they ran out of food in the dining car.

"There's your father, pacing the platform."

"Late as usual," said Michael. "Gee, where'd you get all this stuff?"

"From this little tailor."

"Tut-tut, how can you bear to associate with your poor raggedy family?"

"Now don't squabble, children," said her father. "Let's be thankful we're getting out of here."

"Finally," said her mother, plunking herself down in their second-class compartment, "I can rest."

"Goodbye, Marseilles," called Uschi and blew the city a fond kiss. "It's been fun."

"Hmmm," said her mother.

"I learned a lot of soccer at the camp," said Michael.

"Permit me, ladies," said her father as he brought out a Havana. He unwrapped the cigar carefully and lit it.

"Look at you, Arthur," said her mother.

"A special occasion, Kate." But they couldn't relax. Not yet. There was still a tension in the compartment. The restless feeling seemed to be shared by the others bound for the *Baleares*, whom they met in the corridors and in the dining car. Uschi discovered the sister-and-brother team she'd beaten to the last four quota numbers at the consulate that day and marvelled that they'd managed to get two more. She also saw other familiar faces from the queues, the hotel and the agency, but the rabbi from the consulate was not among them. Relief screamed from all the faces: people so different in their former lives were now thrown together on the last refugee ship. But underneath there also lurked fear — would it ever cease?

The sun was playing across the high rugged Pyrénées; verdant farmland and peaceful villages lay hidden among the hills. The landscape contrasted sharply with the barren camp compounds of their long winter, and Uschi thought of the handsome pilots who had fled for their lives across these rugged mountains only a little while earlier. The train crossed the border from Cerbère to Port Bou. The customs officers, seeing their transit visas and raggedy appearance, made a minimum of fuss. Uschi and her family had crossed these high rugged mountains in far more comfort than any of the Spanish pilots who'd hiked in the opposite direction at night, starving, freezing and risking their lives.

They arrived in Madrid on a hot July afternoon. This time her father treated them to a taxi, which took them to a small hotel. While waiting to hear from the agency they did the tourist rounds. Uschi, proud of the money her father had given her, undertook her private exploration of the Prado with an attractive guide. But Roberto spoiled her enjoyment of the masterpieces, by telling her how much he needed her money to feed his wife and five *niños*. She thought this reasonable and doubled the agreed fee but when she returned to the hotel she had nothing left. Roberto must have taken it, she thought guiltily. Her father wasn't angry but did not give her any more money.

After a week the agency sent word they were to travel to Cadiz to board the boat. Buying tickets in Marseilles had been easy. Buying tickets in Madrid, with Spanish train stock at an all-time low after the Civil War, was a problem. And once more they needed to queue up in the heat, taking turns every couple of hours.

The train to Cadiz was hot and overcrowded. To get a little air, Uschi squeezed herself out to the train's rear. She spent the balance of the daylight hours wedged in between many passengers, winding up in the arms of a gallant middle-aged Spaniard who held her tight and kept her from falling off the back of the train. He continued to smile at her and seemed solicitous of her well-being. In the compartments people were smouldering in their seats while the ticket controller nimbly climbed over bodies stretched out in the aisles. On one of the numerous station stops they bought salamis and soon the smell of garlic wafted through the carriages.

Toward late afternoon Uschi gently detached herself from the man's embrace and struggled back to her family in the compartment. Just when they thought their voyage would never end they arrived in Cadiz and secured a suite in the Hotel Esperanza. Next morning they met more fellow travellers from Marseilles spilling over in the halls, the elevator, the lobby and the dining room. Some had arrived earlier, some were checking in, and dozens were still expected. All were eager to set sail on the mysterious *Baleares*.

Uschi's family enjoyed their nice, spacious suite, their first post-camp luxury after the barracks and the Red Light hotel dormitories, happy to be together again. It was short-lived, and after a week restlessness set in. They'd been permitted only the minimum currency out of France, and the money was going fast. The situation was similar for all the others. With no extra cash, most were quarantined to the hotel dining room and it was not difficult to total the tabs that were being run up.

"Who's paying for all those meals?" said Michael.

"Hush," said their mother, "your father's got a headache."

"And with reason," said Uschi.

"Why don't you children go for a stroll on the boardwalk," said their mother.

"Good idea, Kate."

* * *

The passengers amused themselves as best they could, playing pinochle, fornicating, sunbathing on the empty white beaches, strolling through the picturesque town, flirting and forming passionate attachments that would not last the voyage.

But visas began to expire like yesterday's lottery tickets and nervous vibrations and much gossip about the local jail, a holding institution without habeas corpus, floated through the lobby. "If you're in, you're in for a good long stay," was the word.

"Where's that damn ship? What news from the agency?

After all, they chartered the ship and told us to come here."

After several more weeks of this the man from the agency showed up.

"Oh, he's here is he? What took him so long?"

"I hear he's a real bastard."

The man set up shop on the hotel mezzanine and busily scheduled interviews. Soon screams could be heard throughout lobby and dining room.

"He called me a con artist and fraud man," Uschi's father reported, white-lipped.

"Con man, papa."

"Don't be so smart," said her mother.

"What am I to do, let my family sleep on the beach?"

"So, in your old age, you're turning into a con man, Arthur!"

But her father had lost his sense of humour. "I tried to calm him down, Kate, but the more I explained the louder he screamed. Everyone must have heard him. I have to sit down, my knees are shaking."

"We heard him, all right." said Michael. "Must be well-fed to scream so loud."

"What's he look like?" asked Uschi.

"Shock of curly black hair and tortoise-shell glasses."

"It's Maurice," said Uschi.

"You should have heard him when we came to him with our quota numbers," said her mother.

"I told him I'll repay the damn hotel bill, every damn last peseta, but he didn't seem to hear me, kept on bellowing like a bull." He ran his broad hand, the hand Uschi loved so much, through hair that was now very grey at the temples.

"I've been a soldier in the war, built up a business, dealt with bank and credit houses, suppliers, customers, and no one ever raised a voice to me, or called me a con artist."

"Don't take it so personal, papa, it's his way of operating. All of us passengers are in the same boat."

"Or wished they were," said Michael. Everyone looked at him, astonished.

"That's what I fear," said her father.

"Where's the ship? Did he say what we're to do? What did he tell you?"

"He was very specific. He wants us to travel to Seville where we're to board, and we're to leave the heavy luggage behind for the ship to pick up."

"Oh? When?"

"He didn't say."

"Oh."

"Well, here we are in Spain," said her mother who could be sensible when the occasion demanded. "It's a vacation until we get our marching orders. So let's enjoy it. God only knows what comes next."

Uschi could hear the tell-tale tremor in her mother's voice. It betrayed a fear of the new world, a place she pictured, Uschi knew, as a gigantic slave-labour camp. Her mother tried a smile. "This isn't a bad little hotel. We take our meals, a little exotic to be sure, and we have the sun, the sea and the beach. We could have done worse."

"Many have," said Uschi, thinking of Helmut, and the nice man who gave her his apple.

"That's my girl," said her father.

Uschi adored the beaches of Cadiz — clean white sand, and empty but for a few señoritas with their duennas, older ladies clad in black from head to toe. These ladies seemed to watch in horror — the invasion of barbarians from another world, in scant bathing gear, who actually swam in the water. What would the Prince say? Uschi thought. He'd laugh to see us swimming and dancing, happy, and not worrying about the ship.

Life was perfect. The Spanish boys were perfect, as handsome as the young pilots in camp, so good-looking that she never knew who to admire first. They followed her in the streets, stopped with her at the wonderful shop windows, and even came to the hotel. She simply loved it. She'd worked so hard to get them out of Marseilles before the

dreaded six-months permit ran out, before they were transported East. She thought again: Nothing good came out of
the East. Not the Near nor the Far East. At least not in
the Twentieth Century. She thought about those pious
yogis *Onkel* Fritz had visited — or was it Dr. Siegfried
Heldenheim? She always mixed up the tales of her psychiatrists, "My spiritual fathers." She smiled. She was safe
now, *safe.*

"You're scratching yourself again," she heard her mother
say, "and you were doing fine in Marseilles."

"I was busy getting us out, mother."

"Well, you did other things too, remember François. And
those Arabs."

"Oh, mother."

Her mother frowned. "François was all right, of course. A
nice young man, good-looking too, but those Arabs, the
same as the types following you here."

"They're handsome too. And most respectful."

"Gypsies."

"Mother! There can't be that many gypsies on the face of
the Earth."

"I know what I see."

Uschi looked at her Greek profile and such fair skin in
wonder. What made her apply the word gypsy to such a vast
range of dark-skinned people?

For once her father took sides. Shaking his head, "They
may be well-behaved young men but they're not used to
young ladies going out alone, unchaperoned, so they're
sniffing around you like dogs in heat." He, at least, knew the
difference between gypsies and and the rest of humanity.

But Uschi's body, soft and wide, sent out signals, and
got wonderful responses. These things happened to girls.
Though deep inside she knew it didn't happen to everyone.
At least not in the same way. *Onkel* Fritz had said some
were more open, more finely attuned — and she was one of
them. That last year at home she'd been practically under

house arrest. She'd slept long hours, got up late, and had to be home again at sunset. All that was changed now. Her life was opening up, its first shoots pushing through the ground, and the chorus of male admiration intoxicated her. It was the most admiration she'd ever received, and she could not imagine how she'd ever lived without it. She felt she needed it like food and water. Without it she was afraid she'd wither away as she had at home.

So she loved these young men fervently and impartially, the handsome and the ugly, the young, shy and bold. It confused and tore at her and made her lose focus, but it also wonderfully concentrated her, made her feel more alive. She longed to see *Onkel* Fritz, but he was far away. The commandant, too, was gone.

She wanted to call the Prince, but the Prince was not around very much when things were going well. Who then? She couldn't talk to her mother. And she had never discussed these things with her father. With no one else in sight she had to turn inward again, and out of these depths arose a compassion for both people and the planet. She wanted to live, to love. To survive — so that she could save them.

13

Uschi's ration-free wooden platform shoes with the orange and purple leather tops brought her satisfying attention when she clattered through the hotel lobby. She could walk, run and even dance in these monstrosities. They were infinitely superior to the camp's infernal automobile tires.

The tall, dark, handsome stranger seemed to know her, for he always rose and bowed at her approach. Soon she found herself searching the lobby for him and after a while they talked. He was a medical student at the University of Madrid who had started his summer vacation the minute he saw her at the station, he told her, boarding the train with her family. His name was Carlos and he was so smitten that he decided then and there to forget about travelling home and instead followed the family to Cadiz.

High romance! And people were always calling her a chubby, clumsy teenager. If only Bea could share Uschi's glory.

It was all right, though, she'd get François to tell her. Where was François now? She thought she saw him in the hotel lobby the other day, but she must have been mistaken. There couldn't be two like him. Could there?

Carlos made love to her in a sort of Minotauran maze. It led to one of a long line of rooms, on the wrong side of the tracks, some distance from the hotel. When he discovered she was menstruating he became incredibly angry. And he called himself a medical student! In a profusion of Dr. Vogel's Adlerian theories of inferiority and guilt, Uschi washed him off and decided then and there never to speak to him again. Next day at lunch in the hotel dining room she ignored his meaningful winks.

"Who's the young man?" asked her father.

"What young man?"

"The one over there staring at you."

"Oh? Where?"

"At the corner table, sitting with three blond young men." Her mother's tone seemed to say, "One even has freckles, not a gypsy among them."

"I don't see anyone."

"If you take off your sunglasses, dear. He keeps making the most awful grimaces."

"I never saw him before in my life." She helped herself to more paella and energetically scratched at her heat rash.

The missing ship, it seemed, had turned up. Finally, they were to travel to Seville to board it. This time the trip was uncomplicated. They would go to Seville and leave their heavy luggage behind in Cadiz where the ship would load it. Upon arrival they were lodged in a huge converted château, with a maze of hallways and corridors. Her father did not have to worry about the bill as the man from the agency had made a deal with the management. François seemed to have disappeared.

14

Tamara woke in broad daylight. She squinted at the sun streaming through the open window and jumped out of bed. Her head ached and her throat felt dry. She called for coffee and orange juice and gulped down every last drop. Good God, almost eleven, she'd miss the boat. Rushing into the shower, she gave a nasty thought to Hirsch and his Piper-Heidsieck. Impossible man, she was glad she hadn't spent the night with him after all. But he was kind of nice, too. Sort of sad underneath that veneer. It takes one to know one, she laughed, and then she towelled herself dry and dressed quickly. She didn't really think she'd miss the boat. Better safe than sorry, though, after all Hirsch's talk about people selling cabins under your nose. She hurriedly collected her luggage, broke her second-best bottle of *Nuits d'amour*, and regretted she'd given her other one to the maid. The scent wafted through the suite and made her ill. She quickly closed her suitcases and called for a porter and a taxi.

People were still lined up at the quay. They were remarkably similar to yesterday's hot and thirsty bunch, like desiccated vegetables left on the shelf. Good God, had they been standing here all night? She suppressed a nervous giggle and helped the cabby with the luggage. No one seemed to be around to talk to, or address a request for VIP treatment for the fiancée of Don Xavier Garcilaso de Montalvo. She lit a Gauloise and got in line.

There were bodies in front, and in back of her, none too patient. It was a tense crowd, and as she waited she got this feeling of *déjà vu*. A good part of her last years, before and after Paris, her one glorious moment, had been spent in queues. First at the convent, then in camp, and now, leaving Europe. Drawing deeply on her Gauloise, she gazed at the lady two bodies ahead of her. Xav, at least, would rescue her from the queues.

It was the war. War killed. At the front, at the rear, everywhere. But the queues remained. How many of us in these queues? In good times one queued up for deposits, in bad times for withdrawals.

* * *

"We made it," said the distraught lady in front of Tamara. "I always knew we would. We're survivors. Dimitri had his doubts, despite being a Uvaloff. But, then, he's a scientist."

She smiled at Tamara who smiled back under her sunglasses. The lady's distress seemed ancient — like a wound that had never healed. Certainly not recent, Tamara decided. It clung to her like a tight girdle, covering her slim figure in the worn and slightly soiled Mainbocher suit. A few strands of grey hair had escaped the classic coiffure, but her porcelain-blue eyes glinted surprisingly cool under an aristocratic cranium.

Clearly, Tamara thought, the lady seemed to suffer the after-effects of the revolution, seemed never to have settled

down. She was beached on dry land, so to speak. She still
hoarded an impressive assortment of life-saving equipment
that probably had become irrelevant 20 years ago. Some
flora get chilled pushing too early through frozen ground.
They're not dead, exactly, but not quite living either. They
soak up sunshine and water like healthy plants, store it in
sickly roots, but never quite blossom save for sudden Grace.

Tamara was torn between pity and contempt. Blatant
misfortune always made her uncomfortable. A veteran of
wilful blindness, she usually turned her back on genteel
suffering, discrete poverty. When it shrieked at her in camp
she couldn't cope. Her mother's devout Catholicism was no
help. It pleased her to have the Sisters in the convent
lament her heartlessness, her lack of compassion. She'd
gotten to like the Sisters' image of her as a monster because
it made her seem powerful in a way she knew in her heart
she wasn't. Under the polite smile she'd like to tell them,
"Look here, my good Sister, go chase your tail up a tree."

Gentlewomen didn't do that — didn't declare themselves
in public without allegory or proverb and risk disapproval,
censorship to the point of annihilation. Of course the Sisters thought any deviation from form monstrous. Nuns
tended to see things in black and white. It was their habit.
She giggled.

Guiltily, Tamara made reluctant little cooing sounds at
the hysterical lady. She lit another Gauloise, wondering
how long they'd have to stand under the fiery sun. Any
minute now the lady might break into a more flagrant
display of distress. She recalled battles fought in camp over
the straw in the sleeping sacks, cubes of meat. Here on the
pier they might bring out the firehose — though cold water
would be nice just now. Then take them to jail: the ship
would sail without them. And she was penniless, without
a fiancé to bail her out.

She thought of J.P., the intellectual Latin, and winced. J.P.
had loved her more than the sun and the moon, as he had

often told her. He'd been quite an astrologer, but tight on money. Passion never paid the bills and the French courts tended to be lenient with crimes of passion, though hard on unpaid debts.

She closed her eyes and saw J.P. standing on the ledge. Heaven knows, she hadn't encouraged him to get up there, but then she hadn't stopped him either. In moments of crisis she simply went blank, so she was not too clear on what happened. She knew afterwards she should never have married him — even if he had gotten her out of camp.

"So what could we do?" asked the lady, pushing some stray hairs from her face. "Dimitri was reluctant, but he usually is, and that nice young man assured us it was a fine ship."

Tamara stared at her through her glasses. "A young Corsican, you say? Tall, dark and handsome? Not named François?"

"François, yes. Poor boy. He had to sell potatoes on the black market to help his sick mother."

"But of course."

"A lovely young man. If we had a son . . ."

"You wouldn't want him, Madame, I assure you. So he took you too, the louse. The travel business wasn't exactly his line, I'm told."

"I understand he was in business with some ladies. We really ought to complain to . . . to someone. Only we'd have to leave the queue to complain."

Tamara wiped her forehead.

"We checked it out, we weren't born yesterday, you know. All ships booked 'the duration,' give or take a few years; all shipping tied up, even banana boats. No passage for love or money. And I don't always believe much in love."

Tamara smiled.

"My friend Adelina does. Seventy years old, bless her. Sang at the St. Petersburg Opera. 'Cheer up, my dear, love will come to you.' So Dimitri and I went to see this young man . . ."

"François." I'm getting quite impolite, always interrupting her. It must be the heat, Tamara thought.

"François, every day. Dimitri mornings, I afternoons. I don't sleep well so I am absolutely useless mornings."

Why were people so proud of their uselessness, Tamara thought.

"Dimitri and I took turns pleading with him to let us have the first two available passages. Pleading with him around the clock. Not that we're not used to it. And of course buying potatoes from him."

"Black market prices?"

"No, a little reduced. I like them with sour cream, don't you? And I adore kasha. Very hard to get. He was also interested in my jewellery. A clever young man — what did you say his name was?"

"François. Spread out all over Marseilles with his ladies."

"Ladies?"

"Girls, Madame."

"Ohhhh." The lady put on her sophisticated mien and winked at Tamara. "So one day he motions us into his back room. Not really a room, just some curtained-off space at a waterfront café. It was morning and Dimitri's turn but as usual I hadn't been able to sleep so I'd gotten up early and come with him. A good thing, as it turned out. Two passages had come in. The price was a little high and Dimitri's not very good at haggling."

"A prohibitive price, would you say?"

"Well, we wanted to get out. Had to, my dear. So we fixed it up with him. We're not penniless, you know. I am the Countess Uvaloff and Dimitri's my husband. Oh, *mon Dieu!*"

"What is it?" Tamara looked at her, alarmed.

Madame de Uvaloff plunged her hand into her dehydrated bosom, heaved a sigh and extracted a worn satchel of red Moroccan leather. "One day I shall lose my head, I swear." She touched her head as if to make sure it was securely in place.

I bet she plunges her hand down her bosom several times a day, Tamara thought. The Countess dived into the satchel and extracted a huge black pearl ring, holding it playfully against the sun. Then with nervous fingers she explored the rest of the little bag.

"Put it back, please," Tamara urged her. "If the customs see it they'll take it. In fact, it's not wise to let anybody see it." Since camp she distrusted officialdom. Even J.P., who was a guard. Especially J.P., and his mom. What the officials didn't know couldn't hurt you. Then no one could ask questions, or punish you for wrong answers. Just do it, and ask later. Then she'd smile her ivory smile and open her large green eyes and the matter would blow over. She was lucky in her looks. She lit a cigarette and thought she didn't trust Xav either, the impeccably credentialled rep of a sort of neutral country. She trusted no one.

With fascination she watched the Countess complete the complicated process of pinning the red satchel back into her chemise. "If your jewels could talk," she said politely, "I'm sure they could tell many a tale."

"You're right there, my dear, it would make a whole novel."

"It would be such a pity for these jewels not to reach the new shores." It occurred to Tamara that she was more concerned with the fate of the jewels than that of their owner. She started to laugh.

"Let me in on your joke."

"Oh, nothing." An exasperating woman, she thought, yet a heroic one, too. With her old woman's energy, of which she'd seen too much lately, masquerading as a substitute for life. With her fears and phobias, old and new. The Countess's original fear had been legitimate enough, she was sure, but by now it had bred innumerable offspring.

Was original fear like original sin? Tamara looked at the Countess and saw that underneath those layers of fear was a joyful human being, of genuine gaiety. A little false in spots, she was the tough product of *noblesse oblige,* keeper of a stiff upper lip and all that, but vulnerable for all her composure. Still, that deep joy was a time bomb, ready to go off anytime.

"My husband has been promised a teaching post at a university. His former students have been kind enough to arrange it, but of course we were reluctant, more than I can say, to go. We like it here." She sighed. "But we can't stay. Europe's not the place just now. We like good old fascism. You know where you're at and what's what, the way they do it here. It's a thing the world is coming to appreciate."

Tamara smiled.

"I know what you're thinking," the Countess lowered her voice, "what about the attacks on the Jews?" She looked around at the line-up and bent toward Tamara.

"I hate to use clichés, clichés being the domain of the bourgeoisie," she drew up her lean frame to its full height, "it's all the fault of the man with the club foot. It's a dirty job, as they say in Berlin, but someone's got to do it. Some, in fact many, of my best friends are Jews. They can't be fascists. Although I'm sure some secretly would like to join. And, frankly, all that talk about democracy makes me rather nervous."

"In that case you're not sailing in the right direction."

"We like to eat," said the Countess.

"In that case you are." Tamara tossed her head back and laughed. "I like it here, too. The sun, the blue sky, the happy people. A room to take a bath in now and then." She too sighed. "As long as I smell good I can ignore bread and politics." It wasn't true. She liked and expected a lot more than sun, sky, and a bath, but it sounded good. Straightforward and down-to-earth.

"Tut-tut, *chérie,*" said the Countess, "you want a lot more. But don't feel badly about it. It's your due, beautiful girl. If only I'd met you before, under different circumstances, one could have arranged things."

Tamara looked at her suspiciously. The old dear was sounding like a marriage broker. "Arranged things?"

"Well, there's Igor. And Igor's cousin, Pauli . . ."

"What about these esteemed gentlemen? And how, may I ask, do you know what I want in life?"

"It's all over you. Your face . . . Igor'd like your face."

"Thank you kindly, Madame, but I've made my own arrangements." Absently she blew on her engagement ring; in answer it exploded blue-white sparkles in the sun.

But Countess Olga was busy looking for her husband, whom she presently discovered in the shade of a customs shed.

"Dimitri, oh Dimitri. Over here." Her voice rose easily above the pier's din as she stabbed in his direction with a bejewelled and badly manicured forefinger. He was playing with some harbour urchins.

"He's deaf and dumb when it comes to children. We never had any, you know."

Tamara said comfortingly, "The planet's overcrowded as it is. And from what I've seen of them, you're better off."

"I dare say. What a lovely ring. Engaged?"

"Yes."

"And you're joining your fiancé?"

Tamara nodded, adding, "He's posted in Cuba. A diplomat." It was a mistake.

The Countess's eyes glistened maliciously, "Ah, *la vie diplomatique*! When I was a *jeune fille* I lived with my uncle, the ambassador to the Vatican. In Venice. One day I shall tell you of my adventures."

"I've no doubt you will," said Tamara. She instantly regretted it. The Countess's face had turned sad and the porcelain-blue eyes filled with tears. Why do I always trample on people's feelings? It's that damn egocentricity of mine. As if I were alone in the world, I plough into people, hating to apologize in the wake of the wreckage. Why didn't the nuns teach me? To cheer up the Countess, she said quickly, "There'll be plenty of time aboard to tell our tales."

"And you, my dear, here to rejoin your fiancé. Ah, how well I remember my engagement, it seems like yesterday."

"Mine seems like three hundred years ago."

"When was it?"

"Tamara shrugged. "Only last month."

"And naturally you miss your fiancé."

"It happened so fast. My visa expired," she said bluntly, "and so did my money."

"And so you needed a protector."

"If you put it that way, yes. To avoid a sojourn to the local jail. I'm afraid there's not much room here for poor persons under your good old fascism, Countess."

"Oh, my dear," said the Countess sympathetically. "You wait and see what happens to you in a democracy without cash. They put you in jail just as quick, before deporting you, habeas corpus and all. But don't worry too much, my dear. Pretty young ladies are usually exempt. Dimitri, oh Dimitri . . ."

Tamara grinned. She's right about the cash. Without Xav I'd be lost. Oh, why can't I learn to manage alone? She could hear her mother's voice, soft but firm, "A woman alone is only half a person." It sounded wrong now. With J.P. she'd never felt like a person at all. More like a displaced, frightened foreigner at the mercy of her French guard. Perhaps her mother, in her time, had been right. But her time had passed.

The Countess called again to her husband and he finally responded, waving to her, his nostrils wide and round. His pale blue eyes looked almost rimless as he reluctantly bid goodbye to the children.

Being a husband to a distraught lady must carry its own penalties. Tamara eyed the distracted Count sympathetically and decided his wife wasn't the henpecking type. But who knew what she might do later when she got old and fat? She envisioned herself with a double chin, big pendulous breasts, and varicose veins. Absently, she smiled at Dimitri who pressed his remaining coins into small, grimy fists and ambled over to join them.

A voice from above like the voice of God hailed Tamara. "I see you decided to join us, Goddess."

It was Hirsch.

"What luck for all of us," boomed Steinheil behind him.

Tamara's sunflush deepened. She squinted up at the potential protector from submarines hungry for bodies; Hirsch was a safe bet as a lifeboat survivor. She could see it. Trapped together for days on end, parched by the sun, shivering under the moon, wildly toasting each other with saltwater. More, more, more. Gulping it down. Fighting each other for more, more, threatening to slurp up an entire ocean. Suddenly someone waves a shiny nozzle with a brand-new silencer and they all fall over each other, hands raised, upsetting the balance of the lifeboat, begging for their lives.

Tamara counted the lifeboats. Then the rafts in the shrouds. She was too far away but she guessed she didn't even need ten fingers.

"Count Dimitri Aleksandr Eugene Buzz de Uvaloff," said the Countess. "My dear husband."

"*Enchanté, Madame.*" He kissed her hand warmly. Tamara shrugged at the grinning Hirsch. The Count asked her something but the Countess called, "Where's your scarf, *chéri?*" She rummaged through her deep purse to extract triumphantly another silk square, "A gift from Aline Czapska." He suffered her to wrap it round his patient St. Bernard's neck. When she turned once more to their battered luggage he stuffed it into his bulging and torn pockets with the others.

* * *

The tattered Uvaloff suitcases were crammed with treatises on Count Dimitri's specialty, the domestic habits of the sturgeon. The yellowed pages were transported lovingly from university to university during the couple's post-revolutionary travels through European cities.

Dimitri plunged into a rambling account of the difficulties of rescuing and preserving his research. "Here I was swimming the iced Dnieper, those damn papers on my back in my rucksack. Frankly, I'd wanted to burn them all along." He gave the suitcases a disgusted kick, "But Olushka here wouldn't let me. 'They'll make our fortune yet, *chéri*,' she said. She can be very persuasive. She hates to part with things. So there we were, the papers on my back, Olga by my side. The river getting colder and colder and the ice thicker.

" 'I'm getting a bit tired, Buzz,' she said. When she's tired she calls me Buzz." He squinted affectionately at her and gave her a small poke in the ribs. " 'Keep paddling, old girl,' I encouraged.

"Then the bullets started zipping behind us, to the sides, over our heads. I thought we'd have to dive and get water into the rucksack. Those damn papers would have dragged us down and drowned us. I swear they kept aiming at the rucksack . . . I could practically hear them thinking it contains classified information or at least the grand duchess's jewels. Rat-ta-ta-tat, rat-ta-ta-tat. But it was only these papers on the poor old sturgeon. So we kept paddling away. What else was there to do? Then we reached the embankment and climbed up and hid in the reeds like Moses. We unpacked the rucksack and spread the papers to dry in the sun. Had she let me burn the stuff we could have made it in Igor's old limousine, I told my little helpmate here."

"It's his sense of humour," she smiled. "Those papers are his lifeblood."

"Aw, they weren't even good for a tax deduction."

"In a democrazy they will be. They're great on tax deductions, I hear."

"How many times do I have to tell you, Olushka, you can't believe everything Igor says!"

And there they lay, naked under the semiliterate hands of the customs officer who poked industriously at the Uvaloffs' marvellous and untidy possessions. Dimitri watched them with his detached air. Olga hovered anxiously. All were affixed with a sloppy imprimatur, and the Uvaloffs winged aboard like two tired and dusty angels.

Tamara was treated with that special homage men in uniform pay beautiful women. Even in camp the guards had practically saluted every time she passed them at the F-barrier. They had showered her with food, unsolicited, and the small privileges the other inmates missed so sorely. She was young and these small favours made the difference between survival and a tolerably uncomfortable stay in camp. It had not helped her parents. Her mother became ill and died. Her father's political notoriety made staying in camp risky. In fact, he escaped during a Maquis raid just before her marriage to J.P. Except for her mother's death and her subsequent marriage to J.P., her camp experience might have been likened to a series of visits to the dentist for periodontic treatments. Lengthy but inevitable. Tamara accepted it all with her ivory smile.

She extracted another Gauloise and several brown hands hastened to light it. With grins and bows they unlocked her luggage for her, lovingly pressing tiny keys into the ivory hulk, affixing the ubiquitous exit stamps without ever questioning anything. Their eyes were fastened on her with that caressing sheen men born under the southern sun reserve for women and babies.

"Que le vaya bien, reina," they called after her and she smiled her ivory smile. It died as she became enmeshed in the traffic aboard. She wasn't being mugged, raped or mutilated; she just suffocated slowly in the boiling midday rush. The porters tried to hack a path for her through the hysteria and she blindly pushed after them.

She thought of a limerick by Ruby, "The so-called human race isn't going anyplace and, I declare, we're getting there."

And at a very rapid pace, too. It made her furious, then it made her laugh. But there was no place to stop and laugh so she had to go on inching her way through the bodies. I can't possibly make this voyage, she thought, I'd better get off while I can, and flee these hysterical vegetables. Her eyes filled with tears. She'd run out of time and her fate was with this ship. The crowd swept against her like the tide. Set toward a new life, for better or for worse, her life was now entangled with theirs.

She was pushed against a tall barrel-chested man whose eyes popped at her.

Herr Steinheil pursed his dry lips soundlessly. Mentally he made a four-star entry into his former little black book, watching out of the corner of an eye, to see if Frau Steinheil had noticed.

She had.

* * *

Like ants up an anthill they streamed into the ship's belly all day. The *Baleares* groaned under the distress of 1,000 men, women and children fighting for food, drink and sleep. Luggage, children and spouses found at last, they bedded down in holds still bursting with the harbour's heat long after the sun had set.

But the ovens were hotter. They were filling with remains worth pennies at a chemist's, minus gold teeth. They vomited out ashes, sickly sweet ashes. They spewed moral and physical pollution into the atmosphere.

* * *

SHMA YISRAEL, ADONAI ELOHENU, ADONAI ECHAD.
Hear O Israel, The Lord Our God, The Lord Is One.

15

Uschi had made up her mind to kill herself when they came for them. And she knew they'd come. That morning she'd locked herself into the bathroom. Possibly my last shower, she thought wryly, very much alive. She hated to miss what would happen next. She felt like the heroine of her own play, and needed time to watch herself act it out. Resentfully she came out of the bathroom and got dressed under the watchful eyes of the Gestapo. Her mother rushed around hysterically, taking in the laundry from the back balcony. They told them they had 20 minutes to pack and to pack only what they could carry.

Uschi took her favourite dresses and found her blue suede shoes with the reptile insets, the ones she had long determined to wear when they came. Then they were marched to the nearby station, along the Linden-lined street. Their luggage was searched and Uschi had to empty out her little pocketbook. Uschi did not like it one bit but her father tore it away from her and with trembling hands shook out its contents on the counter. When she had recollected her things she sat down on the bench and expressed her contempt for everyone by taking out her pocket mirror and painting on her best mouth with shocking pink lipstick. The station was black with people. In the late afternoon they were loaded onto the trains and told not to leave or they'd be shot.

Inside the coupés and compartments in close proximity sat the travellers, unable to move much except to get up and stand in the corridors. Uschi was still brooding about the indignities she'd suffered. She could not speak to her father. Later, before her father could prevent her, she got out to get a drink of water. She walked to the middle of the platform and drank.

They did not shoot her. They screamed at her and called her a whore but they did not shoot her. Everyone watched in horrified silence, as Uschi triumphantly reboarded the train. She had made her point. Only cowards were shot. Her father trembled. Uschi did not speak to him again during the transport.

It was during the trip that she met the Prince. She talked to him that whole first day. A dead man shared their compartment. The dead man was covered with one of her family's blankets. It was beige-brownish camel-hair, with white buttons and black stripes and white fringes. Uschi would never use it again. At the border they were told those with more than 100 marks would be shot. Money was thrown down the toilet, banknotes were burned. Hundreds of thousands were destroyed in minutes. Then the men in black got out. The trains rolled on. Now people at the stops came and brought them milk and water and cheese and salami and French loaves. They were allowed out, but were afraid. Greedy, grimy hands grabbed at the food through the open windows. Uschi could not eat with a dead man beside her. She hadn't eaten in days, but she wasn't hungry. She had lost track of time. At night she'd taken to sleeping in an empty first-class compartment with some of the young boys. In the darkness she took off her girdle. Girdles were in fashion and her mother felt girls should wear them. The men in black had looked in on them but said nothing. The others were crammed into the coupés. Once they passed the border the trains stood around in the open countryside for hours. It was very pleasant fall weather. No one seemed to know where they were heading. A red-haired woman got off and walked away. No one stopped her. People said she had relatives in the place. Uschi wanted to get off, too, but the Prince counselled against it. Everyone else stayed on, too.

"The cowards," said Uschi contemptuously, "why don't they run away?"

They're afraid, said the Prince. *Besides, they've no place to go.*

"I'm more afraid of those in the trains than the ones outside."

That's precisely why you should stay on the train.

"But we'll die if we don't run away," protested Uschi. "I hate to be herded around like cattle. Clinging together and not striking back."

Man can survive as an individual only. So be brave, my child, grow up. As for many, I suspect they prefer collective death to lone survival.

16

Tamara got up from her bunk, washed her face, powdered her nose and combed her hair. She found the Countess on the boat deck, dispensing tea with cognac from a large, battered thermos, the jewels on her fingers sparkling in the sun. "Ah, our beautiful young friend. Have some tea and cognac." She poured a cup. "Impossible to get anything on this boat, we shall all starve. Everyone seems quite out of their heads. It's not funny Dimitri." He sat on a pile of luggage under a small sun umbrella, sipping his tea with the mien of relaxing in a Parisian boulevard café, while Olga fussed with the luggage.

"How often has this blessed old thermos saved our hides," Dimitri said contentedly.

"I couldn't do without it. Some more?" asked Olga.

"Yes, please."

They sat in silence, each with their own thoughts. But

then Tamara, trying to be polite, asked, "And how are your quarters?" She saw her mistake immediately but could do nothing about it.

"We can't bear it down there," Olga sobbed, "right over the engines." The thermos shook in her hands and Tamara had to ball her fists to keep from escaping to her claustrophobic cabin. She hardened herself to Olga's untidy sobs and her body grew stiff against the fear that flowed like muddy water from a dirty garden hose. Dimitri came to her rescue.

"We'll be all right, Olushka," he said, and patted her hand. "We always are." Far from calming her, his tender tone elicited a fresh outburst.

"They separated us again. Like in camp. They put Buzz in the men's section, and me in the women's. And he needs me so, especially at night." The Countess' sobs scattered like so many raindrops and were absorbed by the anxious crowds.

Tamara had the feeling that the calm Count could very well fend for himself, might in fact welcome it.

The way Dimitri gazed at her with his round innocent nostrils Tamara just knew she'd been right about him enjoying a little vacation from Olga. She felt some secret mirth at the situation, and a tiny bit of guilt, too. But she'd come too far now to let it bother her. She resolved to help these two bewildered aristocrats achieve better bunks than the burghers. Should she offer to share her cabin? No, there wouldn't be room for two untidy ladies, let alone Buzz.

She'd try barter. From camp she knew that food, beds, and bodies were bought and sold and on board they were practically in the same situation. "I hate to be crude," she told Olga, "but do you have any spare cash?" Delicately, she did not mention the jewels.

Olga frowned and Dimitri looked astonished. Tamara said quickly, "It's a purely altruistic inquiry. No greed in this case. I think we may be able to organize something."

"Fix something up? Make a deal?"

Tamara nodded and the couple smiled at the familiar phrases. "All's well then," said Dimitri as Olga's hand strayed to her desiccated bosom, the home of the Uvaloff fortune. They looked so forlorn that Tamara felt a warmth welling up in her that she'd seldom felt recently. She'd have to concentrate. Sitting quite still, the image of an officer who'd stared at her as she got into her cabin came to mind. She said urgently: "Please wait for me here, I'll do some scouting."

"Not to worry," said Dimitri, "there aren't exactly a great many places to go to." And indeed their view was blocked by a colourful mass of persons snaking about slowly, painfully, as if aching under the burden of physical closeness.

Tamara spotted a familiar white uniform near one of the forward hatches and laboriously pushed her way through. But she was not fast enough. Just as well, she thought, recalling the officer's expression in the cabin. She managed to hunt up another officer and started to tell him of the Uvaloffs' plight. They sat down on the hatch and he was all sympathy and hand-holding. One of his colleagues, small and swarthy, came over and the trio discussed the situation. Serenely oblivious of the traffic around them, they both now held her hands, poked at her arms, waist and legs. It was a worthy cause so she bore it admirably.

Hers was by no means the first such request, they told her. Precedents for cabin rental had been set the night before. A person named Steinheil, however, had decided not to avail himself of the opportunity. It became clear that they were now entering the second phase of negotiation. They were talking price. All three made their way back up to the boat deck. No slouch at haggling, Countess Olga vigorously upheld her end while Dimitri sat by, nostrils flaring in moral support.

And so it came to pass that in the heat of a Seville afternoon on the Guadalquiver River one of the smaller of the Tsar's cousin's jewels and a tiny cabin on the *Baleares* exchanged stewardship.

17

Rhythmic thumping shook the ship with a dull joy as she steamed downriver to her impending embrace with the ocean. The sun dabbled Dali designs on her freshly scrubbed decks, as it did on the green waters and hardened tanned faces. Soon the river breezes began to break up the umbrella of air smothering the ship, and the passengers took deep draughts of the good stuff. The poop deck, with its cool breezes, was the place to be.

Organizers emerged. Graduates from camp, these ersatz Teutons were only too happy to spread a little bureaucratized order.

One thousand passengers, eight lifeboats, 20 rafts, 30 life rings. The rafts hanging over the side of the well deck, the flotation and life-saving equipment all took up space. As did the deck chairs. If they could not organize the space aboard, they could organize the passengers. Three sittings were arranged in the mess hall on the tween deck. This begat the Auxiliary Stewards' Corps. It followed the investiture of the Auxiliary Deck Police — the passengers' response to Fritz Steinheil's epic battle with the chairs. The ADP proudly displayed their bullyhood with dirty white armbands, but the ASC topped them by eating with the crew.

Uschi wanted in on it too, so she joined the stewards and was assigned to the lunch sitting. Her mother told her she was crazy.

"You always say that, mother."

"Just like the postmistress job. If there is anything you got out of that, please tell me. I'd really like to know."

"Plenty," said Uschi darkly.

"Connections? Food?"

"What's the use, Mother, you wouldn't understand." This was the end of most of their arguments. Her mother's need to have everything put into practical, concrete terms filled Uschi with contempt. Her mother was unwilling, or unable, Uschi felt, to allow for emotional or spiritual gains, or for long-range goals that would not necessarily end in things to eat or deposit in the bank.

The assistant postmistress job hadn't been that bad. Uschi, in fact, loved it. Sex enfolded her like a protective cloak. Every morning and afternoon, as she trudged along the main road from her *îlot* to the post office below the F-barrier, she stopped for a little chat with some handsome man behind the *îlots'* barbed wire or with one of the guards out front. Smiles and *"Allos"* greeted her if the *îlot* K guards were on duty at the F-barrier. It never occurred to Uschi that the F-barrier, which separated the men and women, served a purpose beyond her own amusement.

This lasted as long as the sun was up. Uschi loved the sun. But as she watched it sink down on the horizon, lost for the whole night, her life sank with it, leaving her cold and weak. By lamplight she could do nothing. Nothing. All her energies left with the sun.

Joining the stewards' auxiliary was of course a lowering of her status as assistant postmistress, but it might hold other compensations. Maybe another commandant. But one could not live in the past. She frowned. He was still an open blister. She rarely even talked to the Prince about him. She felt they'd left camp too early, she'd only barely met him. And then there was the cabaret. With a troupe of real professionals whose every movement Uschi had envied. The girls were so beautiful, so free and open. And they had so many boyfriends. Everyone had laughed when she auditioned. In the middle of the big dramatic scene, too. She hadn't gotten the part. Uschi brooded for weeks about it.

Why was it people laughed when she was at her most earnest? They'd left before she could audition for the next show.

Uschi was serving soup to *Herrn* Steinheil. She tried to stop him from pinching her bottom, but refrained from pouring the lukewarm liquid down his stout neck.

"She doesn't like me," he complained. He'd managed to sit next to Tamara, two sittings ahead of his family who ate without him. They all sat at long tables on benches.

"I wonder why," said Tamara.

"I don't," said Hirsch, "but let's ask her."

Herrn Steinheil wagged his fingers at Hirsch across the table. "You're just sore I'm next to the most beautiful woman on the ship. In the world," he added gallantly.

"*Sans blague.*"

"Come on, boys."

"Brilliant aren't they?" said Uschi, now serving boiled potatoes, hard-boiled eggs, canned tuna and some nice vegetables.

"Ughugh, vegetables," said Steinheil.

"Good for growing boys," said Hirsch.

"I like them," said Uschi. She hadn't had any fresh vegetables for so long that she'd forgotten the taste. Steinheil was stupid. The women at the hotel had eaten lemons to get vitamins, grateful for anything that could be bought without ration cards. She wished now she had eaten those lemons, so nice and yellow in their skins. If she had, her nails wouldn't keep dropping off.

"Are you joining us for the entire voyage?" Steinheil winked at Tamara. It had cost him a few bills to sit at her table.

"I get off the second to last port," she looked straight into his big face, wondering why he was winking at her.

He glanced at her engagement ring and said with heavy emphasis, "I bet someone's waiting for you."

"You're psychic," she said coldly.

"Someone is always waiting for a goddess," said Hirsch.

She smiled at him. Her engagement was no secret, but she resented Steinheil's knowing smirk.

Again Tamara felt that invisible fence close in on her like a trap. She fingered the ring, played with it. She ought to take it off for a while; maybe it would make her feel free, independent. It was a feeling that sang to her in Seville, before boarding. She felt it first at the hotel, the easing of tension, of the fear for survival. Maybe there was a new life for her after all? Just as she was enjoying a respite between her departure and her upcoming marriage, this fool Steinheil was pushing her right into it again. It would be weeks before she had to face Xav, maybe never if they were torpedoed. She smiled as if asking to be left alone, then got up and excused herself.

"Wonder what she's doing here," Steinheil said to Hirsch, making a broad gesture with his huge hand. "A high-class broad."

"Haven't you heard? There's a war on." Hirsch lit one of his monogrammed cigarettes and blew the smoke at Steinheil.

"There's got to be more to it, if you get my drift. Boy, would I like to get a hold of that."

"Why not make a run for it, old man. Got nothing to lose but time, and of that we've got plenty."

"Excuse me," said Steinheil. Seeing his lady at the top of the 'tween-deck ladder, he got up to head her off.

"Strange bird," said Hirsch.

*   *   *

"What's with Steinheil?" asked Tamara, who had returned to the table for her sunglasses. "Why is he always winking?"

"He's struck dumb before your beauty, Goddess. *Merde.* Sit down, have some more coffee."

"He's the second henpecked husband I've met aboard. Does it worry you?"

"Let's say it's not exactly a strong case for matrimony. Cigarette?"

"Thank you."

"Remember, cabin C, neighbour."

"And how could I forget?"

18

Uschi rushed to the galley in time to see a dirty brown hand sweep molten butter off a plate. The hand belonged to an assistant steward. He had just used it to blow his nose delicately between thumb and forefinger — an old sea custom, no doubt.

Uschi spent her second night aboard on a mattress she propped up on the poop-deck walkway. Berthed to sleep, her body pressed against the softly swaying planks. Above her stars shimmered, while below, in the ship's bowels, her parents and little brother fitfully slept. She heard a tenor's triumphant song and thought of her Prince. Then she herself was asleep.

* * *

"Hi ho, what have we here?"

Uschi opened her eyes into Hirsch's laughing face. His golden moustache and glasses, as he bent over her, glistened in the early morning sun. "What're you doing so far up, sleeping beauty?"

It was the man from yesterday, the one who'd talked to the beautiful redhead on the quay.

"Sleeping, my good man." She stretched luxuriously, sitting up and glancing round the ship. There was a bright morning hush in the air while the river below spread in stillness. The horizon showed the first flush of dawn and seconds later the whole sky was blushing.

"What's the hour, friend?"

Hirsch looked pointedly at the rising sun. "Time to queue up for the first sitting, little beauty. I'd say it's half past five."

"Oh, you're up early by the dial of your Patek watch."

"It's consideration," Hirsch said modestly. "The people in my lifeboat want to be alone."

"*Sans blague.* Does the captain know what's happening on his ship?" Uschi used her stern voice, though she was used to these things from camp.

"The real captain is invisible. Others, however, are not."

"Is there more than one?"

"At least one per lifeboat: elected by secret ballot."

"It figures. Just like the *îlots*."

"Gotta organize. I happen to be in a very busy boat," said Hirsch, yawning.

"On you it looks good."

"A wise guy," mumbled Hirsch.

"But a shame to throw you out so early when you finally can take it easy."

"Sensitive too."

"And the real captain's disappeared?"

"We suspect we're being navigated by the cook. Still, I warmly recommend the lifeboat suites. They're one of the more fortuitous lifestyles aboard. Want me to put in a word for you with our captain? Passengers are also elected by secret ballot."

Herr Steinheil's cookie-cutter face flashed before Uschi. "Thanks," she said hastily.

"Thanks yes, or thanks no? I shall have to introduce you to my captain."

"Thanks, no."

"Don't mention it." He bowed elaborately and clicked his sandals together and Uschi giggled, not at all displeased.

There was something likeable about the man, despite his nasty exterior. Something boyish behind the monogrammed everything. Quickly she checked his sandals.

"Looking for something?"

"No, nothing." Had she seen right? She squinted downward. There it was. On the buckle. ASH. "What's the S for?" She pointed downward accusingly.

"Oh," he said lightly, "you'd never know."

"Wanna bet?"

He gave her a quizzical look and said quickly, "Aside from the company, a decided bonus, think of the lifeboat's fringe benefits. If we sink you're right in place. No need to jump overboard, no fuss, no heroics. Unless you want to be a hero, of course. At any rate, you'd hit the water snug in your blanket."

"And at your side. With a record player. Happily adrift. Unless the boat capsizes. And I'd be all alone, the sole survivor, undamaged, hugging a plank. Some gypsies told me I've nine lives. A triple-protected lifeline. See?" She was almost in tears now.

"Life's not so bad," said Hirsch unexpectedly. "Even for lone survivors. A little beauty like you die? Ridiculous. *Qué barbaridad*. We need kids like you around. Once we get off the ship, you'll see you're better than coffee in the morning. Let's go eat, I'm starved."

He pulled her to her feet and the blanket slipped off. Fortunately she was wearing her pyjamas. The blanket had been too scratchy on her naked body. But exposure never bothered her. In camp she'd often rushed outside the barracks semi-nude. Everyone did it. The guards liked it. Uschi carefully put her prized trenchcoat over the pyjamas.

"Let's go take a shower."

"Later," said Hirsch, dragging her down the ladder. They climbed down to the main deck and walked midship to the entrance to the tween-deck mess hall. Despite the early hour the breakfast queue was way along the main deck.

"What'd I tell you?" said Hirsch.

"I see I have time to go take a shower and get dressed. Hold my place, please."

Before Hirsch could object, she rushed off to her bunk for clothes, towel and toothbrush. Her mother was asleep. She breathed a sigh of relief and softly rummaged around their luggage. If her mother woke up they'd have another of their pre-breakfast tiffs over where she'd spent the night. Her mother liked playing detective, snooping around after her daughter. It made Uschi sick. Quickly she grabbed her things and climbed up again to the shower stalls.

The large shower room below the galley had gratings in the ceiling. They allowed an unobstructed view of two early birds performing their morning ablutions before the entranced eyes of the male attendant and the cook's friends.

Uschi was about to censure them severely but the image of *Frau* Spiegel slapping her over the borrowed glass arose. Pointing out their shamelessness, not to mention their casual attitude, might get her another slap. Surely these dumb ladies must have an inkling they're being observed. Why didn't they use the shower stalls? It offended her to see those women wash themselves before these vile men. In camp she'd encountered middle-aged fiends exposing themselves at the open-air troughs in plain view of the young guards in the guardhouse outside the barbed wire. What are you, the policeman of the world, Bea would say. Uschi shrugged. But she wanted to make the world a better place. Quickly she brushed her teeth at the basin and then went into the peep-proof shower stall and took off her coat and pyjamas. She showered with raw warm river water. Later it would be cold unfiltered ocean water. And there would be no soap to dissolve the salt.

In camp she'd taken chunks of ice from the tap of the trough and melted it on her warm body, drawing reluctant grunts of approval from the middle-aged sex fiends in her barracks. "Ohhh, look at that girl."

"Yes, she's some clean little pig. Who would have thought it."

Uschi sighed and carefully dried herself inside her stall. She put on her fresh clothes, wrapped her soap, towel and pyjamas into a tight bundle, and carried her trenchcoat over her arm. The air was cool and not too many people were about. You might almost call it peaceful, if peace was possible on the crowded *Baleares*. Uschi rushed back to retrieve her toothbrush and saw the naked ladies, not bad for their age, drying themselves with formerly handsome bath towels. They sure seemed to take their time. Uschi stole a glance at the eager faces above the grating. They must have bribed the cook. Money? Not likely. Gauloises, probably. Or Gitanes. Everyone liked strong French cigarettes. You couldn't convince Uschi these two didn't know they were being watched. Hadn't the Prince said, "There's no end to the stupidity of man?" No, that was Gurdjieff.

"Pigs," she muttered and left in disgust. "Dirty pigs." She'd tell the guy with the moustache who was holding her place in line. She liked him. He never told her his name. ASH? She rejoined him halfway down the ladder to the mess hall two decks below. "Thanks for saving my place," she said, slapping him on the back. "You're a pal."

Suddenly she was glad to have a friend aboard, a big brother. Her little brother, Michael, was nothing but a big baby for his 13 years. When he wasn't hungry he was lousy. And she wasn't so sure he was her friend. He'd been strange since the transport. Scared. Frightened. She shrugged and squeezed Hirsch's arm affectionately. "What's ASH for?"

"Allow me to introduce myself, young lady. Alexander Hirsch."

"Good, but what's the S for?"

"A secret. Just call me Alex," said her new big brother.

"Yes, but you're either a spy or it's some horrible name."

Hirsch shook his head and grinned. But he didn't know

Uschi, her determination. She decided to extract it from the purser — even if she had to stay with him all night.

"And my name's Uschi."

"Delighted to meet you, Uschi."

"And what d'you do, man with the secret middle name?"

"I make movies." Hirsch could be astonishingly patient. They had arrived in the mess hall and she cuddled up to him on the long bench. She had plenty of time, she didn't have to serve food till lunch. "I'm very interested in the theatre so I took this audition in camp. Ooff, they were just getting a new show together when we left so I don't know if I got the job."

"You sound almost sorry you had to leave."

"Funny, but in a way I was. Leaving people behind and all that. But I was glad to get out, too. And to meet people like you," she smiled.

"Didn't see you at any auditions, though."

"I fluffed one, and took the last one again. Were you there looking for talent?"

"Maybe."

"Oh, that's what they all said." She remembered the intoxicating creatures, actresses and chanteuses, who had all the men in camp at their feet. Well, never mind, her day would come. "But I was going to try hard," she said earnestly, looking at him out of her hazel eyes. "I would've done well, too, I just know it."

Hirsch liked determination. "Let me get my foot into tinseltown, *Liebchen*, then you can come and audition for me. I'll send for you."

"*Sans blague?*"

"*Sans blague,*" said Hirsch solemnly.

"Here, have some of my bacon."

"It's not a sure thing."

"Have some anyway," said Uschi grandly.

Early morning banter batted back and forth between the long tables and benches like so many tennis balls. The young crowd had taken over and were happy to get going. The older ones were not yet up.

"They have a man in the women's washroom," Uschi informed them, her mouth full of bacon.

"What's he doing there?"

"Ogling the women."

"A male attendant? Did you make it worth his while?"

"Not me," said Uschi, swallowing. "But these two big cows did." She thought of their large breasts and reported joyfully. "Some guys were peering down through the grates." She scratched herself vigorously. "Probably gave the cook a pack of Gauloises."

"Why the cook?"

"The washroom's below the galley, friend."

"Were the ladies worth a pack of Gauloises?" asked Hirsch.

"If you don't like Gauloises," said Uschi doubtfully.

"Do they need help in the women's washroom?" asked Steinheil, who'd just come in. "I'd be glad to volunteer."

"A ladies' washroom auxiliary, LWA. *Frau* Steinheil wouldn't mind?"

"What she don't know don't hurt her," laughed Steinheil.

"Guess where he'll spend his time from now on?"

"The galley?"

"*Frau* S. probably makes him pay for each time," mumbled Hirsch.

"Then those obnoxious kids of hers must have cost a pretty penny," whispered Uschi.

"He seems well heeled."

The sun was fully up now, and the mess hall was getting stuffy. But the heat did not detract from the friendly ambience. There'd be nothing to do all day, and no place to do it. Reluctantly they moved to the main deck to make room for the second batch.

"Let's go listen to my records," said Hirsch. But when they got to his lifeboat it had been covered with canvas.

"Why'd they cover it?" asked Uschi.

"Probably need to keep things under control in the day-time. I think I'll go rest up in my cabin for a bit, get ready for the night."

"Oh, you got a cabin? So why don't you sleep in it at night?" She was using her "little mother" voice. "Get some rest?"

"Too hot. And too lonesome. Once we're at sea it'll be cooler. Want to sleep with me in my cabin?"

She was about to lose a friend. And fast, too, if he was going to be like that. She still held the memory of her commandant. Aloud she said, "I don't see how they carry on like that in public. In camp they were more discreet. Action behind blankets and all. Like a private cabin, if you come to think of it. Their friends held them up."

"But now they're free. Free to get rambunctious. And they're not as scared anymore."

"You're sure? I think they'll always tremble in their boots," prophesied Uschi.

"Only the old ones. The young are almost free from fear."

"It depends on their karma."

"Who told you about karma, my child?"

"I'm interested in these things. And I know the Prince," said Uschi reluctantly.

"The Prince? What Prince? Tell me about him. Like all peasants, I love nobility."

But Uschi shook her head. She hated to discuss Him with outsiders. "It's just as well," she mused, "maybe you can learn from them in your lifeboat." She shouldn't have said it, she didn't like the way Hirsch looked at her, and the Prince certainly wouldn't have liked it.

"Sometimes you startle me, child," laughed Hirsch.

It enraged her. "If the ship gets sunk the ones in the lifeboats will be saved." And this enraged her even more. Where was democracy? Even in the bottom of a lifeboat money spoke. Maybe it was all karmic, as the Prince said. Otherwise everything was a great big hoax, a colossal cheat perpetrated by some higher power on mankind. When Uschi was younger she believed firmly — like everyone else she knew — in a big man with a beard sitting on a golden throne in heaven. He entered everyone's misdeeds into a big fat ledger, handing out annual punishment or reward. It was good, it was simple, it was beautiful. But it didn't really work like that. In camp she'd called fervently on this big man to come and avenge the horrors she saw all around her. But nothing happened. The man never came.

Uschi hadn't really formally renounced the big man but she was very glad she met the Prince. The Prince explained the theory of karma. Cause and effect. If people got what they deserved this time around they sure must have been a bunch of hyenas in their former lives.

"In camp I had a friend with holes in the knees of his pants the size of a fist," she told Hirsch. "And he was sweet, too. And handsome. I can't imagine he deserved such lousy old pants." She wondered what had become of Helmut's baby face, blue eyes, dimples and fair hair. He'd been crazy about her, much to the chagrin of Bea. He might be dead.

"Poor Helmut was starving and all the time those bastards were eating and drinking down at the infirmary. I had champagne there myself," she said shamefacedly.

"Be glad," said Hirsch, who'd been following her soliloquy with utmost interest, "at least some didn't have to suffer."

"If you put it that way . . ."

"Come, let's find some of Steinheil's leftovers." By that he meant the remaining chairs. But he needn't have worried, despite Steinheil's valiant efforts there were plenty left.

They dragged two under the shade of some tarpaulins, hatch tents dropped over the cargo booms, and they got so comfortable that they almost felt like they were aboard a real cruise ship. Except for the milling crowds, and the fact no one came to ask them if they wanted anything to drink.

"Do *you* believe in God?"

"No," he lit a cigarette.

"I used to. Before they came and took us away. My mother still does, but she's so nasty now."

"Of course."

"I'd like to again. I must tell the Prince. Sometimes at night I wonder why He allows little children to be burned in the ovens. Right while we're sitting here talking. I suppose it's their karma. But their karma couldn't be all that bad yet." Her voice broke a little.

"When we were still at home a friend of my father returned. He'd escaped a different camp, much worse than ours. They were talking late one night, and didn't know I was listening. He told my father they played football with little children, making mothers watch. Brains were flying all over the place and the adults went insane."

Hirsch put his arms around her.

"My three little cousins. Two, three and five years old. And their big, ten-year-old brother. They were left behind in the big city. All alone. Their father was shot for stealing sugar. So proud he stood there, calling, 'Greet me my dear ones.'

"One had blond curls, and one brown curls and two had big, brown eyes and one had blue eyes. The ten-year-old also had blue eyes. No one heard from him again. Do you think there's a children's heaven?"

"Sure," said Hirsch. "Sure."

"One day on my mail round — I was assistant postmistress — I thought I'd give Him one more chance. I told the Prince about it. "God," I said, "you've changed and I don't know you now. But if you're still up there, please get us out of here. I'm sick and tired of this place, karma or no karma. Please, God, and I will give you the rest of my life." He didn't do anything. But then I met the commandant and three weeks later we were out."

For the first time Hirsch was silent.

19

"Hi," said Uschi to the fascinating red-haired creature, "where've you been hiding?" But for a brief glimpse of her in the sweltering mess hall, she'd not seen her since the tumultuous embarcation. She gave Tamara an encouraging smile.

"In my cabin," said Tamara. "I didn't know my presence was desired."

"It must be really hot in there. Hirsch doesn't even sleep in his."

"So that's why he stopped knocking down my wall." Tamara lit a cigarette with her long fingers. Uschi watched her enviously. She hid her own grubby stubs, damaged by the camp diet, and curled her stubby toes. She had developed this habit of sniffing at the rims of her fingernails, filled with pus, just before they fell off.

Tamara said, "*Herr* Steinheil recommends my continued presence near the lifeboats, to be on the safe side. There seems to be a shortage, he said." They were loafing on the boat deck, although passengers were not supposed to be near the lifeboats.

"Steinheil sleeps in a boat. Has he pinched you yet?"

"He wouldn't dare." Tamara threw her cigarette into the water and propped her long, tanned legs against the bulwark.

"He dares with me. Everyone dares with me," said Uschi, aggrieved, following the arc of the cigarette before it hit the water. Then, bright-eyed, she said, "I know why they don't dare with you."

"Why?"

Uschi could see clearly what in Tamara caused that rare

Steinheil inhibition, that invisible F-barrier that restrained even Hirsch. "It's that super sophistication of yours. Damn, now I've done it."

Tamara smiled. Uschi fervently wished she had some of it too and gazed at her in full admiration. She wanted to do something, to tell her something to make herself look good. She looked at her hands.

"The gypsies in camp told me I've a double lifeline. Triple, actually. If we sink I might be the sole survivor." Suddenly she felt very protective. "You'd better stick close to me. It's like triple indemnity. *Sans blague.* Out of 1,000 drowning I'd be the only one saved. Out of 1,500, one of two. I'd survive a plane crash, too. Let's see your lifeline." She took Tamara's slim hands into her own. She wrinkled her nose. "I don't think yours is as long, so you'd better stick with me."

"You really believe it?"

"Sure. Touch me. It rubs off, you know."

Smiling, Tamara touched Uschi's arm, realizing she was being offered a rare honour.

"Now you'll survive, too," said Uschi, satisfied.

"I never thought the day I saw you from the pier would bring me such good fortune."

"You looked rather doubtful. D'ya feel anything yet?"

Tamara smiled. "Not yet."

"You will. I didn't want to board, either, but my ma wouldn't let me stay. She never lets me. I was all set to elope with this Spaniard." Suddenly she remembered the rooming house. "One of them, anyway." She sniffed at her nails. "So I let her talk me into coming along. Ooff, maybe it's for the best."

"Probably is," said Tamara consolingly, "but I know just how you feel. I was scared, too. Especially when I saw the ship."

This pleased Uschi. "So what made you change your mind?"

Tamara looked pensively at the young girl. "My visa had run out and so had my money."

Uschi contemplated this. "You'll make out," she said finally, "*sans blague.*"

"I'm not that sure, I've no double lifeline, you know."

When Uschi gave her a shy smile she said, "But I've no doubts about you, *chérie*, no doubts whatsoever."

Uschi liked endearments from older women. She'd gotten plenty from the *respectueuses* at the hotel. But she'd hardly gotten any from the matrons in the barracks. She was glad Tamara liked her. She was beginning to think only the prostitutes did.

"I'm pretty crazy," she said magnanimously.

"Only on top. I detect a good deal of wisdom at the bottom."

Uschi clapped her hands, chanting, "She says I'm not crazy, not crazy, not crazy." She danced between the lifeboats then climbed up on the railing, balancing precariously.

Tamara had seen her sit like that before, but now she was worried. "You get down from there immediately, Miss."

"Ooff. If I just sit quietly, how's that?" She was sitting gracefully, dangling her brown legs.

"You're going to fall into the water, you little monster," Tamara called angrily.

"No I won't, I have perfect balance, see?" She stretched her arms heavenward. "Besides, I'm a good swimmer."

Tamara looked like she was going to hit her and Uschi said quickly, "Remember the lifeline." When Tamara laughed, she said, "It's my will-power. I don't fall in at night, either. I've this perfect place on the poop. My mattress is on this catwalk next to the potatoes. You ought to come by sometime. No one bothers you there. Steinheil can't climb up, hahahahaha. It's nice and airy, perfect ventilation, dry too. Except when it rains." Now there was a thought. She stopped. What would she do when it rained? She shrugged her shoulders. She'd worry about it then.

"I sway with the ship," she sang. "When it falls I fall with it, pressing myself hard against it's planks. Like now, I'm pressing my legs against the rail, see?"

"Get down."

"I can neither fall to the left, nor to the right, nor down, up there on the catwalk."

"Get down, please."

"It's my will-power that makes me so lovable."

"What does your mother say?"

"She doesn't know."

"Oh?"

"She's sick on her bunk all the time. In the daytime, too."

"Poor lady."

Uschi thought about it and for the first time felt a twinge of pity for her mother lying sick on the sweltering deck, way down in that nightmare. "I never thought about it that way." She climbed down from the railing and stood in front of Tamara.

"If it rains or gets cold you could sleep in my cabin."

Uschi looked at her, horrified.

"What's the matter?"

"I . . . I don't know. It sounds so . . . closed in." But what bothered her was the idea of sleeping in a tight space with another woman, no matter how pretty, when she'd just survived the barracks with a bunch of burghers.

Tamara laughed. "I felt tight, too, but now I'm getting used to it. That's funny . . ."

"What?"

"I offered to share my cabin with another woman, an older woman, and she turned me down too."

"What'd she say?"

"I don't know, I didn't actually offer it, I wanted to but she would have been horrified."

Uschi blushed. "Maybe she wasn't used to sleeping with another woman either."

"People want to be free, I guess. And alone."

Uschi sighed.

"She adores her husband, her big baby. Doesn't let him out of her sight. Can't bear to be separated from him."

"Yes," Uschi was getting bored. What was she babbling about? "I'd be the same, any girl in love'd be." She had to see the commandant every night hadn't she? "You see I've this feminine psyche."

"Feminine psyche, what's that?"

"It's a thing that attracts men, and only a few girls have it."

"That's great."

"I wonder. First you attract them. Like flies. And then you worry about them and don't want to let them out of your sight. Especially if you're married."

"This hasn't been my experience," said Tamara. "But you with your feminine psyche needn't worry, they'll stick around."

Uschi thought this over for a while, wrinkling her forehead. "Then why am I holding onto them?" she asked. "Am I afraid they will run away?"

"Not a chance, *chérie*." She sighed.

"You sound so sure," said Uschi.

"Of course." She lit another cigarette.

"Then I better stop. Actually, none's ever had the chance to run. I'm always leaving, or they have to. It's just my fear, I guess. Before I was always staying in the same place, except when I went away to school. But then *Onkel* Fritz said things would change. Now how did he know? We weren't even kicked out yet. And he didn't mean on the outside only. *Onkel* Fritz's my analyst."

She wondered whether he was all right. He'd always been talking of leaving, but the day they came for her family and put them on the transport he hadn't been around. For days she'd searched for him.

"But I still feel very lucky," Uschi said defensively.

"Faith is beautiful. And *I* was the one going to school in a convent."

"Don't you believe in anything at all?" asked Uschi pityingly.

"Nothing."

"Nothing? But you're so beautiful."

"Don't look so sad, *chérie*, I'll manage."

"I wonder," mumbled Uschi, then the gong sounded. "Excuse me, gotta go serve lunch. *Ciao*."

"And I'd better fix my face," said Tamara.

* * *

That morning in May they were to report to the velodrome the Parisians called *Vel d'Hiv*. Her father was supposed to go to the Stade Buffalo with the men, but he had gone to Switzerland to recoup their money. It would be months before they saw him again. The *Vel d'Hiv* was so jammed with women that they were finally told to go home and report again next morning.

They waited for hours. The next day at the entrance they had to turn in scissors and knives — for which they got receipts. Inside they sat around on their suitcases and surveyed the huge building. Mrs. Adler discovered acquaintances from Dresden and Berlin. Gossip raged. Women searched for Nazi spies among the throng. Toward evening they were moved into a box on the edge of the cinder track.

Straw arrived and they had to stuff it into skinny sacks. The air was full of chaff. They slept perched together in the box while the guards marched up and down the long halls.

They could hear the dull detonations of the French antiaircraft. The Germans must be getting closer to Paris. A bomb would have caused utter panic.

They had to wash in the open, in the presence of male guards. Toilets soon went out of order so they had to use hastily built cabins with pointed roofs and holes in the floor.

Breakfast consisted of coffee, grey bread and canned liverwurst. It made them thirsty in the May heat. For lunch and dinner they were given a thick soup of beans and peas. Calls for volunteers made Mrs. Adler carry buckets of water from the open air to the enormous field kettles.

A week full of tension passed. Everyone believed the Germans were approaching. There was no outside news. "God, just think, the S.S. will suddenly replace the French guards." Then they were loaded onto trucks which drove along the Seine and by the Louvre in the sparkling sun. The women cried. Three trains were waiting at the station.

After travelling three days and nights through the countryside, they stopped one warm June evening in Oloron de St. Marie. Soldiers loaded them into open trucks. Standing in the trucks, they shot past cornfields, meadows, pastures and little friendly houses, the blue Pyrénées in the background. After half an hour they arrived at the camp. The iron gate opened, revealing a paved road with ditches to the left and right and barracks framed by little islands of barbed wire. There was a sentry box at the entrance and a plaque with a large black letter "G." A thin female guard with a black straw hat and cape came rushing up and yelled, "Quick, quick, get down, take your luggage and follow me!"

The woman counted them and ordered 60 to a barrack. The barracks were covered with old roofing felt. In the roof were large hatches with wooden drop shutters. On the floor were 60 strawsacks without covers. No tables, benches or eating utensils could be seen. The water was near the camp's main street, eight faucets over wooden basins covered by a roof. This was where the more than 1,000 women in îlot G performed their ablutions — in the open — when the taps were on.

They went to sleep on their strawsacks and woke up to their new life.

Mrs. Adler met some old friends and became fascinated with camp life and the ever-changing kaleidoscope of the women's emotions. Warm embraces and kisses came fast and furious. Tamara held herself apart, refusing to talk to anyone. "I won't be here long enough to make new friends, Mother." Mrs. Adler shrugged.

The camp was built in a valley of damp clay which the rains turned into ankle-deep mud, smooth like an ice rink. The July heat sat heavily in the valley and the women dragged out their strawsacks to sunbathe in the fresh air. But the soil, which never really dried up, penetrated damply into their mattresses. Delighted guards lingered outside the barbed wire.

Tamara sat broiling in the sun and gave herself a pedicure. She'd accumulated a collection of kitschy novels as a barrier against conversation and work. Her one thought was to return to Paris and continue with her painting. She was into what she chose to call her barbed wire psychosis. "Why not paint here?" Mrs. Adler suggested. "Let's see if we can find you some watercolours."

"Why bother, Mother."

"But this is a lovely landscape. People travel to the Pyrénées for their vacations, to rest, to take the cure in Pau, even to paint."

"Under their own steam, Mother. Anyway, why bother?" Tamara didn't really mean to be disagreeable. Everybody, she knew, was trying to survive.

"Why bother? I will tell you, my daughter. We go through certain rituals to keep ourselves sane."

"But Mother, we're all quite mad here."

"That's your opinion. And all the more reason to try. My poor girl, I blame myself for having neglected you. I was too involved with looking after your father. And with our social life. You're at the beginning of your life and you're well on the way to botching it up. I should have given you more of a firmer foundation, and not relied so much on your Nanny and the Good Sisters." Mrs. Adler began to cry and Tamara said quickly, "Oh, Mother, please. No use crying over spilled milk. What's done is done."

But Mrs. Adler would not be soothed. "What will happen to you, my poor little flower?"

"All you have to do is call me your forget-me-not or rose bush and my life will be complete."

"We ought to pray."

"Mother, please.

"How long since you've been to Mass?"

"Mother."

"Didn't the Sisters make you go? Didn't they teach you?"

"Only to smile, Mother."

"My poor child, you're so angry. Be a little patient, things will turn around. The Lord has given us a very good life."

"Until it changed, with those monsters at home creeping up on us and poisoning us bit by bit." She lit a cigarette. "And what about our present situation? Which, by the way, could have been prevented."

"I wonder," said Mrs. Adler reflectively. "We made mistakes, your father and I, I admit. But we did the best we could under the circumstances. When we finally sent you off to Paris we hoped you'd forget the whole mess."

"I don't blame you, Mother, you did your best. But I was old enough to remember, and I'm old enough here in this filth, among these horrible women."

Mrs. Adler got mad. "I don't want to hear you to talk like that. These are nice women. Real people who are suffering real misfortune. Who are you to put yourself above them? What have you accomplished in your life? Tell me that."

Tamara stalked off.

★   ★   ★

By midsummer the women who were able to show visible means of support were permitted to leave. The French were glad to get rid off them, and many settled in the nearby villages and farms. They even visited in the camp.

There was a bit of a mix-up with the Adlers' Swiss money. In the first place there wasn't as much as they had thought.

And, as Tamara's father had explained, the account was in a friend's name; but the friend couldn't, for the moment, be located.

"Probably travelling in India," Josh Adler said in a letter from Switzerland. He was still working on the situation and Mrs. Adler was getting nervous. Tamara was furious and Mrs. Adler found it hard now to deal with her. But at least they knew Tamara's father was safe.

"But we need Father's signature to transfer the Swiss money. If we're ever to get out of here."

"Tamara!"

"I'm sorry, mother."

"I know you didn't mean it the way it sounded. God will help us, you'll see. I know your father will be back for us."

Camp life got duller but more peaceful after the more prosperous women moved out. The Adlers had more space in the barracks and commandeered a nice secluded corner for which some Spaniards made little benches and a table.

Still, Tamara became fretful. "What if the Nazis come here into the unoccupied zone? They won't let us get away twice.

"Patience," said her mother, who had managed to find some eggs.

"I've this funny feeling something terrible's in the air." She was sorry the instant she said it for her mother suddenly was sad.

"No, no, it can't be. The Lord will help us."

"If you say so."

"We shouldn't have sent you to the convent. We failed you, my poor little girl. Whatever happens, don't think of us too badly, we loved you."

They embraced and Tamara felt some of the hardness in her melt. "Don't worry, Mummy, I will never leave you."

Then one cold rainy October evening a huge transport with thousands of Jews from Baden and the Palatinate arrived in open trucks. They came from Karlsruhe, Mannheim, Heidelberg, and a dozen little villages in between. Among the more than 7,000 people were children, the sick, and the old. The Gestapo had arrested them all within two days, and put them on transports at six the next evening.

They deported the entire Jewish population of the German province of Baden and the territory of the Pfalz in one fell swoop.

These people were mostly petit bourgeois and tradesmen. The wealthier Jews and the professionals had been smart enough to hear the music — they fled before the war. It was the first organized deportation of German Jews. The Nazis had made a start with Polish Jews but the German Jews, many of whom had fought in World War I, had been pretty much left alone. Some had even converted. This had perhaps given them a false sense of security. The French government was never notified of the German plan, so the arrival of the transports left them totally unprepared. All sorts of speculations arose as to who these dangerous travellers might be. Since there was no legal precedent for pushing German citizens into France wholesale, the notorious Eichmann had to ride the trains himself and literally talk them across the border at Clermont-Ferrand.

Now the barracks were filled again. Amidst all the confusion the most beautiful fall weather prevailed, with the sun shining hot and glorious, a blue sky nestled against the bright blue mountains in the distance.

Soon they had word that Josh Adler was back from Switzerland. Tamara got them a pass from the *îlot* chief and they went to visit him in one of the men's *îlots* below the F-barrier. How changed he was. He looked thin and unkempt, his rumpled clothes hanging loose, his dark hair turned grey.

"I look like a scarecrow," he said. Still Josh had the old twinkle in his eye, but his wife held him close and wept. Tamara just stared. It was hard to reconcile the harrassed man with the fastidious Prussian who believed in the honour of both the Germans and the French. He's still my father, she thought, the man I love and admire.

"Lice," he said, scratching. Tamara looked round the barracks. "Here's not so bad," said her father. "You should have seen Le Vernet where I went looking for you two."

"We hear Le Vernet's a punishment camp," said Tamara.

"Made the mistake of inquiring about you and was asked for my papers. They stuck me into the camp and it took some doing to get myself transferred here. Believe it or not, this is supposed to be a great place. First thing I've got to do," he said, still scratching, "is to clear the transfer of the money from Switzerland so we can get the hell out of this hotel."

"We'll be fine," said his wife. "First you need to take care of yourself."

"Don't worry, Father," said Tamara.

⋆ ⋆ ⋆

At first she didn't pay any attention to Jean-Pierre. He was an officer who always just seemed to be around. He likes you, was the general consensus. Why me, Tamara thought. It might be any of you. But it soon became clear that Tamara was the reason for his visits. A dark, fierce figure, he had coal-black eyes and the kind of five o'clock shadow that requires careful, close shaves. He seemed obsessed with Tamara, and he bore gifts of food, wine, flowers and perfume. Tamara shared conscientiously. He was a Catholic, she told her mother.

"A gentleman," she said.

"Uh huh."

"What's wrong with him?"

"It's too early to tell, although I must admit he looks good from behind the barbed wire."

"If you marry him you can leave, dear."

"Marry, Mother?"

"In-laws of a French officer can leave, too," said Mrs. Mayer, the barracks chief. "She's a stupid girl."

"Oh, stop it, everyone." But she couldn't help thinking about him. She owed her parents so much, and it was an option, an open door. No word yet about the Swiss money. "You know I would never leave you two here."

"Well, that's fine, but just think about it, dear. Promise?"

Tamara sighed.

In September a second wave of dysentery followed the July outbreak. The old, the weak and the starving were no match. The camp had few medicaments, and its infirmary's only beds were for the very sick. Mrs. Adler became ill.

Tamara and her father took turns sitting by her strawsack. Her mouth was slack, her gums almost white. Tamara chased the flies that settled at the moist corners of her eyes. For a while she smiled and took her hand. Then she merely looked, unseeing.

Tamara could not bear it. Her beautiful lovely mother was being torn from her and she could not stop it. Rage shook her body as she swore, "Let me get out of here and never, never will I allow myself to be poor again." But her mother was already dead. They took her to the infirmary. The bread truck would collect all the bodies in the morning.

Father and daughter walked behind the truck to the crowded little cemetery at the north end of the camp. They'd gotten a pass for this.

Behind them walked people who were neither mourners nor friends. These folks used burials to get *îlot* passes. They stretched their legs a bit along the camp's paved road and perhaps initiated a friendly relationship behind the barbed wire of the men's *îlots*.

*   *   *

Jean-Pierre invited Tamara to join him on his Christmas leave, but she didn't want her father to be alone in camp.

Mrs. Mayer, her *îlot* chief, helped her get passes and as often as she could she took the long walk through the mud and the camp's main road below the F-barrier to visit her father. Conversation would drag. He was even more quiet and brooding than usual. Then he'd abruptly become brisk and business-like, telling her names and addresses and asking her to repeat them several times.

After Christmas, camp life got a notch tighter when the Germans came looking for political prisoners and made the French confine people to their barracks. The search lasted from early to mid-morning. Heated debates began.

"They've no right to do this. We're in unoccupied territory."

"Ha!"

"We're under the protection of Vichy."

"Ha!"

"The French aren't to blame."

"So why is my mother dead?"

"Then whose fault is it? God's?"

"You leave God out of this."

"Who deported us from Paris and stuck us into this shithole, harmless refugees who sought their protection? Who wanted to fight the Boche with them, you tell me? And what if the camp is bombed? We're sitting ducks here, in these mountains."

"Who'd want to bomb us here, we're behind the lines."

"The British, the Germans, the Russians, the Spanish, for all I know."

"Not bombs maybe," said Tamara, "but I've a bad feeling. I've heard things."

"You're talking about the labour camps?" said several women, pointing east.

★ ★ ★

One day Josh Adler was gone. A man she had met on an earlier visit smiled and shook Tamara's hand. He whispered that she should not worry, smiled some more, soberly shook his head at her questions and then, smiling still, made a little bow and sent her back to her *îlot*. During the next few days a rumour spread through the camp that several men had escaped with the Resistance.

Tamara was left with the family jewels, the furs and the furniture in Paris storage, and eventually the Swiss money that had not been able to save her mother's life.

She made up her mind. "Children," she said, "I'm getting out of here."

She married Jean-Pierre in a ceremony in the main infirmary and stopped by the barracks to pick up her belongings. There were tears and good wishes and no shortage of envy.

I never expected to win a popularity contest here, she thought, but a little more feeling wouldn't have hurt. She remembered her mother's counsel about being more friendly, but all that was behind her now.

They went to Cannes for their honeymoon. It was incredible to be free again. Everything seemed different. Nothing could ever be the same again. Tamara got the furniture out of storage and sold it and her mother's furs. She only kept the jewellery. Jean-Pierre was very attentive and took her sightseeing and to good restaurants. He was an ardent lover. But to Tamara it all seemed like a dream, and she still saw herself walking the mudpaths of *îlot* K. She was a married woman now, and had to return to Oloron with her husband. They rented a small villa but Tamara never returned to visit her husband's workplace or her mother's grave. She tried to be a good wife by practising her limited culinary arts and being cooperative in bed. Her days seemed to pass in a fog. She loved the landscape, the pure mountain air, the lovely colours. But the little mountain village made her restless and she couldn't talk to the peasants. One night J.P. came home late and very drunk. When she refused to have sex with him he hit her. For the first time she realized the extent of J.P.'s drinking. Instantly her gratitude evaporated. No man could touch her.

"Don't you dare hit me again," she said coldly, "ever."

"Aha! Getting on your high horse. You weren't so high in camp before I got you out. In fact, you were quite meek, my little mouse. And now you think you come from Jupiter's thighbone, hmm?" He had a bit of trouble with the word thighbone but Tamara was not amused.

"And who are you? A jail guard?"

He hit her with renewed fury. "You think you did me a big favour by marrying me, don't you?"

She moved away from him but he came after her and shook her so that her long red hair tumbled loose. "Answer me. I want to get this straight. You feel you did me a big favour, *non*?"

"Now that you mention it." She recoiled from his alcoholic breath.

"Get out of here, you whore."

"That does it." Tamara ran upstairs to throw some clothes into a suitcase. She didn't notice it was his.

He was watching her from the doorway. "You walk out of here and I'll shoot you in the back."

"Ah! And where'd you leave your service revolver? I think it was on the piano last time." High drama, like in her mother's kitsch novels. She grabbed the suitcase and rushed past him, down the stairs and out the door. Of course he didn't shoot her. Did she really think he would?

The whole thing was over in a minute; she hadn't really thought about it, just acted on instinct. Slowly, defiantly, she carried the suitcase to the station and took the first train available, which was to Pau. She felt light-hearted, as if a great weight had been lifted from her. Almost happy. Action, at last. Her own decision, right or wrong.

Tamara took a room at a hotel. She had some money and by being careful she could live on it for a while. Then what? She went to bed. She'd worry about it later.

Pau was an elegant spa, very lively. A lot more lively than Oloron. It also cost more money. She spent her time browsing in stores and buying little. One day she met Lise, a fellow student from the convent, the daughter of a rich merchant. She'd forgotten she lived at Pau.

"Tam, how are you? Are you here on vacation? Why didn't you call me? How's Paris?"

"I haven't been there a while. It's a long story."

They went to a patisserie and ordered coffee and pastry.

"Now tell me, what have you been up to? You look a little pale and you've lost some weight."

"Yes, finally."

"Where are you staying? You must come and meet my family."

When she named the hotel Tam could see a slight frown cross the cheerful brow but then Lise said quickly, "It's the war. We're all suffering."

Tamara took her wide smile and suddenly the whole story of the *Vel d'Hiv*, the camp and the marriage burst out of her with the force of the Niagara Falls until she heard Lise's voice, "More croissants, more coffee?"

Hadn't she heard anything? Tamara stared at her in horror.

"I must be off," said Lise, looking at her watch. "*Je me sauve.* I'll call you. We'll have tea soon. *Garçon*, the bill."

"I'll take care of it."

But her friend made such a fuss that Tamara let her pay it.

"*A bientôt.* See you soon."

"Sure."

Tamara never heard from Lise — she must have told her parents. What were they supposed to think of an enemy alien who'd been deported to a camp and run away from her husband, a proper French citizen and officer of the army?

Soon J.P. was at the hotel and begging her to return. "Life is nothing without you, *chérie.* I love you so much."

They took the train back to Oloron. Where else was she to go?

* * *

"My friend Bea and I were going to cut through the barbed wire," Uschi told Hirsch. "We'd swiped the scissors in the main infirmary. We practised nights. But then we got released, and never had to." She sounded almost sorry. "Bea's gone to Casablanca, François tells me. I wonder what she's going to do there."

"How come you got your visa?"

"Hustling. I come from a pretty long line of hustlers. My ma's folks were cattle traders. It's in the genes. You should see my ma in action."

"I'm sure I'll have the opportunity."

"She threatened to drown herself in the *Vieux Port* in Marseilles if this guy didn't return with our black market dollars. She really believed she was going to do it. Of course she can swim a little. My ma has only one gear these days. Hysteria. And she lays it on to others. Then she stops and rests up. She's down in her bunk now, thinking she's deadly sick."

"You don't like her much?"

This stopped Uschi. "You know, I never thought about it. There wasn't time. Poor Ma. She's still resting up from her suicide threats. And from all the weeping and howling at the Spanish consulate."

"You're a wicked girl. What does your father say?"

"He bears it. He's some sort of a hero, I think."

"That's all very well, but I do hope your friend Bea is really in Casablanca and doesn't wind up back in camp. I hear something's in the wind. When'd you leave Marseilles?"

Uschi sighed. "More than two months ago. It doesn't seem that long but we've been kicking around Spain ever since. The hotel they put us in in Marseilles was horrible. Fleas, lice and bedbugs galore, just like in camp. Four of us in a room with a little wash basin. It would have suited my little brother. He's opposed to water." She giggled. "We had plenty of chickpeas though. I swear that cook knows 71 ways of making chickpeas. But we could buy horse baloney.

I adore horse. Sort of sweet tasting. And you don't need ration cards to get it. But I'm off the chickpeas and Jerusalem artichokes.

"Poor kid. But you don't look skinny."

"My ma made me beg for ration coupons from men in cafés. I felt like a prostitute but she'd poke and prod till I'd ask them and then she'd go over to their table and whine and whine till they gave them to her." She blushed. "Sometimes I'd eat with this old guy at a black market restaurant. His cousin's a big producer in Hollywood."

"Oh, what's his name?"

"I forgot."

"What about your father? Where was he in all this?"

"He was in this holding camp near Aix-en-Provence and he couldn't get to town too often. He's not that enterprising and they were only letting them out to go to the consulate at Marseilles." Not exactly. The men in camp could go out at least several times a week and report back at night; some even rented apartments in Marseilles. The old guy was swinging all over the place; Uschi just hated to think of him. "Were you in that camp?"

"No, no. One was enough for me. I made private arrangements."

Uschi stared at him. "You're lucky."

"Hey, something's got to rub off of hustling one's life away in the film business. I stayed with a friend."

"We had some fun, too," said Uschi, not wanting to be left out. "Especially with the Arabs." She was toying with her newly grown fingernail. "They used to play mandolins in front of our windows, serenading us. God, were the burghers upset. I guess they figured those Arabs lowered the tone of the fleabag. My ma was the ringleader." Uschi blew gently on her new fingernail. "But she didn't mind eating their food, my ma. That is, when they invited us to home-cooked meals."

"She sounds like a pragmatist."

"Is that what they call it?" This fingernail wasn't growing

in as neatly as the others; it would look a mess.

"I was assistant postmistress. Now I'm a lowly waitress. Sub-stewardess, really."

"Couldn't keep those fingers out of it," smiled Hirsch. "How come I never saw you with your mail sack?"

"You can't be very observant. First the mail and then the audition. Well, I never saw you either. And I thought I knew everyone." Why did she have the feeling again he was pulling her leg? She drew herself up to her full height and gave him a stern look.

"I'm sorry I missed you and your mail sack. I was in îlot E, below the F-barrier," Hirsch said in his best UFA voice.

"I'm sorry for not seeing you, as well. My father and brother were there too."

"Bet you didn't have a special pass."

She didn't like his smile. She threw her head back and the hazel eyes flashed more green in the sunlight. "I'm always going special," she said with dignity. "Want to know how I do this?"

"I'm not so sure."

But her mouth seemed to have taken on its own life. "In Marseilles Bea and I knew these Arabs who gave us cigarettes and fed us. Bea, me, and my ma. And then this Algerian cook promised to smuggle us out in his galley. But then we got our visas so we didn't need him. He seemed to have smuggled out Bea, though. And François's girls. Then my other girlfriend knew another Arab, a big brown one in a costume."

"Kalaoute?"

"Burnip. No, burnoose," she said impatiently. "He'd give her Gauloises. My ma was horrified. I don't smoke," she said virtuously.

"Horrified about the Gauloises?"

"No, the Arabs. When the other Arabs, the ones who invited us to dinner, serenaded us in front of the hotel, my ma nearly died."

"After the dinner?"

"No, she was too stuffed. Before."

"You should laugh more, *Liebchen*."

"Then Bea met a black guy who also brought her cigarettes."

"Ma horrified?"

"We didn't tell her."

"Gauloises?"

"Craven-A."

"Ah."

"Then we got our visas and cleared out. I never get to see the ending of anything." It was Uschi's greatest grief. Whenever she really got into the action she had to leave.

At that moment she remembered the morning, raw and before dawn, when a voice had called sadly, "*Au revoir, Poupée, au revoir petite Uschi.*"

And from inside the truck, squeezed in between her family and the other dense bodies, she'd called to the commandant, "*Au revoir, au revoir, au revoir.*"

She couldn't even see him, it was like parting from *Onkel* Fritz all over again. Why, oh why, did she always have to leave? Why must they always stay behind? She brushed her fist over her eyes.

"Cheer up, sweetie," said Hirsch, patting her plump arm in the bright sunshine.

21

Tamara was pacing the deck. The act of pacing was a triumph of muscle over space, an exercise which enabled her to push away Xav. But soon he was with her again, getting larger, approaching inexorably with every slow knot of progress. Tamara made up a welcome dialogue.

"Here I am, my dear, now what?"

"Now we're getting married," Xav said in his slow, precise way.

She laughed her pretty laugh. To her it sounded tinny. "So simple, really, 'getting married.' Oh sure, I'll make a terrific wife. Decorative. For you, for anybody. Because you know, I perform my function. Do my duty. Don't make scenes, demands. Because I don't love anyone, surely not myself, so it's easy for me. One, two, three . . . easy as pie."

She stopped pacing. What would he say to that? She bit her lower lip. What could any man say? Marriage to Xav had been her aim, the end of her financial worries, security at last! The start of her new life with the diplomatic clique. Talk, talk, smile, smile. The gossip, the interpretation. What did she or he mean by that? What was the real intent behind the broader smile, the lingering lip, the askant finger. Any little slip would be instantly broadcast into the globe's nooks and crannies where those diplomatic antennas were fine-tuned for any tiny aberration. Scandalous potential, oh joy, making the heart race and the blood flow faster. Suppose Xav found out about J.P., or suppose she met another man. What then? Not that she planned to, she'd really had enough. But Xav, whatever his sterling qualities, was no Jean Gabin in *Pepe le Moko*. He tended to cling to people and things and might not let her go so easily. It was the clinging that made her feel so tight, so claustrophobic. Was it her destiny to always wind up with the same sort of man?

Karma was the word Uschi used. With her long red fingernails Tamara lit another cigarette and frowned. Had she not seen a little bit of clinging in that sweet kid? No, she must have been mistaken, Uschi had little to cling about. She seemed so free, so uninhibited, that Tamara refused to accept that camp might have tainted the young girl too. There was too much love in her, too much life. She almost wished something would rub off on her — but it was a luxury a person in Tamara's situation could ill afford. Besides, even if she'd wanted to she couldn't feel anything. Jean-Pierre had killed it. He'd chewed on her feelings like a dog on a bone. She thought of her dinner in Seville with Hirsch, how she almost felt, and smiled.

"Having a little after-dinner stroll?" called the Countess. "We love our little cabin. We must have you for tea."

Tea from Olga's thermos? "When we're more under way."

"It'll be cooler then, I hope."

"Come, Olushka, we'll be late," said Dimitri.

Tamara couldn't imagine what they could be late for. Unless they'd discovered something to do that she wasn't aware of. She sat down and lit another cigarette.

She had not seen it happen, but suddenly she heard cries of "Man Overboard." The cry was taken up by a dozen voices until the deck reverberated with a mounting fear and hysteria that had lain dormant since embarkation. As in a dream she watched the tall man take off his shoes, strip off his shirt and dive into the sea. She held her breath but stayed away from the screaming, shouting, weeping, wildly gesticulating crowd at the rail. The captain must have ordered the ship to stop for they were slowing down.

"O God, do something," she said, almost against her will. Since the convent she'd stopped believing in God, but now she realized that she meant it. All around her people were invoking a deity, passionately, fearfully, guilt moving their tongues. Then she heard cries of "Got her, he's got her." She sat back and lit another cigarette with shaking fingers.

A crew member threw a rope down and from where she stood she could see something being pulled up. The rope seemed heavy now and two, then three crew members were pulling on it. She heard cries of "Make room, make room for them." Then, "He's trying to bring her round." This was followed by a great "Ahhhhh" and a voice saying, "He's taking her to the doctor. The doctor, oh, where is the doctor?" Then, hard by her, almost brushing against her with his dripping burden, she saw the tall, fair man carrying what seemed like a wet bundle. On closer inspection it turned into a little old lady whose messy strands of white hair were plastered against her face. She was very pale and the skin around her eyes seemed swollen purple. The man was barefoot and his wet pants clung to his powerful body. His broad, hairless chest was dripping wet. The aura of cool control around him seemed to calm down the excited mob. They stopped pushing and shoving and fell back to make room before regrouping into new excited clusters. Tamara was fascinated.

They make me sick, she thought, as she climbed up to the deserted boat deck. But the sight of the man, half naked, had touched her. He seemed so different from Xav and J.P. So physical in his solid presence, so reassuring. Hadn't she only recently noticed a similar physical presence? She frowned. It couldn't have been in camp where she spoke to almost no one. At the hotel in Seville? But her memories of the hotel were about thin dark men hanging around the lobby. Then she remembered. It was Uschi, the plump little girl dangling her tanned legs from the rail the day she couldn't decide whether or not to board.

*   *   *

"When you need them, the bastards have a way of fading into the distance. Better you shouldn't need them."

Uschi stirred her orange juice and frowned at Hirsch.

Suddenly serious, he asked, "What's your dad going to do?"

"Haven't the faintest," Uschi said. "He doesn't talk to us anymore."

"He must be plenty worried. God, I'm lucky to be alone."

Uschi looked at him in surprise. It was the first time he admitted to a problem — it was nothing short of miraculous, she told the Prince later.

"Ah, you think I'm a cold fish. Being bored with people's aches and pains doesn't make me blind, you know. I note the discomforts of the good bourgeoisie ejected from their witless lives as well as anyone."

Recalling the slap in the face from *Frau* Spiegel, the notary's wife, Uschi grinned.

"I don't happen to think suffering ennobles mankind," said Hirsch. "I never pretended that this unfortunate interruption of my professional and private life has widened my horizon, made me a better man."

He finished his drink. "Suffering ennobles those who want to suffer."

"The saints?"

He didn't listen. "Nobility was never my ambition. It's usually a cover for things you don't have, can't get and don't want. In our case, in the camps, cooped up together for any length of time, good people get greedy, angry and stupid. Also more religious! But it rarely makes them think. As with age, whatever they were when they got in, they got more so when they got out."

"What d'you mean?"

"Well, people are always saying 'it's his age.' Well, what's it got to do with age? They develop a certain way and they continue to do so, and they atrophy along the way. Age only shows it more."

"I guess they haven't the energy to live any longer. If they get more rotten all the time there's not really any point saving anyone is there? Like when the resistance fighters risk their lives raiding the camp and they refuse to go?"

Hirsch laughed. "With gorgeous girls like you I'm all for it. One's supposed to give one's fellows a chance, being imperfect and all, but in reality, bah."

"And artists like you?"

"Naturally."

"If we eliminate them all there won't be any left but you'n me — and I don't know about you."

"I tell you, sweet, it's best to eat a lot of good food and drink a lot of good wine while waiting to resume life. And try to make plenty of francs, marks and pfennigs."

"And make love?"

He laughed.

"I don't believe you. You sound outrageous." But secretly she thought he was right.

"No, my little cuddly, I'm sure you don't. You want to clothe me in your shiny knight uniform, don't you? But look at yourself. Take a good look. Somewhere inside you there's a junior Hirsch. A narcisist. That's why we like each other."

Uschi smiled. She agreed with about almost everything but his materialism. Was he really like that?

"I don't believe you for a minute," she told him, "you're nothing but an old softy, afraid someone will make you cry." Then she felt rotten for saying it. It seemed sort of dishonest, hanging in the air between them. He might not be as insensitive as he made himself out to be, but he was pretty bad, of that she was quite certain. Maybe it was his way of playing it down. Maybe he was ashamed of it. Nevertheless, he seemed more accessible and considerate than a lot of the good burghers aboard. If insensitivity had that result, then she was all for it. Or maybe he was less desperate, and so he could afford a certain amount of magnanimity.

"Are you that nice to everyone?" she asked him.

"Me, nice?"

"Pardon me, but I thought you were being nice to me. Maybe when someone doesn't assault me I think he's being nice."

He put his arms round her and patted her on the back. "Poor kid, you've had a hard enough time and here I'm giving you some more. Next time I get out of line, slap my face or something."

"You're OK, Alex. Really. You're not so bad." She didn't know why she had this need to pretend he was really a dear, sensitive man talking tough to hide his feelings. His frequent insensitivity didn't make him a monster in her eyes. And the commandant's torturing Spaniards didn't make him one either — at least not to her.

"Personally, I never really suffered," Uschi told Hirsch in a loud voice. "Except when they put me to work in the typhoid barracks." She wrinkled her nose.

"Typhoid barracks?"

"Most of the time those chicken coop windows were down, lest the old women got cold and caught something. I mean *more* of something. As if it mattered at that point. There they were lying like corpses on their stinking straw-sacks. I had to comb their wispy white hair every morning, and when I saw their white mouths I knew they'd die. No doctor ever came to see them. Then I was glad because they would cart them off in the truck after they delivered the bread. I suppose I shouldn't have been glad but there was one less to comb, one less to wash. After a while I got sick and they let me off." She kicked the chair savagely. "Ouch. It wasn't very noble of me."

"You did the best you could. Suffering with them wouldn't have helped either."

"You think so?"

22

At high tide the *Baleares* steamed through the gulf and past the cape into the open sea. The rough waters tossed the ship up and down. A steady wind blew north-northwest, clouds covered the sun.

The decks were empty of passengers, making the ship, but for the cluster of deck chairs, look like an ordinary, freshly painted freighter. The mess hall was empty, too. This cheered up the crew, paid and unpaid, who practically wallowed in all that unused space as in a well of hot sulphur springs. With the seasick prostrate, fear, for the moment, had been defeated by a handful of survivors.

"How can we persuade them to stay sick?" Hirsch asked the second engineer.

"Not the gorgeous redhead, please."

"You mean my neighbour in B? Have another drink."

"You mean you saw her first?"

"Not necessarily. And probably . . . I'm a reasonable man.

"Probably?"

"Aw," said Hirsch, "probably nothing. She doesn't like me. Besides, I've seen more starlets than you'll ever see, even if you went to the movies every night. You have my blessings."

"I drink to that," said the engineer.

The *Baleares* plunged on, her decks deserted. At intervals a patch of bright sun found its way through the clouds and streamed down on her new white paint. Far across the water she gleamed bravely, a plume of spray at the bow glittering briefly in the fitful sunlight. She wallowed in her slow rhythmic progress through the grey-green sea.

Tomorrow the seasick would be up again, and fear would stalk the ship — a fierce lioness on the loose, ready to disembowel the weak and hang their carcasses from the bow.

* * *

She must have dozed off on deck. When she opened her eyes she saw the tall fair man who had rescued the old woman. He was sunning himself nearby in his blue boxer shorts, smoking a cigarette. She smiled sleepily. Blue-eyed men seemed to wear blue shirts. But not really having known any, she wasn't too sure about their underwear. When the man saw she was awake, he reached for the pants he'd hung over a lifeboat and stepped unhurriedly into them. He was not in the least embarrassed and smiled at her with a wide easy smile that seemed to suggest that he found the world a pleasant place. With his sky-blue eyes, his short, brown sun-bleached hair, firm chin, and tanned, leathery face, he was the most handsome man Tamara had ever seen.

"I'm sorry I hung out my pants to dry, but you were sleeping so peacefully that I didn't want to disturb you."

"There's so little room on this ship," Tamara laughed.

"And every inch counts. I'm Gil Smith, second engineer." He held out his big hand.

"You're the one who rescued the old lady. Smith?" She put her hand in his.

"My father was American. White trash. My mother black Portuguese." His blue eyes twinkled, deepening the laugh lines in his face.

"I've never met a black person, but you look pretty white to me."

"Oh, people are people, and when you work on ships you meet them all."

"Including people like me."

"Nothing wrong with that."

"It could be debated."

"O.K., let's debate it."

"I'm Tamara Adler."

"Tamara. Tam. It has a ring to it."

She laughed and shook a cigarette out of her case. He got up and lit it with his gold Dunhill lighter. She wondered how he could afford such a thing on a Spanish crewman's pay.

"A gift," he said, as if psychic, and for a moment she got madly jealous. But then she thought: what's it to me? The Corsican François who sold her the cabin had one too. And he was a pimp.

"Excuse me a minute," he said, "don't you go away, be right back." He moved with the grace of an athlete, with his deep chest, broad shoulders, narrow waist and long legs. What touched her most of all was the way he looked so quiet, so comfortable with himself, giving the impression that wherever he went was the place he most liked to be.

He returned shortly. "Like a cold beer?"

Tamara was not one for beer but to refuse him seemed inhospitable. "Sure. Thank you." He offered another cigarette and lit it with the Dunhill.

"Gift from a passenger?" she couldn't help saying.

He laughed. When she kept looking at him, he said, "You wouldn't believe it."

"Try me."

"Well, Tamara, I met a lady in Shanghai; you might say a Countess from Shanghai."

"You do get around."

"A sailor's fringe benefits. And you, going to New York?"

"Only to Cuba."

"Friends there?" He smoked his cigarette and glanced at her engagement ring. It sparkled in the sun. She played with it and suddenly wanted it off. The ring seemed so out of place on this ship. "Engagement ring?" He bent toward her and she felt this free-flowing electricity coming from him. Almost involuntarily, she leaned back to protect herself. He smelled of the sun and freshly baked bread and maleness and she thought of Xav and J.P. One heavy, one lean and nervous: both so tight, so unlike this tall fair giant. And she felt her world could never be the same again now that she knew it held a Gil Smith. Then she remembered the wet bundle in his arms. "The little lady you saved, how is she?"

"Fine, thanks."

"How did she fall overboard?"

"Quite a trick for someone as old as that. I think she got too near the rail, got dizzy and lost her balance."

"And you saved her. You're a hero."

"Her time wasn't up yet." He smiled broadly.

"A miracle. Do you believe in fate?"

"Sure do."

"We make our own fate, for better or for worse, I guess."

"That's why you have the anxious look?"

"Do I? I'm afraid I have to watch my step around you."

He grinned and nodded.

"I never realized," she said, more to herself. He smiled broadly as if to say, "Come on, lady, relax." Then he said, "You take yourself too seriously, we all do. Sorry. But I've got to get back to the salt mines."

She looked at him questioningly. "I'm the fellow who drives this tub. Most of the time anyway." He laughed with his white teeth and got up and climbed down from the boat deck. He looked back up and waved at her.

She stared after him and thought: Gil. Like Gil Blas, the Spanish hero. So I have an anxious look. And all the time people tell me how glamorous I am. Well, he's different. She was curious when they would meet next. It was not easy to keep out of each other's way on a crowded little ship.

*   *   *

Uschi snuggled close to the hard planks. She lay flat on her back. The sea was wild near the cape, white foamcaps gurgling, rushing, swelling, bursting, endlessly, endlessly. A dirty green beneath a dark green horizon, watery bands of aqua and green raging with jealous tongues into the white foamcaps as if seeding destruction itself. But the foam, indestructible, seemed eternal. It rose easily, mockingly, to the crest of each wave until the bands, raging, licked up white foamsoup beneath a faint blush of dawn and divided, came together, and broke again in an unending game of heavenly landscaping. Now the whole sky broke into a faint blush. A rainbow of dirty green, grey and dark green bands spanned the horizon above the *Baleares* as if to encourage it to hold out against the sea which seemed to yearn to engulf it.

Thank God for the storm, Uschi thought. For once she was not feeling the least bit guilty. In truth, she didn't feel so great but she was determined to enjoy having some space to herself. There wasn't really that much room on her little poop deck, but enough to imagine herself alone. She lay nice and cool, thanks to the high wind that blew steadily around the cape. None of the good burghers crawled over her, inquiring, whining, complaining. She shivered and drew her mother's mink higher up on her chin. The sun gleamed malevolently behind a film of cheesecloth. Uschi wiped her exposed face.

"Be careful, *Liebchen*," said Hirsch, "this sun packs a nasty punch."

"Go away and let me die in peace," said Uschi weakly.

"Here, cover your face like a good girl." He gave her his shawl.

Uschi did not hear him. She was watching a fishing trawler tossing lightly on the waves. Like a nutshell, it danced nimbly up and down.

"Up and down like life," she told the Prince, "only up's nicer. But no matter, people don't ever like where they are. That's been my experience."

At your age!

"Sure." She hugged the planks, feeling their support for her body, helping her go with the ship's movements. She felt very sick now.

It grew quite dark, more stormy, and very cold. Even the stars cast little light.

The Prince will come and carry me off, she thought, as she lay fighting the darkness and the cold. Then she fell asleep.

PART TWO

23

The Baleares sailed past the cape into a tranquil ocean. Most passengers were up and on deck again, jamming the mess hall below and stuffing themselves to make up for the meals they'd missed the past few days. Uschi was serving lukewarm soup at lunch, her attention distracted by a feeling that was like frantic elves rushing to and fro under her skin, attacking her very red and rapidly swelling face. From what she could gather, the elves' activities began the day she was lying seasick on her mattress, her face exposed despite Hirsch's warning.

"Damn," she cursed, almost dropping her plates. The elves seemed to have produced a bed of blisters that were preparing to burst and dribble down to her chin and into the soup. Uschi wiped them off carefully with her upper arm, balancing the plates but, ooff, it hurt.

It was also unbearably hot. Feeling the eyes of everyone in the mess hall upon her, she quickly set down her plates and fled up to her mattress on the poop deck. But the sun blazed down so hard that she had to escape to the shelter deck.

"What'd I tell you," Hirsch said. And she couldn't answer. She glared and replied, "I wish to reflect in solitude." When that didn't work she lost all composure and screamed, "Va-t-en, fou-moi la paix, go away, you fiend."

Hirsch knew when he wasn't wanted. "Be back later, Liebchen." He patted her plump arm soothingly, "Hope you feel better."

During the rest of the day Uschi dozed in the shade of the aft awning, sometimes waking and sipping the ice tea someone had thoughtfully placed near her. She talked to the Prince. Mostly about the heat. Her head felt dull. After dinner it got crowded under the awning and she climbed up to her mattress under the stars.

Does it hurt a lot, little one?

"Yes."

I'm so sorry.

"I should have listened to Hirsch."

Yes, said the Prince.

But Hirsch had made her feel guilty again. She felt the same ridiculous guilt she felt as a young child, when she'd played on the cement border of the dung heap in her grandfather's little mountain village and had fallen in. The neighbourhood children laughed at her horrified attempt to hide her dung-coated body from her grandmother. She felt this same guilt float up from deep inside like an enormous puffed cotton ball soaked in vinegar. It smelled sour, like festering pus. She tried to laugh but the movement split her blisters open and made her wince. The Prince watched her so silently she did not notice his large, awesome presence.

Don't avoid, little Uschi. Don't run off, stay and face it. Fight. Fight for your life. Be brave and earn your survival. The others died. Many more will. But you were saved. Don't feel guilty. Remember: you are truly saved only if you survive wholly, in body and mind. Body and mind are one and both must be healthy. It is not your fault that you survive while others die. There are reasons. You may be able to do things they couldn't . . . He hesitated as if he wanted to say something very important, but then continued more casually. *Be cleansed and guilt-free, free from shame also. This world needs no more cripples. Go, and live.* He struck her on the shoulders as if knighting her.

Uschi wept. Not in frustration, but with a tremendous sense of relief, an impending sense of freedom. She could taste the soaring she'd do. Joyfully she stretched herself, despite the pain of her burnt blistered face.

"You win," she told the Prince softly.

We win, he said, *we win, Liebchen.*

"Will I ever be pretty again?" She took a little pocket mirror and looked at her torn face.

He laughed merrily. *Good often comes from bad. Turning poison into medicine. People pay for sea salt cures to peel their boring old faces. Imagine yourself with this nice new skin . . .*

"Yes," she said, feeding on his voice. It was like the wind whispering to Moses on the mountain. She'd hung onto his voice during much of the transport. She'd forgotten what he'd said; remembering only his voice, whispering in her ear.

In truth, she couldn't recall much about the last few years. Almost nothing before camp. Time seemed to have rushed by her; there was this haze over everything like cheese-cloth: it muted colours and blunted images till her life became one formless, anaesthetized lump. Her memories were without sharp edges. Everything blurred and ran together, except for a few remarkable episodes, which stood out in sharp relief. These she could recall without real discomfort: most related to her own experiences, rather than to any of the people she'd loved. There was *Onkel* Fritz, and Bea and Helmut and the commandant and even *La Tigresse*, all lumped together in the pain of separation. Especially the commandant. Of course he tortured people . . .

But he'd been good to her.

"He didn't really torture that many. Just a few Spaniards. And not often. He didn't like Communists. And a few prostitutes."

Beware, child, you're not serious. And you're not cynical. Not at your age, hmm?

"No," she said.

*   *   *

Tamara sat topside leafing through one of those dumb women's magazines, wondering how it had gotten into her

163

luggage. It must have been among her mother's things. She sighed. She could not bear to think of her mother. She'd been closer to her father but she missed her. She pushed her huge sunglasses higher up the ridge of her nose and scowled at the magazine's advice. How to become the perfect woman to attract a man. She tossed the magazine aside and closed her eyes.

She lit a cigarette and took a deep pull. Perhaps she should try to write an article for this ridiculous magazine. Catching men was her specialty; she didn't even have to do the research. And it would be nice to be independent, to not have to bother with Xav anymore. She began to experience a feeling of lightness and the kind of slight pain you get when you finally use an atrophied muscle. She tossed her head back and caught sight of the lifeboats. There didn't seem to be too many. She frowned. Not enough for this mob. What if they had an accident, were torpedoed? Even running without lights at night they were a fine target for the U-boats.

She laughed bitterly and went to the railing. Was there anything worth surviving for? She leaned over and stared into the green-cresting foam. Far below the waves broke on the side of the ship, each crest spreading out in a lacy pattern that was rapidly drawn astern and swept back again toward the middle. She had lived so fast these last few months that she felt like the waves had swept away her feelings. They rolled inexorably, like a newsreel. One reel after another. She looked harder and the shifting foam seemed a sharp metallic green. It paused in the trough of a wave and J.P.'s plaintive face stared up at her. Then someone grabbed her hard.

"You all right?"

"No."

"You look like you've seen a ghost."

"Maybe I have." With shaking hands she lit another cigarette. "I . . . I must have gotten dizzy."

"Here, let me help you." The man put his arm around her waist and led her to a deck chair.

Only there did she recognize Gil Smith. "It's you. I must look a sight," she said, smiling wryly and gesturing toward the discarded fashion magazine.

"D'you really want to know?"

"No."

"You like a drink?"

When she nodded he said, "Stay here like a good girl. Be right back."

She closed her eyes and sank deeper into the chair, feeling very tired, suddenly, as if she'd been running. He returned with a thermos and poured two cups of tea laced with brandy.

"Drink up, that's a girl."

"Oh, this is great, the best thing I've had since I've come on this godforsaken ship.

He frowned slightly. "Oh, she's a good little ship, nothing wrong with her."

"It's the passengers, you mean?"

He smile broadly. "Could be."

"Oh, a diplomat, too."

He smiled some more. "Ready for another?"

She nodded and held out her cup.

"Good."

He pulled her chair over. "Here's where I say, 'You stick with me, kid and there'll be more.'"

"Careful, I might take you up on that."

"That's what I'm hoping for."

"Along with the tea, it's probably the best offer I've had in a long time."

"Things that bad? Where are you sleeping?"

"Oh, I'm one of the lucky lottery cabin winners."

"Then you must be rich."

"If not for those damn Swiss."

He looked at her. "I've got a large shoulder to cry on."

She looked at his massive torso and smiled.

"I'm off at midnight. And I forgot to ask for your phone number the other day."

"No phone, shower or service in this cabin. She scribbled *cabin B* on a page of her white notebook and tore it out for him. "If you don't get a dial tone just knock in person. It's what my neighbour does."

He folded the page into his overall pocket. "Who's your neighbour?"

"An eccentric film director from UFA in Berlin."

"Hirsch."

"The one and only."

"Speaking of the devil." He laughed and pointed in Hirsch's direction.

"Goddess! I got tired of trying to knock down your wall. And with my friend, the engineer. *Ciao*, people, *ciao*."

"*Ciao* to you, too. What's the second *ciao* for?"

"One for each, Goddess. I'm impartial with the sexes."

Tamara decided she liked Hirsch. She supposed everyone eventually liked Hirsch. He was so smooth, almost glib in the way he knew so many things. But one could sense something deeper beneath that sophisticated demeanor. If you had time. She sighed. Time was something she didn't have.

Lately she'd felt that she was trying to outrun time while it chased her down like a police hound.

"Want a quick drink," Gil asked, "before I vanish down into the bowels?"

"Sure, *amigo*."

Gil gave him his cup. "Unless you want to come down with me?" He looked at Tamara.

"Why not," said Hirsch. "Let's have a look by all means, we have plenty of time."

"Come," said Gil. He pulled her up from her chair and then helped her down the ship's ladder. Hirsch followed. As they climbed down in to the engine room's dense heat the sound of a thousand quivering vibrations rose up and enveloped them. It all made Tamara feel quite ill. She did not like machines.

Gil looked pleased and held her hand.

"Like a ballet," said Hirsch, "a thousand nuts and bolts winging in rhythm, every nut attuned to the other. It's more than one can say for people. It'll make a nice background. After we hit the iceberg."

"I see you like it," said Gil.

"Why not."

"Sounds like hell to me," said Tamara.

"But then goddesses don't like these things," said Hirsch.

"You're right. I despise machines." Things that moved, mechanisms that made irrational noises, filled her with horror.

She sighed and grabbed the exit ladder.

"Don't go," said Gil. "Stay and talk to my big baby."

"You don't mean Hirsch? Ta-ta, I'm going up."

Gil's blue eyes crinkled with laughter as he lifted a grease can over a valve and bent his head down to listen to the engine beat.

"Tell daddy where it hurts."

"True love," said Tamara.

"The best kind," said Hirsch.

Tamara imagined the can turning into a fat penis. It ejaculated oil into the crevice.

"Ta-ta for me too," said Hirsch, climbing up after her.

"See you later," Gil called after them. He smiled straight into Tamara's green eyes.

It was good to be up on deck again, breathing in the hot air. It was still cooler than the air below.

"I was getting claustrophobic."

"I sort of got used to it when borrowing my friends' yachts." Hirsch yawned. "How about a little nightcap, neighbour?"

"Why not."

* * *

Tamara sat staring into her cabin mirror. It was a bad mirror, not the sort she was accustomed to. But no matter, she didn't really see herself. She saw her father, tall, in his tennis clothes, full of life. Then her mother, cool, elegant, in her ermine coat. And then her governess and the nuns. She was trying to talk with them and she failed. One after another. She thought of Gil and his big babies, the machines. She had no experience with his kind of humanity. Tamara's heroes had nothing to do with machines, did not oil them or anything. Tamara's heroes had money, and power. She shook her head. There were no heroes left. She put her head into her hands. You'd think a man who talked to machines would be cold, distant. But this one seemed so warm, so human, and it touched you. He reached out to you and filled you with warmth, made you relaxed and loose inside. In his presence she never thought of the Swiss money. Her fiancé made her feel tight. But Gil Smith seemed to have a soul. Didn't everyone? His was different, out in the open.

She looked into the mirror again and saw herself smiling. Something was wrong, unfamiliar. "For heaven's sake," she said to this face, "you aren't dead yet." She began to brush her hair with quick light strokes and continued staring into the bad mirror. And then her voice said, "What's wrong with a little shipboard romance?"

* * *

Next morning Uschi's face was the size of a small football, more raw than leathery.

Go see the doctor, Liebchen, said the Prince.

Uschi frowned. Fortunately she did not see Hirsch. *Go!*

"Bet he's nothing to give me. Just like in camp. They're always out of everything, so why bother."

You've got something better to do?

"No!"

The doctor's office on the cabin deck was besieged by a horde of women who wandered in and out, whining and complaining. They paced the deck and peered into his adjoining cabin. Its curtains were tightly drawn.

"Bet he's sleeping."

"He's out getting cigarettes."

"He's with the ugly brunette, the tall one with the big nose."

The sea air must have done them good, Uschi thought. She hadn't heard them complain so heartily since they'd been home with their families, berating their husbands. During the transport they'd been numb. In camp, subdued. Most of them. And later, in the hotel lobbies waiting for the ship, they'd been tense. When they stop complaining watch out, the commandant had said. Once they stop they die. It had certainly been true of the typhoid barracks. But those were old. Thinking of them Uschi felt a pang.

The doctor escorted the tall ugly brunette out of his cabin and a sigh went through the waiting crowd. Uschi compared the brunette's hook-nose to that of the witch in Hänsel and Gretel. But she had to admit she had a fine body, one of those tall lithe jobs she so envied. Like Tamara. Except Tamara was beautiful.

"Ciao, querida," said the doctor, patting the ugly brunette's shoulder, restraining himself, "come see us tomorrow." He beheld the crowd and twirled his British, sandy moustache. The ugly brunette blushed and drew herself up haughtily against the women, stalking off on her red wooden platforms. The air was suddenly electric with women's laughter. Uschi forgot her dignity and laughed, too. The doctor's buck-toothed smile spread, infinitely content with the female attention that floated toward him.

The doctor slipped the thermometer into Uschi's very dry mouth. She sat still, looking up at him out of the hazel

169

eyes that were buried in her swollen red face.

"We're showing a little temp, *querida*," he said kindly, patting her round suntanned arm. "Unfortunately, we've nothing to give you. *Lo siento.*"

Uschi shrugged.

"You'll be all right, *querida*. Hold out your hand."

He shook some aspirins into her sticky hand as if they were gold pieces and said, "Keep it clean, keep it clean."

"On this ship?"

"Come see us tomorrow, *querida*." He smiled and gave her a little pat on her bottom. "*Ciao.*" She decided to smile back but he'd already turned to his next patient, a small pretty blonde. When he saw her hesitating on the threshold, he said, "Patience, patience, I don't think there'll be any scars. Until *mañana*, then."

Dismissed! She scowled silently but could not help wondering why he bothered to flirt with a wounded woman who had a ruined face. She thought of the ugly brunette. Maybe he liked wounded, ugly women. The old desire to compete had crept into her misery. But entrapping him was a process too exhausting to contemplate.

On the shelter deck, she sat brooding about the restoration of her beauty. It was something she both anticipated and feared. The Prince usually told her she was pretty. Personally, Uschi thought pretty women were silly. Handsome was better. Brünnhildes were handsome. Was she a Valkyrie? Would she ever be? She felt more like Joan of Arc. Powerful. Uschi had felt powerful ever since she beat up her brother Michael. It was a brute power, she felt; not at all like the feminine power she discovered when she met the commandant. To know him her slave was intoxicating. But to beat up Michael was good, too. Maybe there was hope for her as a Brünnhilde. She could become a superwoman, a Valkyrie, and ride, sword drawn, into the flames. To live. That was the secret. Not to die. Dying was too easy. Everyone got in on the act. Uschi had seen it over and over again. Like the Prince said. The trick was: *To Live.*

But she needed a reason to live. Beneath the chaos in her mind, well protected and nurtured, there was a huge, orderly demand for a reason to continue living. She wanted an explanation for a crazy universe. Since her prayers for release from camp had been so promptly answered, she half believed again in a God who took care of his creatures. It wasn't the wise old man from her childhood, but some infinitely calm mind, orderly like the Prince's, that set guidelines. Things couldn't be left unguarded, unattended, for people to destroy, to create chaos. God, people were dumb. The Prince said that refugees had no roots. They were uprooted. Rootless. Uschi didn't believe it. People had always been dumb, she thought. She frowned and scratched her nose delicately. There must be a reason, a good reason, for why she'd been shipped around like a truckload of Jerusalem artichokes, why she'd wound up seasick on her back and suffered from sunstroke. Things had to fit, neat and tidy, like the Sunday crossword. She thought of Hirsch who had tried his best to protect her, warn her, about the sun. To no avail. He should have dragged her off someplace and given her a good paddling. Uschi frowned. How had her past influenced her present fate? As far as she could make out aboard the *Baleares*, it had all happened to make her better, wiser, stronger. Uschi was glad to suffer for this noble purpose but she wanted to suffer beautifully. She could not bear to have any part of her become ugly. Disgusted, she looked again in her pocket mirror to see her swollen face. She'd have to hurry and get pretty again, or at least handsome. Ugliness was not something she could permit. The Prince was against it, too. Uschi felt very keenly that she could not bear permanent ugliness.

She was sure she could not be touched, mutilated, or destroyed unless she let down the barriers of will that kept her inviolate. She might be knocked down temporarily, like now, with her sunstroke, but deep inside she knew she would ultimately prevail. The Japanese say: fall down 99 times, get up 100 times. And although she didn't know the word for it yet, Uschi understood that she was a survivor, one who could ride into the flames and emerge, unharmed. She fanned herself with a dirty handkerchief and crawled deeper into the shade. Even when she was besieged by "love's swift errors," as she was with the commandant, Uschi would follow her own timetable. She felt a little dizzy.

* * *

A little before midnight Tamara heard a knock.

"Hi," said Gil, looking scrubbed, and grinning from ear to ear.

"You're early," Tamara said. "Please, please come in."

"I rushed through my watch. Couldn't wait to see you."

He smelled of good soap and aftershave. She looked at him, happy. What a good-looking man he was. His blue shirt matched his blue eyes; his smooth tanned skin showed through the open collar.

He found a place to sit down in the crowded little cabin and brought out his pack of Gitanes. "May I?"

"Please do."

"Nice dress."

"A little number I picked up at the Seville market."

"On you it looks good."

"Thanks." She was used to compliments, but from him they sounded special. "Would you like some brandy?"

"Fine. Cigarette?"

"Not just now. It's a little stuffy in here." She sighed and with a wave said: "All my worldly goods."

"Lotsa stuff," he responded consolingly. As if to say, lots of people have less.

"Much is my mother's. She died in camp." Tamara was saying this to a man she barely knew. Maybe it was the way he listened, his strong face focused on her fondly, a softness in his eyes that made them seem velvety as he sat quietly, comfortably open, accessible. He didn't hide behind the walls she was used to. The comparison would be ridiculous, of course, and she didn't really want to measure him against other men, but she felt that before her sat a real person. A person with problems like other people, but someone who could deal with them. He didn't ignore problems, didn't escape in an alcoholic haze or hide behind diplomatic small talk.

She started to flash her ivory smile but stopped. It seemed out of place with him.

"What is it? You look distressed."

"I was going to smile at you," she said, and really smiled. "But I guess I don't know how."

"You're doing it."

"It's not my old cover-all smile. It's . . . it's different."

"Well, if it makes you feel better, I'm glad. Nice brandy."

"I wish I'd met you sooner," she said, brushing her long hair back. "Come, let's take a stroll, it's stuffy in here."

Outside he took her hand. She hadn't felt so light in years and she wasn't going to worry about anything tonight. Tonight she wanted to be happy. From the lifeboats came much laughter and the piercing strains of a tango. An empty beer bottle hit the deck near them and made her jump.

"Hoodlums," said Gil. "Let's go up to the bridge."

"Can we?"

"Sure. You're with me, kid."

"That was Hirsch's boat. Also his tango. I hear it through my wall but I bet he has more fun with the gang in the lifeboat. Besides, the boats are cooler than our cabins."

"You don't have to be on the defensive. It's OK with me — and you had the money to pay for it."

"No matter how I got it?"

"Well, you got it, so why agonize?"

"You make it sound so simple."

"That's the way I like it. No complications, no headaches."

"All you have to say now is life's too short."

"Simple doesn't mean trite, you know."

"Or boring."

"You're really afraid of being boring?"

She nodded, then shrugged and began to laugh.

* * *

The bridge was dark except for a small hooded lamp over a shelf near the chart room. An officer nodded to Gil. Then he smiled politely to Tamara and suddenly seemed to remember something that needed to be done on deck. Both of them were silent. They could see a sliver of the moon. He drew her close and kissed her, gently stroking her thick red hair. Slowly he ran his hand over her back and when she pressed close to him he fondled her breasts. She could feel his penis strain against her thin dress. Although there was no one on the deserted deck she felt uneasy. As if reading her mind, he said, "Want to go to my cabin?"

"It's not stuffy?"

"It's starboard, there's a nice breeze." He led her down to the cabin deck.

"Oh, it's so much cooler." She looked around. "And bigger. So uncluttered. Cigarettes, pipe, books, bottles."

"Want to move in?"

She giggled and he filled a glass of brandy for her.

"Mmm, it's better than mine."

"Only the best for you, Tam. Let's drink to *amor y pesetas*."

"I'll take the money."

"You're welcome to mine. Relax, you look tense."

"What'd you expect in a strange man's cabin?"

"Want me to rub your neck?" He did it before she could answer.

"Oh, that feels great." Outside she could hear the waves beat softly against the ship's hull, as if accompanying the music from the lifeboats. She felt his hand lift her against him and she went limp in his arms. Her mouth and crotch were moist, and she arched under him as he penetrated her hard. The shock almost cut her breath and she clutched at him.

"Come on," he said, "come with me, come, come."

"Yes, yes, yes."

She lay still under him, her body suffused with a fierce, soft warmth. She gazed at him and said dreamily, "You've got to be one of the most handsome men I've ever met. Hairless and tanned, despite your black Portuguese mother."

He grinned and said, "Built like a wooden Indian." He got up to rinse himself at the washbasin.

"You don't have to worry about me," Tamara said from her luxurious perch in his bunk.

"Just a seaman's filthy habit."

"A girl in every port, eh?" No wonder, she thought, he's a perfect specimen. She remembered the skinny, leathery J.P., with his five o'clock shadow. And Xav, the impeccable Latin. "Whatever," she said. "Give me a cigarette, you handsome devil."

He had this wide, good-natured grin as he lit one for her and his eyes twinkled.

"Come here," he said. And grabbed her again.

24

The invisible captain brought the *Baleares* safely into Lisbon harbour. They anchored in the Tagus Estuary and hordes of small boats swarmed around her like sharks, disgorging natives bearing tschotchkes, company agents, customs officers, and quarantine officials. The coastguard came aboard to prevent any of the passengers from darkening Portugal's shores.

Uschi and her new friend Hirsch sat taking in the scene from the hatches, fanning themselves in the stale hot air with Uschi's straw hat. Uschi was chilly despite the heat.

"Poor child, these extra people are cutting off what little oxygen we have." Hirsch was blowing perfect smoke rings into the still harbour air.

"Someone get me off this ship," cried Uschi, gingerly touching the blisters on her face.

"If only I could, *Liebchen*. Just the same, please leave your face alone."

Both looked in distress at the tumult around them. "Not that I wouldn't like to get off myself," added Hirsch, "but here we are."

"Damn." Gingerly she blew her nose.

"Here, take my last hankie. Soon I'll have to do my own laundry like a bloody Chink. It's come to that."

"Don't call them that."

"What? Oh, don't mind me, *Liebchen*. I'm just an old fart. You could use a little rest." He put his arm around her. "Here, lean on me."

"How can I rest when there's no place to lie down and nowhere to sit?"

Hirsch nodded as they watched some passengers climb into a motor launch.

"D'you see what I see?" Uschi gripped his arm.

"I see." Hirsch expectantly lit another cigarette and got up.

"Quick, go ask what's up."

"Exactly what I'm thinking." Hirsch grabbed a white-uniformed officer and inquired politely, "And where, may one ask, sir, are these fortunate ladies and gents motoring towards?"

The officer shrugged.

"That's it, I'm off," said Uschi, poised to leave Hirsch's restraining presence for one of her odysseys.

"Oh no you don't." Hirsch tightened his grip on her. "You're in no shape to go off alone. We'll do this together."

Further diligent questioning elicited that those in the launch needed to visit the local consulates in town to have their visas revalidated because they'd expired during the *Baleares*'s two-month game of hide-and-seek with her passengers.

"My visa's OK," said Uschi regretfully. "I'm on my mother's. Hers is OK too."

"So's mine."

"So who knows."

"Ooff." They looked at each other. "Let's go."

They left with the next launch. No one questioned them because they simply acted as distressed as everyone else in the visa-revalidating queue. Acting distressed had become second nature.

"You can relax now."

"I am."

"So why d'you frown?"

"I always do," said Uschi happily. She let her hand slide over the side of the boat, touching the soft warm waves.

Looking distressed was Uschi's forte, it was an exercise in which her mother, that mistress of distress, had achieved Olympian feats during the last two years. *"Celui qui fait l'âne ramasse le foin,"* was her father's comment on what he described as her mother's emergency face. *The one who plays the donkey gets the hay.* And her mother sure put the hay to good use. Still, Uschi wondered what her mother would do in the new land — provided they got there. Would she be able to drop her act? Or had she been at it so long that it had become a second skin? "Stress or no stress, the question is: Will she be able to climb out of her groove and start playing a new tune?"

"What are you talking about, child?" asked Hirsch.

177

"My mother."

"She bothers you?"

"Plenty."

"Lots of time to talk about her on the ship. In the meantime let's enjoy ourselves, shall we?"

"Sure," said Uschi, who was in the best of spirits. "I love it here. I love all southern cities."

The launch delivered them to a flight of stone steps still wet from the tide. "*Terra firma*, Mother!" said Uschi.

An elderly Portuguese gent from the consulate briskly organized the group and led them off across Praça do Comercio, a large square on the waterfront, through an archway into an area of narrow streets and alleyways. Their guide herded them off toward Rossio, a tree-lined plaza with fountains, hotels, restaurants, sidewalk cafés, flower sellers and bookstalls.

To Uschi the people in the streets seemed serene. Their poise contrasted favourably with the anxious postures of her fellow passengers, who resembled a sort of diplomatic mission from a strange country: a little band of emissaries from the land of fear. But here there was no war. And no fear, as far as Uschi could see. Certainly the pace was different. And there were yellow streetcars too. Like in Marseilles, but smaller.

Uschi squeezed Hirsch's hand and whispered, "Let's get away from them."

"OK, *Liebchen*." They lagged behind and then left the group to its visa problems. Wandering off into the sunshine, Hirsch smiled faintly, taking in everything silently.

"What are you thinking about?" asked Uschi.

"I'm writing a film." He looked at her and grinned broadly. Uschi frowned and pursed her lips.

"Oh."

For a moment she thought he might be making fun of her, but then she decided he wasn't. Uschi smiled and slipped her arm in Hirsch's. They walked briskly in the beautiful sunshine and after a long while came to the tiny streets and narrow alleyways of Alfama, the old Moorish quarter. Donkeys passed, loaded with bundles; women carrying laundry smiled at them. They had to step into a doorway to let a small tramcar go by. Wandering back to Rossio they turned into Rua do Ouro, one of those charming little streets with jewellers' boutiques. Uschi danced along next to Hirsch, hiding her peeling face behind her large hat. Out of the corner of her eye she noticed with satisfaction the men who ogled her plump little figure. She lifted her head and threw out her bosom. "Guess who I am?" her walk seemed to cry out, "just guess." Her self-centred absorption was broken by a delicate filigree fan; it was made of a deep gold and Chinese red lacquer, from Macao.

"You like?"

She nodded ecstatically.

"What are we waiting for, let's go get it."

She tried to tell him the fan was far too delicate for a Brünnhilde like her, but he dragged her into the boutique and made the sales girl get it out of the window.

"Oh thank you, Hirsch dear, thank you very much." She kissed him enthusiastically and almost lost her straw hat. The fan was the most precious thing she'd ever owned, she assured him, with the possible exception of the little duck's head umbrella her uncle had given her.

"Give me your hat," he said, and put it on.

"No, I need it." She snatched it back from him and popped it on her head, fanning herself with her new fan to hide her scarred face. "Oh, look." She danced happily around some painted earthen pots, embroidered blouses, skirts, linen, and wickerwork baskets.

"Let's go get it."

"God, no, where'll I put it, our suitcases are stuffed."

"I like to see you stop frowning, *Liebchen*. Want another fan? Look, there's a pretty blue one."

"You don't have to buy me more stuff, Hirsch. I love you

anyway." She grinned broadly and adjusted her hat. Safely, from behind her new fan, she peered at the world with her marvellous hazel eyes. Her face might have been hidden, but her plump bottom was highly visible and soon a cortege of local virility trailed after them.

Hirsch smiled. "You've sure got drawing power, *Liebchen*. And I shall put you in my films." He gave her a pat. "It's your fat little behind."

"D'you think so?" she said happily. The men were all so handsome. She'd love to gaze into those soulful brown eyes and hold their young masculine hands. Thank God she wouldn't have to make a choice. They wouldn't be here long enough. In Spain she'd had to decide. Wrongly, as it turned out: she'd picked the one lemon. She pushed out her lower lip in disgust and tried not to think of the rooming house in Cadiz.

How much nicer it was to coast, wait, and dream her dreams. But then, she also liked the suspense she felt before choosing. When she dared herself. Would she or wouldn't she? Suddenly it seemed safe and all right to have picked a lemon. One couldn't win all the time, the idea was to take a chance.

"A centavo for your thoughts."

She smiled. "Marry me."

Hirsch laughed. "I'm flattered. But no thank you, I've enough troubles."

She gave him what she thought was her Giaconda smile. "I'm serious."

"I'm tempted, sweetie, but I just got out of one jail and what I need is a little rest and recuperation." He sighed. "Maybe I'm getting old."

"Oh," said Uschi, disappointed. "I thought you'd be happy."

"And I would be, under other circumstances. If you were older; if I hadn't been married before. And if I hadn't gotten into trouble with the ss, and been kicked out of UFA . . ."

"If there hadn't been a war. If we weren't together on the *Baleares*. If we hadn't been always hungry in camp," she continued his litany.

"Speaking of hunger, let's go eat."

They ordered lunch in one of the cafés on the Rossio. A breeze from the river brushed Uschi's hair. They drank Madeira and Uschi said, "White bread, with real butter," and stuffed her mouth full. Then they had *caldo verde*, *espetada*, and a bottle of Boal. "It must be a hundred years old," she gulped ecstatically, then started to cough.

"Oops, easy does it."

"My first real meal in a year."

Hirsch raised his glass. "To your first real meal."

She had another coughing fit.

"It went down the wrong way." He gently tapped her on the back. "Good thing you met your Uncle Hirsch."

She nodded. It wasn't really her first meal. There'd been good food at the commandant's. And at Pau, the elegant spa, after they'd left camp. Uschi giggled, recalling eyes popping at the sight of her waddling around in her automobile tire clogs. She'd almost forgotten the meals with the old guy at the black market restaurant in Marseilles, and all the other stuff. She frowned between bites. She knew that this was different: there was no connection between eating with Hirsch and sex.

"And people always say there's no free lunch."

"What are you talking about, *Liebchen*?"

She gulped down more green wine. "And I don't have to sleep with you?"

"Now that's a turnaround. Twenty minutes ago you proposed to me."

"I meant marriage."

"Ah." He looked at her fondly and kissed her on the forehead and she withdrew a little. How was one to behave with a nice man who bought one things and didn't want sex?" She felt like kicking him in the crotch so that he'd get mad and hit her or something. All this niceness made her feel guilty. In confusion she stared at her fingernails. They looked more terrible than ever. Hirsch looked too and she hid her hands under the table. "I'll grow new ones."

"Let me see."

"No, I don't want to."

"OK, I won't insist. Didn't anyone feed you at camp? What about your famous commandant?"

"Sure, first class." She was now sorry she'd told him. He couldn't understand. No one could. She bit her lower lip. "Ouch."

"You're bleeding."

"It hurts." The sunshine turned grey for her and suddenly Hirsch sounded almost cruel, bent on exposing the pain she was trying to hide from herself. The commandant was a bad dream, a foolish thing she'd done a lifetime ago. Something to be ashamed about. "But he was nice. Even if he tortured Spaniards," she said, almost in tears.

"The bastard must have been scared for his hide."

"No one really knew him."

"And you did?"

Uschi frowned. "More vino?" asked Hirsch. She shook her long, straight, sun-streaked hair. For a brief moment she was afraid of Hirsch. All that talk about the commandant could give him ideas of his own. Even if he had rejected her marriage proposal and the idea of sex. That's the way men were. Inferior. Uschi got very mad and looked at Hirsch probingly. Maybe the refusal of the marriage proposal, and of sex, was an act. A test to see what she'd do. Now, maybe, he'd really show his face and ruin their friendship. The fact that she liked him was no reason to go to bed with him. She'd loved the commandant, but she'd hardly liked him.

"Look at your admirers across the street."

"Ooff." Indeed, some of the youths who'd followed them hung around on the sidewalk while others, more bold, had claimed nearby tables.

"You're becoming a star. Soon they'll want your autograph."

"I love them all." Uschi brightened, a queen smiling at her vassals. "They're so full of life, so happy. The others, our kind, are grey, mummies. Shrivelled up like old coconuts. These," she pointed at the youths next table, "are like the sun. I love the sun." Ruefully, she touched her burned face. "When we arrived in camp there was this gorgeous October sun. It kept us alive."

Hirsch smiled and offered a cigarette. She shook her head and leaned against him. She felt a little tipsy.

"I stood in that sun with the gypsies. We stood at the fence, watching people go by, talking to the guards. Sometimes we stood leaning against the administration barracks, with the sun warming the metal wall. All day long that October sun shone on us as if it would never go away. It warmed everything. And the air was so pure you could taste the ozone. I had terrible skin then, but my skin got so pure up there. Feel." In her eagerness she dropped her fan and grabbed his hand. Then she remembered. "*Merde.*"

Quickly she shielded her face again. "I'll show you before we get off the ship. When I'm healed."

Hirsch patted her hand. "I'm sure you will. And you're right, the air was great up there. After all, the place is near Pau. People spend a bundle in the spa to breathe that air. Something's got to be good in that place."

"You should have seen me at Pau with my auto clogs, I was a riot."

"You bet."

Uschi closed her eyes and dropped her fan. The wine felt good in her body. And as long as the sun blazed Uschi could never die. She could live forever high up in those mountains, on that small piece of earth — even when it held so many, locked up together, prisoners and jailers. Above them, in the wide open sky, her spirit could soar high in the beautiful air. Her body could dance to the gypsies' *castañuelas* beneath the sun's radiance. She could mourn each dying ray with the gypsies, as only women in twilight can mourn for their lover. And then came the winter.

"The gypsies locked themselves inside their barracks all winter. They never came out. Never opening those chicken coop windows. They breathed in their own stench like the women in the typhoid barracks. They laid out their cards and boiled things on that awful stove. All day long."

"They had plenty of time, what'd they boil up?"

"Dunno. I never ate with them. They got it from the Spaniards. Everyone got everything from the Spaniards. Everyone was always rushing to the stoves, simmering apples and chestnuts with snow. Stuff like that."

"Like what?"

"Apples and chestnuts, it wasn't bad." She looked at her terrible fingernails again.

"Dessert?" Hirsch called for the waiter.

"Chocolate mousse," cried Uschi. "With whipped cream. God, I haven't had whipped cream in years."

"Flan," said Hirsch. Then the waiter suggested morgados, almond cakes, Barrigas de Freira, Madeira honey cakes, and natas. Not too much?

"*Ess, mein Kind.*"

"God, this is so good it might make me orgasm. If I could orgasm, that is."

She bit her lip. Now she'd done it again.

"Want to change my mind about eloping?"

"Where to?"

"This isn't a bad place, we could stick around here."

"Can we come back tomorrow?"

"We'll try."

They went through the narrow streets, across the Praça do Comercio, down the stairs, and caught a return launch with a group from the consulate. Uschi trailed her hand in the warm water again and looked back at the city. Maybe she could wait for the commandant here, with Hirsch. He'd have to come out of camp one day, maybe soon. She was beginning to like this city and she hated the thought of going back to the *Baleares*, to her parents, and ending up in God knows what awful new place. Her mother was always saying that they'd have to work there. Work. Work. Work. She'd never really worked but she didn't think she'd like it much. The new place was sure to be alien to her, as alien as this city seemed familiar. As Spain had seemed familiar, as the gypsies had. Strange to others, but familiar to her.

"I'm almost tempted to stay. But my Ma would kill me." Uschi was being dramatic. She also wanted to see what lay ahead at the end of the trip. It was the same urge that had made her decide against suicide the day the Gestapo came for her family. She quoted Gibran. "But as she descended the hill a sadness came upon her and she thought, 'How shall I go in peace and without sorrow? Nay, not without a wound in my heart shall I leave this city.'"

"Sounds corny to me."

"Not like Brünnhilde. Riding into the flames."

"So that's your thing, eh?"

She looked tenderly at him. "We'll always be friends, won't we?"

"And I'll make you a star."

"Shake."

*   *   *

The *Baleares* was crowded with swarms of peddlers, customs officers, and white-clad quarantine guards.

"I feel like the stuffing in a Christmas goose," said Countess Olga.

"The stuffing's as good as the goose, *chérie*," said her husband, "if not better."

"And as hot as fresh out of the oven."

"The contained can't be cooler than the container."

"Dimitri, it's too hot for physics."

"Buddhism," said the Count, removing his pipe.

Spotting Uschi and Hirsch, the Countess cried, "Where have you been, children?"

"How'd you know we've been somewhere?" asked Uschi innocently.

"You have a well-aired look that I find absent on this ship."

"Lunch," said Uschi, still somewhat tipsy.

"Visas," said Hirsch.

"Visas? Luncheon? Where? How?"

"In a divine open-air restaurant on the Rossio."

"At the American consulate," said Hirsch.

"Congratulations, I'm happy for you. Dimitri, oh Dimitri, where is that man?" Her voice easily overcame the hawkers, customs officers, and guards as she plunged in among them. "How can you lose someone on this ship?" she asked no one in particular as they all began to look for him. "Bodies, bodies, but very few amusing bodies. I must get off this ship for a breath of fresh air. Look what it's done for Hirsch and little Uschi. Dimitri, oh Dimitri!" She dived into a knot of gamins. He was there, handing out coins. "There you are, Buzz. Look into the lunch-and-visa situation, quick. Hirsch and little Uschi have been to lunch at the American consulate. And I always knew there was something wrong with our visas."

"Oh, I know the consul from Budapest. When I was teaching at the university. Give him my best regards."

"Thank you," said Hirsch.

"I know they're adorable and we never had any, Dimitri," Olga was trying to extricate him from the boys, "but I simply must get off this ship for a moment."

"What's happening?" asked Tamara, who'd joined them.

"You see these bedraggled happy persons reboarding the ship?" said Hirsch.

They looked toward the gangway.

Tamara nodded and Hirsch said, "They didn't get their visas today so they'll have to return to the consulate tomorrow." He grinned. "One more hardship in their quest for a new life. I'm off to my lifeboat." He lit a cigarette. "I predict we'll be in the harbour for a good long time."

"I feel a chill coming on," said the Countess. "Dimitri, please take me to our cabin."

"*Sans blague*," said the Count.

"Ahhhhh," said Tamara, and they hurried off in different directions.

"They do catch on," said Hirsch, pulling on his cigarette. "They're not so dumb."

"Camp alumni," said Uschi.

"Were they in camp?"

"They had enough credits for graduation."

"I like you, brat."

Uschi pretended to be overcome and blew her nose into Hirsch's last clean monogrammed handkerchief. "Want to elope?" She threw her arms around him.

"I didn't say I loved you." He drew her tight to him but she immediately felt uncomfortable. As soon as she could she freed herself.

To distract him, she said, "You're crazy about her." It was patently unfair.

"The phony red-haired goddess?"

"She's nice," she said defensively.

"Not exactly my dish."

"You must have changed your mind."

"Come on, I'll buy you something." He dragged her over to where the hawkers had spread their wares.

"I can't be bought, you know." But then she cried, "Soap! Saltwater soap." Ruefully she rubbed the crook of her arm. An accumulation of a week's dirt had collected there. The saltwater showers only made it worse.

"I haven't sat in a hot tub for two years."

"Any hot tubs for sale?" asked Hirsch.

"At the bedbug hotel in Marseilles four ladies were washing in the sink every morning."

"Delightful."

"If you like four naked ladies."

"I do."

"Four of them?"

"All."

"Damn, my ma." Uschi pointed at her mother, resurrected and promenading, inch by inch, on the arm of her father. Sure, at least, if not of terra firma, of a stationary ship in port. She was followed by Michael and complained heartily about her seasickness.

"I'm glad you're better, *Maman*." Uschi gave her a dutiful kiss. "This is my friend Hirsch. We went ashore for lunch." She was sorry she said it, for her mother's face took on her well-known look of instant alarm.

"I hope she didn't bother you?"

"Not at all, she's a delightful child."

But she was not that easily assuaged. "I hope you didn't get into trouble again, you know what a time we had getting our visas. If anyone knows you left the ship . . ."

"It's quite all right, *Madame*. It was my idea, actually."

"You're sure? It sounds like one of her ideas. Well, she won't have to annoy me much longer. I'm not going to be around forever."

"You'll survive, *Madame*," said Hirsch politely.

"Of course she'll survive," said Uschi's father.

"Ah, Ma, there you go again," said Michael.

"I should be so lucky," mumbled Uschi.

"What did you say, you ungrateful girl?"

"Surprise us, *Maman*."

"I'm playing cards up on the mast." It was the first time her little brother tried to compete with her and Uschi looked at him, astonished. He pointed proudly to the masthouse tabernacle where the booms were stepped. So, he was finally beginning to let go of his father's shirt-tails?

"Then you're nice and out of the way up there." She looked briefly at the little platform at the foremast and gave him her nod of approval. She whispered into his ear,

"I'm sleeping up on the poop deck among sacks of potatoes — but don't tell anybody."

Her brother considered the relative merits of their abodes and decided his was superior. But he said generously, "So you have potatoes to eat."

"You're getting to be a wise guy like your papa."

Her little brother looked proud. He had a little colour, Uschi thought, the sea air must be doing him good. He'd easily been the hungriest, scrawniest, lousiest boy in camp. Uschi urged him to wash, comb his hair, brush his teeth every time she saw him. He had been reluctant to do these things even at home.

"Are you brushing your teeth these days?"

"Oh leave him alone," said her father, fondly tousling Michael's hair.

"He's going to lose them, Papa," said Uschi jealously. He never tousled her hair. "I mean his teeth."

"Well, at least we're rid of him high up there on the mast."

Her father laughed and put his arms around them both. Uschi felt better.

"There's a bunch of us up there," said Michael importantly, "girls too."

"Girls?" Her little brother grinned. Up to now he'd hated girls.

"Come, you two. Let's have a look at what there is to buy." He put his arms around them and winked at Hirsch. "Nice meeting you, *Herr* Hirsch, and thanks for taking care of my little girl."

"Where are you sleeping these days, Papa?"

"Oh, down with the men, but don't worry, sweetie. It's not so bad. And it's close to the women's quarters so I can take care of your mother. A husband's duty."

Uschi knew he didn't say it to make her feel bad. But she did. She always did. It made her feel so guilty. About everything. Guilty for breathing. Guilty for being on this ship, getting away from their captors — when at this moment her friend Bea might be in mortal danger. On the other hand, Bea might be having a great time in Casablanca with François's girls. And adorable Helmut. Uschi knew she ought to be down there looking after her mother, listening to her complaints and making soothing sounds like any dutiful daughter. But she'd rather die than descend into the bleak, suffocating holds. She knew she'd die as surely as she'd have died in the typhoid barracks. It was ultimately a question of the survival of the fittest: the typhoid women or Uschi. And, though she dared not think it, she knew it in her heart: Uschi or her mother. She scratched herself nervously and stopped feeling guilty long enough to see her father enjoying his sea voyage in his own quiet way. They were far from immediate danger and money worries. She could tell he was having a good time by the way he enumerated some of the ship menus. Uschi loved her father's capacity for enjoyment. Simple things made him glad. Things like having butter for his boiled potatoes again. Uschi said earnestly, "I can arrange for you to eat with the ascs."

"And what's the asc, my daughter?"

"The Auxiliary Stewards' Corps, Papa. I'm a member."

"Of course."

Uschi looked at him curiously. Was he making fun of her? "So you'll eat with us."

"I'll be honoured."

"Me, too," said Michael.

"No one's asked you."

"Now, Uschi," said her father.

"Next thing the whole ship'll want to bring their dependents. There'll be a riot and old man Steinheil will throw us all overboard."

"I see you've met the important passengers."

"I've met his lousy kids," said Michael.

"You're right," said her father, "we can't all come to the — what was it?"

"ASC, Papa."

"Perhaps you can make an exception for your brother though. He looks a little hollow to me."

"OK." But she was annoyed. Here he'd brought her little brother into the act again. Couldn't she ever do anything with him alone?

Her father flicked the ashes from his cigar and the wind guided them onto her bare toes. They were still warm but didn't burn her. She stepped back from her father and he smiled and put his arm round her. "Don't begrudge him the food, child. He's a growing boy."

"He never does anything by himself. And I was the one who made the effort to get into the ASC."

"He went out with the boys in camp to buy eggs from the farmers."

"That's different. He didn't do it on his own. He just tagged along like he always does." She really hated Michael now.

"He's so young," said her father, defending his only son. "Give him time."

"He'll always tag along," Uschi said stubbornly, "it's his nature. He never sticks his head out, the turtle. But he's quick to grab the credit."

Michael gave her a nasty look and she knew that at the first opportunity he'd be sure to snitch on her again.

"Come, come, children, no fighting now. It's a beautiful day so let's go and buy something nice."

Uschi could see her father enjoying a sort of anonymity away from her mother, even though there was not much privacy on the ship. In a way he reminded her of Count Dimitri — enjoying his quiet, good-natured inner world. Why had they both married such God-awful women? No, the Countess wasn't that bad. If only her father'd married someone like her. Shyly, Uschi touched her father's arm; he put his arm around her again. They bought more salt-dissolving soap.

He also bought candy, perfume for her mother, the most darling native doll for Uschi, and a football for Michael.

"Oh, Papa, what's he going to do with it aboard?" cried Uschi jealously.

"He can use it when we land."

It was the first time her father had mentioned the future and it frightened Uschi.

When her mother raved about the new land it seemed unreal, as far away as the bogeyman of her childhood. But her father's words made it terrifyingly concrete. It was like the time she had finished kindergarten and had to face the big school. She'd sit for days in a corner of her room brooding, building it up until it became so big she couldn't talk about it with anyone. Even though she generally talked a lot, she knew she hoarded the important things deep within her, afraid someone might ferret them out and destroy them. Once or twice in her early childhood she had tried to tell her mother about something really important. But her mother was always too busy; or worse, she laughed. Once, when her little brother got sick, Uschi's mother sent her away to her grandmother's farm. Uschi wouldn't eat there. Even when she returned home she would have no food. Her mother stuck her into a little dark room in the basement and tried feeding her through the barred wooden door. It was like a jail. Uschi spat out the food. On another occasion the doctor said, "You're going to lose that child, better look after your boy." Her mother had fought for her like a madwoman, according to her father.

Among the goods for sale were a pair of the most hideous wooden platform shoes. They were orange and more monstrous than her tire clogs. Uschi didn't really want them.

"Wouldn't you like those pretty sandals over there?" her father asked mildly.

"You're walking like a peasant already," said her mother.

Uschi swore she'd absolutely die if she couldn't have the orange shoes. Her father bought them. Uschi knew he would. He always did in the end, because he liked peace in the family. Uschi felt triumphant.

She remembered the huge battle she and her mother had had the night before the Gestapo came. Her mother, Uschi felt, had wrathfully neglected to pack any of her pretty shoes: especially her favourite blue suede walking shoes, the ones with the crocodile insets. When she discovered them sitting in the closet, forlorn, she'd hurriedly put them on. As soon as they got to camp she found the rubber clogs. The blue suedes were prized away in her luggage.

"If you'd packed my shoes I wouldn't walk like a peasant."

"If you'd packed them yourself you'd have them. You're a big girl now. I couldn't think of everything in 20 minutes."

"You took the laundry in."

"Well, I couldn't let it hang out there."

"Girls, girls," said her father.

The truth was that Uschi had been so busy considering suicide, and then with changing her mind and taking her last bath, that she'd seen no point in packing at all. When she came out of the bathroom she found her blue suede shoes and her favourite blue dress with the red polka dots and matching little jacket she'd designed herself. Mechanically she'd dressed in front of the intruders. She'd never forgive them. But even now, through layers of rage and her desire for revenge, Uschi could see her stupidity. She shouldn't have lost her head. A sudden dreadful sense of guilt made her fumble and drop her new fan.

"What happened to your face?" cried her mother.

"My face?"

"Look what she's done to herself again. That girl will be a nail in my coffin yet."

"I should be so lucky," mumbled Uschi.

"What was that?"

"Nothing." Uschi balled up her fists so she wouldn't talk back to her mother — or kill her. Please, shut her up; oh, shut her up.

"Leave the child alone," said her father, touching her mother's arm. "Please."

Her mother moaned and put on her martyr face.

"I don't want the shoes, Papa."

"Come on now, you're my great good girl. Wear them and enjoy them." Gently he thrust them into her hands. "Have you seen the doctor?"

"I'm much better, Daddy, really I am. He said I'll be fine."

"That's good to hear. Don't be cross with your mother, she's upset."

"Oh, Daddy, she's just feeling sorry for herself. Again."

"She'll calm down once we're settled in."

Again there was the reference to their future. "She never wanted to go anywhere," said Uschi accusingly.

"You and I know we can't always do what we want. She'll just have to make the best of it," said her father sadly. "And you're my good big girl."

It made Uschi proud when he depended on her. The last few weeks in Spain he'd given her their money since she was the only member of the family who could speak even rudimentary Spanish.

* * *

Every morning now people queued up on the gangway to get a place on the launches that would take them to have their visas renewed. They were happy to get off the ship; it was sweltering hot in the estuary, even at night. Still, the atmosphere aboard had lightened considerably. Uschi's mother felt much better so the family ate together. Her mother insisted on it, but Uschi was on her guard. She saw her mother as a tigress, always ready to pounce. She was feverish again and felt defensive. She coped using a trick she was very proud of. She pretended to be her own secretary, a nice, polite young lady who guarded the reception area while Uschi was out to lunch. Even Michael noticed her new politeness and wanted to know if she was sick with her blisters.

Not sick, she told him, merely thinking.

"You sound pretty sick to me."

"You're too young to understand." And when he pointed at his forehead, she added, "No, I'm not crazy, stupid."

"Are you two fighting again?" To escape one of their mother's harangues, they answered quickly, "No, *Maman*."

But Uschi felt like a coward, hiding behind imaginary secretary and her little brother. So very unlike Brünnhilde. She missed the Countess, who didn't seem to be around much lately. The Uvaloffs must be ashore. They would be having a great time, browsing and visiting their friends. They had friends everywhere, she thought enviously, and were certainly too busy to think of her on the hot, crowded ship.

"I'm so sorry," she said in the voice of her imaginary secretary to one of her mother's complaints. Her mother looked at her, astonished. Uschi noticed, then, that her mother seemed like a beautiful, ooff, really beautiful, delicate middle-aged lady. She was very insecure, frightened, and burdened with an unmanageable daughter. She also seemed so alone, so fragile, such a far cry from Brünnhilde, that Uschi almost felt sorry for her.

"She's frightened," she said to the Prince.

Sure is, Liebchen.

"Why's that?"

She's in a scary situation and she has no faith.

"But we all are. And I do?"

Sure do.

"Then how can I help?" cried Uschi, overcome by great waves of pity.

Be nice to her.

"I'll try," she said doubtfully, mapping out her new Being-Nice-to-Mother campaign.

You could pray for her.

"I don't know how."

The way you did in camp.

"On the orange crate?"

Yep.

25

At night the coastguard thoughtfully volunteered free Portuguese lessons to the girls, and soon happy couples were seen practising near the lifeboats. So intent were all hands on learning that no one paid much attention to anyone else. Soon a few enterprising young officers came on board and insisted on dancing to an old phonograph in the mess hall, their white uniforms limp with perspiration, crushing against their partners' long gowns. Uschi and Hirsch were peeking down from above.

"They're nuts," said Uschi.

"Sure are," Hirsch replied, lighting a cigarette.

"Sweating down in the holds when they could be nice and cool in one of their swinging nightclubs."

"It's all the new flesh."

"Some romantic you are." Uschi was disgusted.

"Want to elope, *Liebchen?*" He gave her a little pinch.

The dancers surfaced, wrinkled and hot, promenading round the crowded main deck arm in arm. The girls were willing captives of the romantic officers.

That night the Uvaloffs returned laden with gifts for their friends aboard and next morning 500 more bewildered passengers swelled the breakfast queues.

"They sneaked them on in the dead of the night. They caught everyone catnapping," Uschi complained to Hirsch.

"I see you had a conversation with the Countess."

"She saw them. You know she can't sleep."

"You'll make a fine reporter, *Liebchen*.

"They brought one with them. He's here with us now."

"Who're we talking about, *Liebchen*, you lost me."

"The American reporter. He came with the Uvaloffs. He's still sleeping." She frowned. "Except I'm not sure he's a reporter."

"Oh, nowadays everyone's a reporter. Unless they're a starlet."

Uschi's face lit up. "Maybe he's a spy for the MI5."

"You're one romantic little girl. How'd you know about the MI5?"

"The Uvaloffs." Her attention was riveted to the six live oxen that had been tied to the pad-eyes opposite the mess hall entrance. "They just smuggled them aboard."

"The oxen?" asked Hirsch.

"The passengers. So the tales about staying in port to renew all the visas were nothing but a red herring."

"We're in a fascist country."

This time Uschi hit him. "Do those animals look slightly seasick to you?"

"Only a little unbalanced in their psyches."

"Their psyches aren't going to be slaughtered."

*   *   *

The coastguard moved off, making just a little more room for the 1,500 passengers, six live oxen, disgruntled crew, an American reporter and the invisible captain. After a hot, stagnant week the *Baleares* steamed out of the Tagus estuary. The hawkers in their little boats gave them an enthusiastic send-off. That night *Herr* Steinheil, invigorated once more by the cool sea air, led another attack against the deck chairs. Some still had people in them. In the morning much splintered wood could be seen on deck.

Uschi stopped being a waitress. She was preparing herself for her future as a star. She also liked eating with the other passengers. Her connections in the galley still got her choice portions.

"Too bad they had to take on the extra 500," she told Tamara at breakfast.

"What 500?"

"I don't believe it. The 500 passengers they sneaked aboard last night. Didn't you hear Steinheil raving?"

"Oh, I thought I heard a commotion."

Uschi could have sworn she blushed. "Your cabin isn't soundproof," she said suspiciously.

"You're right. I do see some strange faces. And they got them all on while we weren't looking?"

"Well, some of us were, for all the good it did. They must be making a bundle on this trip."

"Here we're talking about money again," said Tamara.

"I wouldn't know about that," said Uschi, "but I can't stand sneaks, and these people have no morals."

"You mean the ship company?"

"Them too."

*　*　*

"Touch me," said Tamara. "Oh, harder. Ohhhhhh . . ."

Her breath came in short, sharp gasps. "You make me feel so . . . so alive. Listen." She pulled his head close to her heart. "I've been cold so long," she whispered. "So cold." He penetrated her and she felt him almost like a shock of rebirth. It was something so new, so unexpected, that she clung to him in wordless bliss. She ignored a tiny voice from far off that repeated, gurgling like a river, "Watch out, Tamara, watch out." She cried, "Let's be happy, oh, let's you and me be happy."

"Yes," said Gil, "yes my love."

They lay on a bed of spare canvas from the hatch tents, half hidden by the private shadows that mingled with the shadows from the lifeboats.

"And to think that only a few weeks ago I would have

198

looked down my nose at you," she pulled his ear.

"You did."

"Had I met you anywhere else; at the hotel or at a restaurant or someplace. And I didn't."

"No, sweet, you looked right through me."

"How could I? With that dripping old lady draped over your arm?"

"You could have fooled me. Ouch! Stop tearing my ear off." He grinned at her with a mischievous twinkle in his blue eyes. "Happy?"

"Let me think a bit. Give me a cigarette."

"*Si?*"

"Of course. I don't know how I'll feel tomorrow, or the day after, life being uncertain and all that, but for now, *si.*"

"Let me put it this way. When I met you, you seemed depressed. Are you better?"

"None of us is getting any better. Suffering makes men wise, they say, but frankly, I haven't noticed fresh outbreaks of wisdom around here, have you?"

"Oh, it's around if you know how to look for it."

"Wisdom among the survivors?"

"They're tough, they make out. It's the others, the ones who stayed behind in the camps you've got to worry about. Look at it this way. These people here on the ship. They may be damaged but they're alive. Life is good. Life is not to be despised."

"You sound so pragmatic."

He laughed. "They say pragmatism is for those on the way up while principles are for those on the way down."

"How clever, darling."

"I've been around for a while and seen a few things. We usually get the things we deserve. The lovers, the leaders. In the end we deserve what we get. We may not like it, but . . ."

"And the environment, outside pressure doesn't change us?"

"We change if we want to change. Age, job, family has nothing to do with it. Change is an effort of the will."

"*Merci*, I've no will."

"Ohhh, you've got plenty of will, but I suspect you don't want to change." He looked at her and laughed. "You like yourself just the way you are."

"Really?" Tamara's smile faded. "Which way is that?"

"You're the type of girl who likes to travel first class and I doubt you're going to give it up."

"You may be right." She stared at him and turned on her stomach, cupping her face in her hands. "But I'm not alone. They're all staying in their old ruts. They don't really mind a little suffering so long as they can stay the way they are. Look around this ship, this collection of monsters, complainers, and accusers. Even bullies like Steinheil, they're all former dreamers. I can feel their fear, their greed, their envy — hanging on to every last bit of their miserable lives. But when it comes to striking out for new shores, *adios*, *muchachos*. They panic and cling to their pasts."

"Don't be too harsh on them, sweet. They do the best they can."

"And you?"

"I've got no complaints. You gotta look at life the way it is — not the way you'd like it to be. The sooner the better. Everyone's got to face his problems. Rich, poor, smart, dumb, old, young. You gotta face the music: no cheating, no discounts, live right or pay up."

"*Merci*. In that case I'll be getting a big bill. With interest. Why did they always let me get away with things? Let me be phony? They could have insisted I be real."

He stroked her back. "Maybe they didn't care; then again, maybe they took you any way they could get you."

"They wanted me like I was, all right, else they could have picked on some other girl."

"You're a real cool cookie, my sweet, always able to figure out a way to get what you need."

"I'm scared out of my skull most of the time."

"Hardly surprising, under the circumstances."

"Do you think people see I'm scared?"

"Probably everyone."

Tamara thought about it for a while. "It's that obvious?"

"Sure. I told myself, 'There's a girl trembling with fear.'"

"So tell me, why am I smiling like an idiot child?"

"To cover up, my sweet."

"Apropos of facing the music. Rumours in camp said lists were being drawn up for people to be transported east to work in labour camps. I heard all of our camp will be shipped out soon. No one will be left. Anyone not trembling with fear has got to be crazy."

He put his arm around her, "You're safe now, Tam, you're safe with me."

She fell asleep in his arms.

*　*　*

Tamara had the dream again. J.P., naked and drunk on the window sill. "I can fly," he cried, "like Daedalus." He spread his arms wide, winglike, and dived. She woke up with a start, and said, "I'm sorry, believe me, so sorry. I just couldn't move. I felt paralysed. I never wanted it like this."

"What's the matter, sweet? You were screaming."

"Nothing," she whispered. "A nightmare."

*　*　*

On the poop deck the Prince said to Uschi: *Man can be free anywhere, here on a crowded ship, in camp, in prison. It's not easy, it requires constant vigilance. It's a never-ending fight against outer darkness and inner confusion, my child. But even when the facts are ignored, they're sure to be cited by your friends, your neighbours.*

"To drive you insane, especially if you can't run away."
To prove to you they're right.

"It's hard," Uschi observed drowsily, "to be a saint on a crowded ship."

26

"Ah, love, *des amours*." Countess Olga wagged a bejewelled finger at Tamara who lay in a deck chair close to her.

"You've seen him?"

The Countess smiled. "I've seen you, *chérie*. It's all over you and believe me, I know just how you feel." She smiled again and dabbed more Nivea on her lacerated skin. "You've met the man of your dreams." She sighed. "I know how it feels. For me the only one was Dimitri. Even if he never noticed the skinny *Backfisch* next door. Dimitri, you see, was our neighbour. I was heart-broken when he married, and swore eternal celibacy."

"Olga Capulet."

"Fortunately for me they divorced after a few years so I got my chance at him. Of course I'd filled out in all the right places by then." She sat upright. "I like your young man. Don't look so startled." She pulled her floppy purple sunhat deeper over her face, pushed up her sunglasses and wiped off the excess Nivea. "There's nothing wrong with being poor, my dear. Dimitri and I have been poor, it seems, forever. It hasn't often been champagne and caviar, even home-made, but we've had our moments. Who knows," she continued pensively, "maybe we're coming to the age of the spirit? Yes, the spiritual aristocracy."

"I hope you have it over the intellectuals. I've never really met a smart intellectual. Rich, poor, businessmen, politicians, diplomats, film producers, they talk smart but they act dumb."

"My opinion exactly, my dear. It's called being human. Talk, talk, talk. So much sound. So much less than words can say . . . Shadows in the silence . . . echoes in empty caves. But I'm waxing poetic. I see you've taken off your ring."

"It was a little tight. But I put on my mother's, see?"

"It's very beautiful. Diamonds, rubies, and emeralds. Engagements are made, engagements are broken."

"It's not that simple. Xav has been very good to me and I'd hate to say, 'Darling, I'm sorry but I'm off with this sailor, please don't be angry.' " She bit her lip and lit another cigarette, but she could not avoid the sense of impending disaster. "Love conquers all, including a lack of cash, d'you think?"

"We never missed the money, Dimitri and I. As long as we're together we're fine."

"But you're artists, you two."

Countess Olga seemed pleased.

"And I'm all alone," Tamara continued. "After I lost my mother I was scared out of my skull. I felt so helpless, so poor. I'd do anything to save myself. I wasn't going to die and I wasn't going to wait till they called my number and sent me off on a transport, so I married J.P." She inhaled smoke in great agitation.

"No one will blame you. You did what you had to do," said Madame de Uvaloff.

"I blame myself."

"You mustn't. It's all behind you now and you're off to a new start. We all are," she said, sitting up straight in her chair. *Noblesse oblige*, she thought, squaring her shoulders, wondering how this beautiful young girl could be so destroyed by the camp that she had to cling to a man, any man.

"You know," she went on reflectively, "I've lived a long time and I've learned a few things. And sooner or later we all have to stand on our own feet."

Tamara walked over to the rail and felt ill. She could just see Xav's refined moustache quivering, fed up with her. His own fault. What did a career diplomat want with her, a five-and-dime princess? She dug her long red fingernails into the rail. Life's like *noir & blanc*, black and white. Play your games, ladies and gents. And what about the Countess's idea of Gil as the new aristocrat? At least he was too smart to live off others' baloney. She turned around and saw him talking to Olga. He must have come topside for a break. She strolled over and he kissed her tenderly.

"Isn't she beautiful?"

"So I keep telling her."

"It's strictly in the eye of the beholder," said Tamara.

"Aw, you're too hard on yourself, luv," Gil patted her back affectionately. "Beautiful and smart, too. What more can a man want, eh?"

"Exactly what I've been telling her."

"Come on, people, my intelligence has been safely concealed so far. Oh, I don't mind. A brain's supposed to be bad for a woman."

"Nonsense, my dear, I've been smart all my life — well, much of the time — I've had my dumb periods, but smart's my trademark. People love me for it. Why, we've practically lived off it." She touched the jewellery bag in her bosom.

"I like it when you look mysterious," said Tamara.

"Yes, tell us."

But the Countess would delve no further into her exploits, so Gil whispered, "Let's go to your cabin."

"Much too hot."

"Let's go anyway. Excuse us, we need some air."

"Ah, *des amours*." She wagged her finger and her rings sparkled in the sun.

*　★　*

Uschi stared fondly at Tamara's long tanned legs. She held a cigarette between her tapered, red-lacquered fingers. The smoke drifted past Uschi's nostrils and made her cough.

The American journalist walked by and doffed his panama. "Morning folks, name's Bickersen, Harold Bickersen. Call me Harry." It was his policy to be democratic with the civilians. When Uschi smiled at him he stopped and offered her a Camel. Uschi refused.

The girl watched the journalist climb up to the captain's bridge. He had some nerve. The bridge was strictly out of bounds to the passengers. Gil appeared. Uschi stared at the man with the blue eyes, even white teeth, crooked smile, and saw he was in love with Tamara. She herself hadn't felt a bit desirable of late. Her messy, burnt face saw to that. She'd welcome any little compliment today, especially from the handsome sailor. But he did not even offer her a cigarette.

Every morning now she'd draw her pocket mirror from under her mattress and ask earnestly, "Mirror, mirror on this ship, who's the ugliest on this trip? No, no, a thousand times no, don't tell me."

"Why must you be so beautiful?" she called to Tamara. The redhead came over and kissed her.

"You're a dear, dear child."

But Uschi withdrew and said grandly, "I'm a woman." Then she stuck out her tongue.

To her surprise, Gil said, "So we've noticed." Uschi blushed all over. He had noticed her. Even in the face of formidable competition! So her love for him wasn't hopeless — not that hopeless, anyway. She preened herself and threw him her shy little girl's smile. Flirting with him made her feel secure, as secure as she'd felt with the commandant. Part of her realized it was a game — she hardly wanted a man of her own. It was too anxiety-provoking, and she'd only have to part with him, the way she'd had to part with everyone she'd known in her short life. Nothing permanent for Uschi, only little games.

It was a safe bet that she only fell in love with the

commandant because she felt in her bones they were about to leave the camp. Each meeting could then be dramatized as their last.

He really was afraid they'd shoot him. On Wednesdays the Boches sealed off the camp and searched out political prisoners. They were carted off in trucks and never seen again. No one was allowed out of the barracks till the trucks departed. Each time the commandant died a little. The non-politicals felt relatively safe. They were an odd lot. Much of Europe was there. Border populations, gypsies, Jews, members of the International Brigade, and young pilots from the Spanish civil war. All in danger, on the periphery of final, mass solutions.

"Got to go, girls," said Gil after kissing Tamara on the top of her red hair. "*Adios, muchachas.*" Tamara took his ice-beaded bottle of beer.

"You love him, don't you?" Uschi asked her.

"Without him I feel like mud. I've this fear of dissolving if I stand still. Into nothingness — six feet under." She almost whispered it, toying with her beer. Only the safety of the ship allowed her to make this admission. She twisted her mother's ring as if it were a talisman.

Uschi felt another great wave of pity well up in her and shyly touched the older girl's arm. "But you're so beautiful."

"What's it matter?" Tamara almost shouted.

"A lot, I think. When I feel beautiful," said Uschi, beginning to feel superior, "the whole world's mine. *Mine.* I can see clearly, then, everything. All I have to do is think of something and I know I can get it. And I also know how to get it, and that I will never cease to exist." She threw out her arms wide, and lifted them high as she danced round Tamara in great exhilaration.

Tamara almost retreated before this burst of energy. Uschi saw it and said quickly, "D'you feel ugly right this minute?"

Tamara nodded. "When I feel ugly," said Uschi, "the way I feel every morning these days, I close up, withdraw, shrink. I close up like a flower at night to protect myself from the passers-by. But then I look up at the sun and it goes away. I can always make it go away. He has taught me how."

"He? Who? Hirsch?"

"God, no. A friend."

"Can I meet him? Is he aboard?"

"He's here but you can't meet him. Only I can. He's mine, all mine." She began to dance around her again, laughing. "Sometimes," she confided, "I've this feeling — you musn't laugh — that I'll live forever. On and on and on. Even on this lousy ship, even in camp, even during the transport. I feel nothing can stop me, I'll be up in the stars, the sky, the universe, the milky way." Again she spread her arms as if to embrace the sun. I'm just lucky, don't you think?"

"Oh you darling." Tamara threw her arms around her and kissed her and they laughed.

"Having fun, girls?" Steinheil interrupted. He'd sneaked up behind them and pinched Uschi's bottom. She kicked him in the shins and he said, "Ouch, you little vixen."

One day, Uschi promised herself, she'd kick him where it really hurt. Just to be on the safe side she took a few practice aims at his retreating back.

"Got to go," cried Tamara, "I'm having tea with the Countess. Use my chair."

* * *

Hirsch sat near the forward lifeboat and saw a man come down from the bridge. Ah, here's my little girl's spy, he thought, his director's eye casting him as the perfect fit. He smiled at the newcomer expectantly. The man walked over, lifted his panama and said, "Harry Bickersen."

"Alex Hirsch." They shook hands. "I hear you came on in Lisbon."

"Yeah, and I had a hell of a time getting on this bucket. Cigarette?" He offered Hirsch a Camel.

"Ah! American. Thanks." He flicked his monogrammed lighter and drew deeply, "We all . . ." Hirsch exhaled deeply, "had a hell of a time getting on." He smiled wryly. "Beggars can't be choosers."

"You've got a point there, pal. As for me, I'm going back home to see what's cooking. It was more urgent for you, I suppose?"

"Yes, a matter of life and death," said Hirsch.

"Death. Yeah. Plenty of that going around. Ha! We've seen some of it. And I guess it'll get worse before it gets better."

"What were you doing in the port, may one ask?"

"I was snooping around a few German shipping companies. You'd suppose all the Nazis have gone home to Papa but a few were still lurking around."

Hirsch nodded. "You look like a professional snooper. You're not a spy, are you?"

"God forbid. Don't even think it. I could get shot! Nope, I'm a reporter. Look . . . Here's my press pass."

"Very impressive, especially in these times. Which paper?"

"Well, I'm a stringer for this morning paper in Columbus. My hometown, Columbus, Ohio. But I'm really freelance. In this business you have to hustle. So now, with us getting into the war and all, I thought I'd better head home and nail down a staff job."

"Is it that time in America?"

"Well no . . . not yet, but damned soon, I think. I hear things. I've got my sources."

"What d'you know that we don't know?"

"Awww." Bickersen thrust his hands into his pockets, grimaced a little, and cast a glance over the horizon.

"I sort of had you typecast, even without the trenchcoat."

"Oh, really," Bickersen seemed pleased. "Well, it's in my suitcase. My good luck coat. It's been to Spain, Ethiopia, and Cairo. Never travel without it."

"Glad to hear it. Had any good adventures in port? I always love a good story. Let's have a drink some time. I happen to have some nice Courvoisier."

"Sure, happy to oblige. Now what can I tell you? Oh yeah. Egypt! In Cairo for instance, there is this area where Europeans seldom venture . . . Well, there's a street there where . . ." On the deck above them the door to the radio cabin opened and the radio operator whistled to Bickersen.

"Oops! Excuse me, pal. But I've some business to take care of."

"Understood."

With a quick efficient movement Bickersen bent and snuffed out his cigarette on the edge of his shoe. Hirsch recognized the gesture. A soldier's trick, he thought. The reporter tucked his unfinished cigarette in his shirt pocket and bounded up the steps two at a time.

"Duty calls." Hirsch called out and stared after him, thoroughly bemused. He saw a night scene, a waterfront street with wet cobblestones glinting in the lamplight. A dark sinister figure in a trenchcoat moves through the fog. Fog machines, thought Hirsch. In Hollywood they were, no doubt, very superior. He began to worry about his brandy supply. But then he figured Bickersen was probably a beer man.

27

Uschi broke out in hives. The attacks came unfailingly, every afternoon at four. Red welts waltzed over her exhausted little body, making her stagger to the infirmary in a daze. It never occurred to her to go see *el señor doctor*. More peripatetic than ever, he rushed all over the ship and reminded her of a boy from her kindergarten days who was always going missing. She felt so tired and ugly that she didn't even want to talk to the Prince.

The male nurse, small, thin and swarthy, seemed to wait for her at the door. He guided her past the few male patients to what she took to be his inner sanctum. He stripped her and helped her up to the table, half crazed with twisting and scratching. His deft fingers tore chunks of cotton into strips and carefully place them, vinegar-soaked, over the ugly red ridges that grew out of her flesh. Uschi lay there, wordlessly submitting to his vinegary ministrations and the odd stray hand that touched breast or crotch.

Uschi's indifference began during childhood. She'd often felt, as she was about to fall asleep, that she was melting, dissolving into pure energy. She felt free of her body then, able to escape the planet's energy field into an unknown void: to become one with the cosmic energy or what she imagined was God. At those glorious times she was not Uschi, lonely Uschi, but one more particle of cosmic energy, a bodiless being free to soar in bliss. Above destiny, above birth and death. From early childhood on she could feel this gravity pressing in on her, bringing her up sharply against the limitations of her five senses, the inability to completely feel, see, taste, smell, hear and touch.

When she came back she felt she was lying on her bed, that the bed wasn't on top of her. Most peoples' beds were on top of them but they didn't know it, she wrote in her diary. Most don't sit on chairs, the chair sits on them. It was a yogic saying.

The time she had measles her bed rotated while she was in it. Slowly, round and round like she was on a spit — she went up and down. It was as if the bed and Uschi were fighting for control. And it was a stand-off. When she got too weak to go on fighting the bed she called out to her parents and clutched at their hands. She and the bed, however, went right on fighting. When their war ended she got well again. In truth, Uschi never became reconciled to living trapped in her body. From time to time she tried to escape up to the Prince's Maia but in the end she was always forced to return to her body. She was condemned to feel with her finite senses. Her conversations with the moon, sun, and stars were only a small consolation.

The nurse's voice seemed to croon over her, but Uschi paid no attention. His hands touched her breast and strayed toward her crotch in a not-too-unpleasant way. Uschi aimed to please, too. She lay very still while the man's voice seeped into her consciousness. He was telling her a list of things not to eat or drink. Especially not the salt pork, the pride and joy of the mess hall. Uschi nodded at each item, but concentrated on Maia. This is how she spent her afternoons. The rest of the day she huddled in her shaded corner under the awning of the aft well deck, shuddering and shaking and scratching herself bloody. Often she merely lay with her eyes closed, and rarely bothered to wash, brush her teeth, or eat. Hirsch brought her tea, water, and juice. Had she been one of the old ladies in the typhoid barracks Uschi would have thought her time was up. She'd even forgot her daily dialogue with her pocket mirror. Still, she could tell from the way people tried not to look at her as she stumbled from the infirmary, that she wasn't a pretty sight.

Days later the male nurse finally smiled and said, "You're better, *querida*."

She thought she detected a note of regret in his voice. On her way up to her mattress a gallant passenger tried to lift her across a roped-off partition. He almost dropped her when he saw her face close-up. Uschi persuaded him to put her down and sat on the planks and laughed and laughed. At least from a distance she looked good again.

"Aha! You're better, *Liebchen*," said Hirsch. "Here, I brought you something to eat."

"How do I look?"

Hirsch grinned.

"No, tell me."

"You look like you could stand a bath, but don't let my judgement sway you. Here, comb your hair." He held out his silver-backed comb to her.

"My mirror, where's my mirror? Damn." She found it under her mattress. "What'd you bring me to eat? I'm not really hungry."

But she ate with a hearty appetite and drank a lot of tea. Eventually she went to sleep. Hirsch watched her for a while and left her in a deep, healthy sleep. Next morning found her in the shower with the soap her father had bought for them. She washed her hair, towelled it dry, put on lipstick, and applied mascara around her marvellous hazel eyes.

We're back in business, she thought. Her skin was now nicely tanned. It had healed and glowed with a satiny sheen. So Hirsch had been right. She must visit *el señor doctor*. The man had never seen her true beauty. He'd have to wait, Uschi was in no hurry.

*   *   *

They were on the high seas now. Fortunately, the weather held. The little ship was more crowded than ever, and most passengers were out on the decks day and night.

"With 1,500 souls aboard a 5,000-tonner," Hirsch said to Uschi, "she could tip over if we all moved to one side."

"Why'd you call it she?" she was circumventing the subject of danger.

"What?"

"The ship."

"That's what they call her."

"Her! Why not him?"

"A tradition. She bears us in her patient belly, on her patient back, our floating mother."

"Baloney, a bunch of planks nailed together, and I can call it *it* if I want to.

"Poor Willies I to VI are seasick, the whole bleeding lot of them, they've been sick ever since they came aboard."

"The oxen?" Hirsch pointed to the six animals standing manacled to the pad-eyes near the rail, kitty-corner from the mess hall entrance.

"Poor Willies, they remind me of my ma — except she's on her bunk and not tethered to the rail."

"I'm delighted you've recovered your sense of humour, *Liebchen*." He patted her on the shoulder.

"Too bad you don't like it."

"On you it looks good."

Uschi shrugged. "OK. Let me tell you my dream."

"Shoot," said Hirsch, resigned.

She gave him a sharp look.

"You know I love you, *Liebchen*. And I don't call you a maniac, although I may have thought it, at times. You're just a normal, healthy, growing young girl, and more fun than a boatful of starlets."

"Forget it then."

"Some iced tea?"

"Please." Even her stomach was better, icy things didn't bother her anymore which was good. Ice was the hallmark of civilization, she thought.

Her face was healed and she looked lovely again. She'd lost some of her plumpness, which was a pity in Hirsch's eyes, but she'd get it back. Girls like Uschi looked plump for a long time and then suddenly become marvellously slim. Butterfly things. "You don't go to the infirmary anymore?"

"Infirmary?" she said with such puzzlement that for a moment Hirsch thought he'd been imagining it.

As usual, Uschi was hazy about recollection. It seemed like she'd blocked it out. There'd been so many things to block out these past two years. Would she ever be strong enough to recall them?

28

Uschi kissed Hirsch tenderly, stroked his elegant moustache and crooned, "Teddy baby, Teddy, my dearest little teddy bear."

"I must be going daffy." Hirsch freed himself from this sweet insolent little mother who treated him like her favourite doll. "Listen, you little terror, you want to sleep with me, I'll risk it. You want to elope, that's OK, too. But let's have no more of these foolish scenes, I'm not your teddy."

"Yes, sir."

"Sorry, kid. I'd like to help you out. But you're a big girl now and you can't drape yourself around every man the way you do and get away scot-free. Even if you sleep with him. Especially if you do. Damn it, I hate to be rough with you, with your sensitive little soul, but you're on your way to a new country. To swear by a new flag — although I wouldn't recommend it. But it can't be avoided. Look, you're lucky you're not a man. You don't have to fight."

One flag, another flag, he thought. A collection of moons, stars, suns and stripes. Those with more stripes thought themselves superior. And their leaders, clever, well-intentioned fiends or simple fools as the case may be, whose nefarious manipulations suck the life out of all their sheep. And what do they do with all that blood? Die on the golf course. Hernia, cancer, heart attack — eenie meenie miney moe.

He held her a little away from him, and gently brushed her untidy, golden-streaked hair from her high forehead. "Poor kid, to grow up in this age. And yet, and yet, with any luck you might just make it. You may be the sole survivor of this sad lot. Yes, you may become the symbol of this new age."

"Me?"

"Having started so badly, you're so much wiser, stronger. You'll replace the leaders, then."

"Ooff, thank you." Impulsively she threw her plump arms around his neck.

Hirsch, the starlet specialist, he thought wryly, branching out into political grooming. He looked at her almost reverently as she stood before him — she was infinitely frightened, grateful, defiant, and insolent. Yet she was solid, very solid. And just a little bit wise.

*　*　*

Hirsch and Harry Bickersen sat in the lifeboat, listening to a scratchy tango from a nearby gramophone. "Another cognac?"

"No, thanks, I'll stick to my beer."

"Well, it's more refreshing," Hirsch was relieved to conserve his dwindling stock.

"Now you were saying . . ."

"Where was I? Oh yes. In South Cairo there is this obscure area where Europeans seldom venture. And with good reason. Cairo's colourful tapestry is strangely muted there. The market crowds, barking dogs, prayer calls, and squalling infants blur into the far-off murmur of traffic, punctuated by the backfire of antique buses or the distant clang of a trolley."

"I like the prayer bit," said Hirsch, seeing a tall mosque on a Hollywood backlot.

Bickersen was in his stride now. "There, if your guide really knows his stuff, and barring any 'accidents,' you'll find yourself standing at the head of a short and shadowy street overgrown with gnarled palms. It comes abruptly to a dead end. A house blocks that end of the street. A mouldering, decrepit warehouse. In its shadow is a café known only to the underworld of Cairo and to corrupt local cops who look the other way.

"My guide would go no further and pointed wordlessly to the end of the street. He pocketed my dollars . . ."

"Hard currency."

"He takes the money and scuttles off without counting it. Turning at the next corner he casts one nervous glance over his shoulder and, poof, vanishes like he was swallowed by the fog.

Hirsch is sceptical. "Fog in Cairo?" he thinks, but he doesn't interrupt.

"Suddenly I realize I'm alone. Or am I? In this racket you learn caution early. Did I tell you I was poisoned on bacon and eggs, at breakfast with this lovely blonde? But that's another story . . . Like I said, you've gotta to watch your step, and be lucky, or it's bye-bye Baden-Baden."

"Baden-Baden?"

"My favourite spa. Also where I was poisoned, compliments of the lovely blonde. But that's, as I said, another story. Anyway. This backstreet is giving me the creeps. There's no one around, and in Cairo that's a bad sign. It's quiet. Too quiet. I'd like to weasel out but I know I can't afford it. Can't turn back now. I'd never be able to hold up my head again back home in the Press Club, or in any other press club. With a shrug I move on. A man does what a man has to do."

Hirsch nodded emphatically. "Another beer? Some ham?"

Bickersen tilts his bottle up for a long swallow. With a pensive look he continues, pausing only to nibble on his slice of salt pork. "This is the real Cairo. No tourists here. The rats foraging in the gutter pause as I pass. Nothing moves but their small beady eyes. A signboard looms above me. Its gilded letters gleaming in the dusk. I get out my flashlight. The sign's all Arabic except the word CAFÉ."

Hirsch seems to have a question. He opens his mouth.

But the American couldn't be stopped. Not now. "Inside a ceiling fan slowly revolves. Its polished mahogany blades send dim reflections racing round the room. There is brass and lacquer and fretted screens and murky corners where phantoms lurk." Harry pauses for effect. With narrowed eyes he continues, "Phantoms — or — something else? Behind the bar, wearing a fez, is a thin Arab who'd been polishing glasses. The Arab is now motionless, staring at me. He inclines his head, almost imperceptibly, towards the beaded curtain at the back of the room. There, on an antique Chinese throne of red lacquer, sits a beautiful blonde and . . ." Harry smacks his palm with his fist. "I can't believe it. I squint, but it's true. It's the blonde from Baden-Baden."

Hirsch seems enthralled.

"She rises, takes a few steps towards me, and shudders. She's recognized me. Her high-necked dress is slit at the sides and a dragon embroidered in blue silk creeps across her breasts."

Hirsch leans forward intently.

"The silken dragon undulates with each breath. Its sequin scales shimmer. Its red jewelled eye flashes in the light, winks at me. She takes another step towards me, and shudders again. With a flash of her creamy thighs she glides swiftly into the shadows, leaving behind only the faint scent of sandalwood and cloves. Something's going on. I don't know what it is, but it's not good. I can see she's frightened. I try to recall the things we said to each other the night before the breakfast. Suddenly I realize how tired I am. Too many cheap hotels, too many run-down booze cans. I must have frightened her. Who was she going to warn?" Bickersen saw that there was one more bottle left and took another long swallow. With narrowed eyes he stared at Hirsch, "There had been too many questions lately. Questions without answers. Answers long overdue. I knew it in my gut. It was *my* can of worms, my hot potato. Even if it cost me . . ."

There was a commotion outside the lifeboat and Steinheil's cookie-cutter face popped in. "Ouch, there you are, guys. I told my wife I'd find you here. Oh, *Jaaa*, yes, I'd love a beer, thank you." And before they could prevent him he'd climbed in and sat down and grabbed a bottle. In the next lifeboat the tango is stuck in a groove and repeats the same phrase over and over. "*Jeepers, creepers . . .*"

"I loved your story, Harry, but don't let me keep you," said Hirsch, throwing him an exasperated look. "We can continue it some other time. I think I'll turn in for the night." And, ignoring Steinheil, he hauled out his nightgear and went to sleep.

⋆   ⋆   ⋆

"Gil?"

"All right, all right, I'll stop it."

"Good God, must we always talk about that child?"

"Got any more beer, love?"

Tamara handed him a cold, sweating bottle and said almost defensively, "Not that I don't like her. You can't help it, she's all over you."

"She's charming."

"She's charming."

"Poor kid, she's had a bad time."

"I've had a bad time, too."

"You're bigger, darling."

"I wonder."

Gil laughed and hugged her. "She looks so lost that you want to take her into your arms and hug her. And you're jealous, my darling."

"God forbid."

"Just a little bit?"

"Best get her a boyfriend, everyone else's got one. Been near a lifeboat lately?"

"Been too busy with a red-haired lady." He kissed her.

"Doesn't she hang around Hirsch?"

"They're friends. He's way too old for her."

"How d'you know?"

"For one, he's still after me."

"The man's got taste."

"Oh? You think so?"

"My engine might conk out one night while the guy's knocking down your wall."

"God forbid," said Tamara, remembering Hirsch at the quay in Seville. "If he hadn't coaxed me aboard I'd never have met you. And your engine." She kissed him.

"He had ulterior motives."

"No, I do think he had my best interest at heart. Underneath all that dazzle he's pretty decent. Look at how nice he is to Uschi, poor kid. As you say, she needs a friend, there is something so vulnerable about her."

"Then, again, we might be wrong, my sweet. Our little girl likes to play games. Underneath she's not nearly as playful. I think she's quite tough. The complaining is part of her act."

"Probably got it from her mother. She's been sick down there in the hold the whole trip. I only saw her once, in port. A martyr. Her father, too, a little bit. Maybe the little brother, too. It's contagious, a family of saints, a shipload of martyrs."

"You think it's an act?"

"No, they suffer, all right. But it's also a mask. From behind it they can strike like cobras. They're dangerous, all right, those martyrs." Tamara put suntan lotion on the long graceful legs she'd propped up on a chair. "Ever see the mother?"

"Got no time for the other passengers, *querida*, but now my engine calls."

"I know, I know."

"Jealous?"

"Madly. And here she comes."

"Hi, everyone," said Uschi, "can anyone join?" She looked at Tamara adoringly.

"Sit down and keep me company. Gil's got to go to work."

"In ten minutes."

"Are you two having a good time?"

"The best."

"Lovely."

Uschi hoped to resemble Tamara when she got that old. She wondered if Tamara enjoyed sex and thought she must. But she couldn't ask her in front of Gil.

"Maybe one day I'll be like you," she said shyly, "sophisticated. When I get to be 28."

"*Merci*, I'm only 24."

Gil said, "*Hasta la vista*, girls, and *ciao*," and kissed Tamara.

Uschi looked envious and the two laughed. They watched him go down the ladder.

"You like him?" asked Tamara.

"He's great. He reminds me of . . . someone."

"Not good old Hirsch?"

"Hirsch's really very nice," said Uschi loyally. "Once you get to know him."

"He's nice to you."

"Oh, sure."

Why does she appear so open, thought Tamara, so vulnerable, when she's really closed off? There is this barrier, this wall with "no trespass" signs.

"That mysterious friend of yours, he's aboard?"

But Uschi wouldn't tell. The Prince hadn't said anything one way or another about about making his presence known. Still, she'd better play it safe lest he escape her like all the others.

"Do tell me about your Prince Charming?" Tamara insisted but Uschi shook her head.

"Oh, very well, I suppose it's the camp. It hasn't done wonders for me either."

Uschi was relieved they'd gotten off the Prince, and she was eager to dissect Tamara further. "What has camp done to you?" There was a mixture of compassion and sadism in her voice.

"It's robbed me of my parents, my illusions. It's made me more hopeless, more . . ." she groped for a word, "desperate."

"And before camp you were a great optimist?"

"No." Tamara nervously flipped ashes from her cigarette.

"So what'd you expect?" said Uschi contemptuously.

Tamara gnawed on her lower lip and mumbled, "I just seem to come apart under pressure."

"No kidding, who doesn't?"

Tamara looked at her distractedly. "You must think me a complete ninny."

"You've got lots of company," said Uschi solemnly. She felt inspired. "Pressure has the opposite effect on me," she said in ringing tones. "When I saw them flying apart, going to pieces, giving up, I despised them, I thought they disgraced themselves. I wanted to try, really try, to be strong, and win. God, I hate losers."

Tamara impulsively kissed her. "You're a brave girl, a little heroine, keeper of the flame."

Uschi looked embarrassed and delighted. "Trying, I guess, is like winning. Camp's made me do that. If you try you feel in control. If you give up things control you. Stay cool, that's my motto. My ma says I'm heartless and it's probably true, I despise the burghers who don't try."

She looked so defiant that Tamara laughed. "I'm sure you're very good at it."

"That I am. If one of them had gotten in my way I'd have killed him." She thought of Steinheil. "Or kicked him where it hurts." She looked shrewdly at Tamara and said, "I don't think you were really desperate. You're too beautiful and too sophisticated."

"Want to bet? So you were never desperate?"

"Sure I was. For survival. Life." She balled her grimy fists. "To go on and on, no matter how wretched, bloodied, torn, sick, just go on. Never stop, cease, give up."

Tamara tossed her cigarette into the ocean. Her voice felt raw as she said, "You go on for all of us." Then she took Uschi into her arms and held her close.

29

Countess Olga lay with her eyes closed, large sunglasses shaping her face into something of a doll's mask. From afar her fine features still looked youthful. Beads of perspiration formed on her upper lip. She opened her eyes and looked at her husband who sat nearby in the shade, working on an old *Times* crossword. At his feet lay the file of papers on which he'd work later. She sighed.

"Dimitri, darling, would you like a drop of nice ice tea?"

"No, thank you, dear," said Dimitri, hiding his irritation.

She couldn't leave him alone. She suffered from a nameless angst. She feared he'd die if she turned her attention from him. Her constant worry put him under a great strain. He was so impractical, she thought, the darling, chain-smoking his cigarettes through his black filtered holder, working in his lab. Although she was the much younger partner she felt more like his mother than his wife. And now on this trip, with weeks of nothing for her to do, no arrangements to make, no connections to wangle, no differences of opinion to arbiter and Dimitri busy with his work, for the first time she felt old. Her hands lay empty, without energy. The diamonds, for once, did not flash in the light. The prospect of weeks without challenge had made Olga lose the marvellous sustaining force that had made their flights through Europe, from university to university, seem like one glorious spy adventure. They felt strong then, in their love. They gloried in each other's strength, rejoiced with their friends, the other exiles, climbing high in the mountains.

And now it seemed over. They were sailing toward a new country. Dimitri to his work, and Olga to nothing. She felt tired and wanted to sink into a vale of peace. The mountain tops had become too high, and beckoned only to the young and strong. It seemed to Olga she'd lost the fertile imagination, the wit that could tackle a new country. Others would have to do it for her. She sighed. Dimitri would have to fend for himself. Her tired eyes had seen another country, a place far off where people did not grow old, did not have to twist themselves into pretzels. They simply loved each other till they were ready to move on to a newer, higher plateau of life.

"I'm thirsty, after all, *chérie,*" said Dimitri. And for once she told him, "The thermos is in the cabin."

"You're not feverish, *Madame?*" Pulled out of her musings, Olga found herself staring into Uschi's searching eyes.

"No. No, my dear child, not at all." She patted her arm, touched.

Uschi grinned and retreated awkwardly, according to the principle of keeping a distance between herself and the burghers. With the Countess, however, she was willing to make an exception.

"When I was your age, poor child," the Countess left Uschi standing on one foot, resigned, "life was a round of parties, *pique-niques,* romps in the woods."

"I used to ride in the woods on my bicycle," said Uschi, pleased, "behind our house." They lived near a huge forest. Uschi had spent endless spring afternoons there addressing trees in French verse instead of doing her homework.

"What lovely times we had," said the Countess, smiling. How she'd adored it all, the discussions, the politics, always politics. "We were political animals then. Talk over lunch, dinner, coffee, till late into the night. Like a never-ending chess game." She smiled. Most of her friends had been chess masters. Well, some. With those beautiful minds.

"I must tell you this story sometime," the Countess said to Uschi who'd been shifting her weight to the other foot.

"Ooff, there's Hirsch," Uschi said, and excused herself.

When the Countess returned home from Venice her neighbour Dimitri was in the throes of a divorce. Her life was complete. She waited out the divorce. And then Dimitri married Olga. Soon after their marriage they had to flee. They went to Berlin, then to Vienna and Budapest and Sofia. Then back to Berlin and finally to Paris in a last, harrowing escape. They were young and full of courage. Life seemed a great adventure, a capital joke, and they laughed at material discomforts as long as they had each other, a roof over their heads, some clothes, food, vodka, cognac, wine, caviar and chocolate ice cream. But with the passing of the years things seemed to lose their flavour. All she really wanted now was a roof over her head and peace. She recalled with difficulty her youthful ambitions. After studying art in Paris she worked as a designer at the salon of Princess Vogeart's, one of her mother's friends. As she lay there in her deck chair basking in the sun behind her glasses and her floppy hat she thought how amused her friends would be to learn that she didn't give a fig now what she wore, as long as it didn't take too long to put it on.

She drew her raw silk shawl around her, one of her last treasured possessions and a gift from Prince Sergei, whose sister, Irina Roubetskoy, was one of her dearest friends. Dimitri sat bareheaded. Without thinking she said, "Please put on your hat, darling, you'll catch sunstroke."

Dimitri searched his pockets for the hat, handing Olga the thermos with ice tea and cognac he'd gotten from the cabin. Not finding it, he shrugged and returned to his papers.

She looked at him closely. Every day her anxious eye seemed to detect a tell-tale sign of impending deterioration.

Her heart quaked at his slightest cough. And as she sat watching him play with his papers and books, she sometimes got the feeling that he was ready to die, as cheerfully as he had lived. He had no hold on life, she felt. No, that wasn't quite it, either. He did not cling to life the way others did. But by not clinging he seemed to thrive. Live every day as if it were your last. Yet his readiness for death, his openness toward it increased her angst, made her restless during the day and toss in bed at night. But she daren't tell him. At night, when she finally woke him with her fidgeting, she'd say, "It's my liver, darling," or "I ate too much." Actually she only pecked at her food, too busy with his. The thought of him leaving her alone on this nasty planet drove her mad, and she fervently hoped to be the first to go. The Countess shivered in the sun and drew her shawl more tightly around herself.

30

The boil on Uschi's arm was the size of a small ostrich egg and the colour of an unripe lemon. It had a pulse of its own.

"That doctor's never there when you need him," she whined to the Countess, sounding like her mother.

"Tried his cabin?"

"No."

"Stop frustrating the child, Olga," said Dimitri, puffing his pipe. "She'll only find a bunch of women coming and going. A female specialist." He chuckled.

"Here, let me look at it, *chérie*." The Countess took Uschi's arm but Uschi snatched it from her with a yell.

"It hurts that much?"

Uschi nodded, hiding her arm behind her back.

"*Alors*, we must bathe it, my poor *poulet*."

"Where?"

"I have a collapsible bowl from the time Dimitri got shot at. At the border. Women coming and going. Ridiculous. Come." She pulled Uschi along by her good arm.

On a hot plate the Countess boiled water, into which she dropped boric acid. When it cooled she carefully bathed the ugly greenish thing. "There's my brave girl. You must be patient, *chérie*, it's not ripe yet."

"Ooff," said Uschi doubtfully. For the past two years people were telling her to be patient, smile, keep a stiff upper lip . . . Brünnhildes were not particularly patient. Brave, yes. She had this urge to charge into the good doctor's cabin, yelling, "Let's get a move on, old boy. Enough with camps, curfews, queues for visas, ration cards, ships, breakfasts, lunches and dinners. All that stuff might sound exciting to the readers of memoirs, but I want to live now."

It was true, she thought. Fighting fear year in and year out snatched away your life — made you feel out of breath, but afraid to breathe in deeply. Around the Countess, Uschi allowed herself the luxury of disgust, a luxury she couldn't afford with her mother.

More than anyone, her mother was the reason behind Uschi's positive demeanor. Her artistry in promoting the tiniest slip-up, the most inconsequential mistake (if mistakes were inconsequential) into a major disaster, made Uschi tell herself every day, every hour, that every thing was A-OK. And getting greater all the time.

After a while this meant Uschi began to conceal her ills even from herself. When she couldn't do this any longer, like with this ostrich-egg boil, she convinced herself that what was happening to her was for the best; that she'd understand later, looking back, say, from the exalted vantage point of 24. But admitting it to herself didn't mean admitting it to her mother. That would be no practical help whatsoever. By the time her ma'd recover from the shock and get around to helping her, Uschi thought, she might easily be dead.

"Hi ho," she said weakly to the Countess, feeling a sudden burst of love for this nice woman who didn't berate her or want to go to bed with her.

"We'll have to leave it like that, _chérie_. It'll open in a day or so. We'll bathe it again later."

"OK. Thank you very much." Sadly she followed the Countess back to the well deck and sat in a chair in the shade under the awning, nursing her arm. The Countess was smearing her face with Nivea. "Want some?"

"No, thank you," Uschi said listlessly. If only she could just get rid of this thing, ride off somewhere, escape this ship, her endless round of calamities. She just wanted to run away and never come back. Never face boils and hives and male nurses who touched her crotch. She shifted uncomfortably. Here everyone counselled patience. Hirsch. Her commandant. Even the Prince. It was so easy for them. Damn, if she could just throw herself off the ship and be done with it.

She gazed brooding into the waves and saw Hirsch winking at her a few chairs away. She winked back. But it turned out he was winking at Tamara, offering her fruit from an enormous basket that must have cost him a bundle at the purser's. Uschi hadn't seen fruit like this in years.

"Lovely," said the Countess.

"The pears?"

"The pears, too. You sound so cross, _chérie_?"

"Me? Cross?"

"It's your arm, of course. Poor child. Wouldn't you like one of his lovely oranges? _Monsieur_ Hirsch," she called, to Uschi's horror, "may this poor child have one of your delicious-looking apples?"

"You said oranges," yelled Uschi in a rage. But Hirsch was there with his basket.

"I'm sorry, ladies, I was going to pass this around as soon

as this lovely here made her selection." He held out his basket to the Countess who called, "Dimitri, oh Dimitri, come look at this treasure."

Carefully she selected two pieces for Dimitri and one for herself. She let Hirsch urge her to have another. But Uschi wouldn't take any, petulantly declaring she wasn't hungry. When Hirsch looked at her arm she hid it. He returned to his chair near Tamara and she hid again behind her sun hat.

"Dear man, so dashing and so attentive. He reminds me of a young Dimitri."

"As usual, he's making an ass of himself. The Goddess, as he calls her, detests him. Besides, she's got a boyfriend aboard. And she's engaged to a rich diplomat."

"Don't be cross with him, Uschi. He's so fond of you."

"Him? Of me?"

"Anyone can see that, can't they, Dimitri?"

"Sure thing," said the Count, not looking up from his book.

"He didn't get *me* a basket," said Uschi.

"But you told everyone you couldn't eat a bite, *chérie*. No wonder, with that arm. Would you like some ice tea?"

"No, thank you. I'm not thirsty, either." Uschi retreated to the poop deck to brood about Hirsch's basket and the implications for their relationship. She didn't know why it annoyed her. It wasn't as if she'd ever sleep with him and she'd forgotten that she wanted to elope and run away with him only two harbours ago. The poop was too warm so she moved under a hatch tent. Rocking herself to and fro, she pretended to sit on her orange crate, her security blanket, in the camp kitchen. She sorely missed her crate.

*　　*　　*

Tamara lay with her long legs propped up against the main deckhouse. The sun felt glorious against her closed eyes and she imagined Gil's face, the cleft in his chin and his deep blue eyes. It was so real that she could almost hear him laugh. There are people whose voices make your spine jump, and there are those whose timbre is velvety and soothing. Gil's was like a smooth drink. Xav's like a gnarled old tree. There was another voice she still hadn't forgotten.

Jean-Pierre Perpignan belied his voice. Short, tough and leathery, he was the sort of man who vividly regretted his lack of height, was almost obsessed by it. "Two more inches," was his clarion call, "just two more lousy inches and the world could have been mine."

It was beyond Tamara. Beautiful herself, she could only marvel at his obsession with height.

"I'd even have settled for one and a half," he lamented heartbroken, addressing an unkind deity, pouring himself another cognac.

"What about Napoleon?" people told him.

"Yes, what about Napoleon," he said wrathfully.

Standing just over five feet five inches, he was barely as tall as Tamara when he flashed his eyes at her, eyes like dark, smouldering coals. The only thing J.P. did not complain about was the size of his penis. He was extremely proud of it and thought that it should make Tamara very happy.

Tamara had no opinion about it, but quickly found him a demanding husband. In fact, she came to avoid sex whenever possible. Night after night he'd pump into her with drunken heaviness, all 140 pounds of him. Sometimes she felt her life was spent laying under him, withdrawn and silent, her vagina dry and tight. She felt then that maybe she should have stayed in camp and taken her chances like the others. At what price freedom? She laughed bitterly. Being assaulted each night by one's husband was certainly not freedom. But she was alive. And the people in camp, only God knew how long they'd live. One day the Germans would return, and they'd ship them east like the Jews from Poland. Tamara had overheard enough from J.P. and his colleagues. No matter how much she hated her present life, a life was a life. She feared death more than she feared J.P.

When he was drunk he'd stay up all night and hold forth. He wanted company and would not let her go to sleep. He'd shake her awake, saying, "Wake up, wake up, you're not going to sleep on me, *chérie*." And then J.P. would pace the room in his briefs and uniform cap, pointing an accusing finger at the God he held responsible for his lack of two extra inches in height.

One night her husband announced, "I will fly." He put on his cap.

"Where's my bottle of Remy Martin? Where'd you hide it, my love? I can't talk on a thirsty stomach but I tell you, food will grow on the trees, big giant trees will shoot up into the sky and give us nourishment and sustenance. Ha! We'll fill the world with nectar and ambrosia. We'll wipe out hunger when we grow wings to fly up and pluck the fruit. Everyone will be happy. Have a little slug, huh? Just a little. No more hunger, I say." At this point J.P. felt his wings expanding.

"Tonight I feel like a bird, *chérie*. Come, feel my wings. Like Daedalus and Icarus, *non*?"

"I'm going to bed, I'm sleepy."

"That's the trouble with you, *chérie*, you sleep too much. Wake up, *chérie*. No time to go to sleep when your husband's growing wings."

When Tamara didn't answer he took the pitcher of ice water from the console and threw it over her. "Hah, I knew that would wake you up, sleepyhead! Look at my wings, *chérie*."

She jumped out of bed, ready to attack him. But then she remembered that he was drunk and that she owed him, perhaps, her life. She bit her lip, but he was rapidly using up her quota of goodwill. She put on a dry nightgown and changed the wet sheets. When she went into the living room J.P. was opening the window and climbing onto the ledge. "Ah, here you are, *chérie*, look at my lovely wings."

He spread out his arms and stood, quite naked, his cap on his head, looking like some skinny scarecrow and teetering unsteadily.

Tamara laughed and then got alarmed. "Get down, you fool, you'll scandalize the neighbours and break your neck."

J.P. fluttered his arms in the mild night breeze and lifted one leg. She grabbed at it but he continued to wave his arms wildly and tried to kick her off. "Buzzzzzzzzzzzzzzz," he called gently, "Buzzzzzzzzzzzzz. Daedalus here I come."

"You mean here you go," she said furiously, using both hands to give his leg a great heaving yank which propelled both of them backward into the room. He rolled on top of her. As usual, she thought. Now we'll have one of our darling sex scenes. But he took her leg and studied it thoughtfully.

"A nice piano leg. Definitely."

"Let go of my leg."

"Perfect for fine tuning. Lie still now. One little touch, and it's fixed."

"Ouch."

"I need to fix it."

"You're hurting me."

"Then lie still." He twisted her leg till she cried out, "Let go, let go, you're drunk."

"That, *Madame*, is a matter of opinion."

"Ouch."

"Just one more little turn."

"Stop it, you hear."

"Please, pretty please."

"You're hurting me, you beast."

"All true love hurts. Just a little bit tighter."

"Stop it, Jean-Paul," and she pushed him so hard that he fell sideways with a look of great astonishment. By the time he righted himself she'd gained the door. "Good night, Jean-Paul, I'm sleeping in the guest room." Tamara locked herself in. She thought of calling for help but then hoped she could protect herself against him. I should have let him jump.

In the morning he faced her smiling at the breakfast table. "How pretty you look, my sweet little wife." He got up and kissed her but she turned her head away and poured him a cup of coffee.

After that their life together continued uneventfully. Yet something in Tamara was waiting for the other shoe to drop.

* * *

When she was calm Countess Olga could clearly discern the fear and greed of the other passengers. Most came from the camps. It was easy enough, or at least not too difficult, to behave in a civilized manner when there was plenty of food, drink and space. Security. Crowd rats together and they attack each other. But these were people, humans. Where they should love, they hated. Where they should be kind, they feared. They were soaked through with this fear. Dimitri, thank God, was free of it. So was that dear child, Uschi. So open, so fearless. In spite of that mother. No one should have a mother like Uschi's, *sans blague*. She could hear the child's eager voice. She laughed, "*sans blague*," and Dimitri said, "Something you want to tell me, dear?"

"I was thinking of Uschi's mother."

"She didn't strike me as that funny," he went back to his book.

"No, no, of course not." We're free now, she thought, all of us. The people aboard have been turned into passengers, refugees no longer. But can they ever shake it off? First-generation citizens of a new land, a land chosen in despair, somewhat belatedly willing to accept them. They were survivors, finally free. Still, they were branded with their fear as surely as with any numbers tattooed on their fore-arms. Countess Olga was willing to bet that if people did not see the tattoos it would take only minutes to sense them.

When she was free from her own angst, which was less and less often now, she tried earnestly to pray for them. Sometimes she succeeded, often she failed. Her biggest failures came at night when she tossed restlessly in their tiny cabin while Dimitri lay quietly snoring. She had more luck in the daytime when the sun dipped the landscape in a hopeful gold and made her feel secure. As if in God's care. Then she was able to laugh at her fears, offering them up as a sacrifice, discarding them as one discards a pair of old, comfortable shoes.

The trouble was that one could never be alone on this crowded ship. Had she been able to be alone she would have been happy. "Never you mind," Dimitri would say, "true freedom comes from the inside."

"You're so right, *mon cher*," she'd reply, but she never really understood. And she continued to pray for the passengers. Inmates who were their own jailers, their uniform a fear-tattooed forearm. In time it was overgrown with foolish pride. The cause of the fear might vanish, but the effect lingered on.

"This fear will poison the planet," said Dimitri. "Instead of loving, they fear."

"No love at all," said Countess Olga, "no love. It makes them destroy every little green thing they touch. They grasp at the Earth's greenness with deadened hands and contaminate every leaf and flower, every river and every newborn thing that hasn't been immunized against them."

"Don't forget stupidity."

"And greed," said Olga. "They'll end up killing the planet."

"What's left of it. If we ever get out of this war."

"They survive, but in body only." Countess Olga could not help herself, she too was caught up in the general fear — it overcame her like an addiction. One whiff of it and she was hooked again. Oh, she was clever, all right. But her cleverness could not save her because the fear was utterly emotional. And when the Lord said, "I will destroy the righteous with the wicked," Countess Olga was resolutely on the side of the righteous. Righteous and clean like the child on her family's estates in the Ukraine. But when things got out of hand she joined the wicked. She flew apart, her teeth shattering with fear as with a fever, her own dormant angst rising and making her the leader of the pack, surpassing them all. She was the cleverest, the most sensitive, the shrillest of the chorus. At those moments Dimitri was the only one who could stop her, bring her back to herself. So distraught was she with the effluvia of evil, her eyes maliciously gleaming, that friends who remembered her innate kindness could only avert their eyes. Yet had there not been one who said, "Fear not?"

*　*　*

The voyage continued. Couples made love in the shadows of the lifeboats. No one but the invisible captain seemed interested. He was rumoured to peer down on them nightly with his pelorus.

"What'd you mean at night, it's dark, and what's a pelo—"

"Pelorus."

"A dirty word? You don't mean binoculars?"

"It's a dumb compass," said Hirsch, "and everyone knows there's no lifeboat action in the daytime."

"You're pulling my foot, Uncle Hirsch."

"Anything wrong, Little Miss? You're acting a bit strange this morning."

"Me? Don't be dumb, Hirsch, everything's wonderful. I hate busybodies. Don't you? Such bores. In camp people were so busy surviving they never bothered being busy, I mean body."

"Pretty soon now, Miss, you'll hit civilization again, and you gotta drop that survival business."

"So they won't attack me anymore, huh?"

"I didn't say that, exactly. But you have to learn to trust a little."

"And you're a great truster, I guess?"

"In my own way."

Uschi thought this over for a while, then said, "I will talk to the Prince about it. Now you'll have to excuse me."

Hirsch gave her a sharp look, "What have I done now?"

"Well, few people aboard go around buying fruit baskets for friends."

"You're jealous, my child. For your information, the purser made me an offer I couldn't resist. Tamara happened to be around, so I gave it to her."

"A likely story."

"You didn't want any."

"I wasn't hungry."

"Jealousy won't get you anywhere. How's your arm?"

"We're bathing it, it's not ripe yet."

"Let me see."

"No!"

"I'll get you a basket too, and as soon as your arm bursts we'll celebrate with the *Veuve*."

Uschi threw her arms around him happily. Hirsch snatched the arm and looked at the hideous boil that had now assumed a greenish yellow colouration. "Watch it, you're hurting me, Hirsch."

"I'm sorry. Have I ever harmed you, *Liebchen*?"

"No." She could tell he was hurt.

"OK, then. And I'll keep the champagne on ice for you."

"Whose ice?"

"Mine."

31

It seemed Uschi's moment of celebration might never come. The ostrich egg on her arm throbbed so dangerously that at night she had to bed it down separately, a pulsating poisonous fetus that made her body pregnant with its own negative life. When she finally brought herself to show it to *el señor doctor*, he said absently, "It isn't ripe yet, *querida*, it isn't ripe."

Uschi woke up on her mattress on the poop deck. At first she thought it was the moon which had grown big and golden during their voyage across the Atlantic. Then she knew it was her arm. Something hammered away in there and was about to happen. It's time has come, she thought, putting on her raincoat and climbing down the ladder.

The ship was in a hush, lights extinguished to hide them from the U-boats. She pounded on the doctor's cabin. For once he was there, and when he saw her arm he quickly pulled her into his adjacent office. He gave the tiniest squeeze to the green egg and out oozed the nastiest green-yellow pus Uschi had ever seen. She watched it with great satisfaction, feeling as if all the nastiness and horror of the last two years was seeping out of her. Then came the blood. Thick, dark, dirty red blood. It came for a long time, uniting doctor and patient in the abortion. When it was all out she felt hollow with relief, thoroughly cleansed. As if all the poison of the planet had left her. Not through any surgical intervention, but of its own volition. It would find no more place in her life.

"Poor arm, it'll be scarred forever. Ooff! Better my arm than my face." She laughed with relief.

"Do not worry, *querida*, it will be OK." The doctor was cleaning and bandaging it.

It turned out that Uschi was right, however; the scar became a "souvenir of evil," as she was later to put it.

"Thank you *señor* doctor, she put on her raincoat over her pyjamas, "sorry to have bothered you in the middle of the night."

"Oh, don't go yet. No bother. No bother at all. You need a drink, doctor's orders."

"No, no, thank you kindly, I promised Hirsch, we'll have the Veuve, he's got it on ice for me." But the doctor put his arm across her shoulders and guided her to his cabin. Uschi felt a little dizzy, but unresisting, as usual.

"You're a little pale, *querida*. Gently he pushed her into a chair and poured her a cognac. She took a little sip. It wasn't the Veuve but it felt warm and clean. The doctor fixed himself a whisky and added water from the carafe. "Here's to your health."

She giggled and held out her glass to clink it. It was nice sitting in his cabin and having his full attention. Time between them seemed pleasantly suspended, the tiny cabin creating it's own sense of privacy, the ship still and its passengers far away.

It was almost like being with the commandant again. Only the way the doctor sat, slowly whirling his glass between his freckled fingers, seemed a little awkward. Underneath the British moustache she could see a little boy peering out. Uschi felt it was her duty to put him at ease.

She took a deep breath and crooned, "I expect you're tired now. A doctor's work, ooff, is never done." He just sat there. To remind him of his excellent counsel, she drew his freckled hand to her soft face: "Look, all healed up."

Uschi had this overwhelming urge to make him feel good.

"Do you like my new face?" she groaned invitingly.

The doctor's hesitation ceased. He grabbed her and pushed her onto his bunk. Uschi watched him closely, wide-eyed, letting his kisses wash over her. She decided he was no commandant. (Had she really felt good feelings and love for him a moment ago?) Because she felt nothing now that she thought he was in her power. She continued to look at him in his passion, her wide hazel eyes filled with a mixture of pity and fear. It was the same pity she felt for the male nurse in the infirmary. The fear came from beholding a passion she did not share. Still, a part of her laughed at those fools who grabbed at flesh without knowing spirit. The good doctor certainly did his share of grabbing. A sense of danger crept up on her but she pushed it aside with an effort of will. She did so need to be desired by this man who'd conquered so many beautiful women. As a doctor she supposed he wouldn't get her pregnant.

Up on Maia the real Uschi asked in a loud voice, "What's going on here?"

But the doctor's blue eyes met hers, resting in them in a sort of curious ecstasy, and almost brought her back down. For a moment she found herself responding to him.

Then Uschi said to the Prince, "What's he doing to her?"

He's mating with you, said the Prince pointedly. *You, you. One day soon, my child*, he said in his soft voice, *you will have to face responsibility.*

"Yes, sir," said Uschi crestfallen. But then she became more animated. "God, he sees her like the others, a bunch of delicious hot dogs! I do seem to offer a little more mustard for him," she giggled. "Ouch, he pinched me, the idiot. I don't see why she's putting up with him, this passionate vegetable, what's she getting out of it?"

Perhaps you should try to find out, said the Prince. *It will prevent much repetition.*

"I'm sure glad to be up here, Prince, and I don't see how she let's him, I let him, get away with it. The whole thing's a complete waste."

Yes, said the Prince amiably.

"Besides, he's not the commandant, not even Hirsch, and certainly not you." She looked at the Prince adoringly.

Exactly.

* * *

Uschi sat on the doctor's bunk, reflectively sipping a mug of hot chocolate. Her new lover had gone on his morning rounds. They'd made love again, and he'd patted her plump arm and left. Sleeping with him seemed to have its advantages: the hot chocolate, for one thing, and a nice breakfast in a cabin.

Hirsch would be queuing up alone for his breakfast. He'd have looked for her on her mattress. He'd want to know where she'd slept, and with whom. She could tell him she'd slept down in the holds with her mother but he wouldn't believe it. If she had to sleep with somebody on this ship, why not with him, her good good friend. It was very embarrassing, she thought guiltily.

Of the two, Hirsch was the more attractive. He was funnier too. The doctor smelled of a not totally unattractive mixture of garlic and sweat. Her Prince was quite odourless.

This morning the doctor had been more affectionate, minding her arm. She could almost overlook how he'd consumed her. He was beginning to recognize her as Uschi in a myopic sort of way, a little apart from his mob of women.

Strangely enough, this morning she hadn't been on Maia. Even with the commandant she'd almost always gone to Maia. To tell the truth, she'd felt nothing with him either, or very little. "You will, *Poupée*," he'd said, "when you get a little older." And now she'd never see him again. Uschi almost cried. She'd have to become responsible. The Prince was right. Did taking responsibility mean not missing people so much?

Uschi stirred a little and took another sip of hot chocolate. Luxuriating, she let it roll against her tongue. Then she lifted the porthole and locked stares with a crew member who was trying to peek in. She beat a hasty retreat, almost spilling the mug on the bunk. It was stifling in the little cabin and she threw on her pyjamas and raincoat. She waited till the man left and sneaked out. She did not stride out proudly like the ugly brunette but hunched over, pretending to have stomach cramps.

Uschi took some fresh clothes and stood for a long time under the salty shower, washing off the doctor's sweat with sweet salt-dissolving soap.

* * *

"Where've you been, wench?" As predicted, Hirsch was in bad humour. He stood alone in a line of burghers. "You weren't on your mattress."

"None of your business." Immediately she regretted it. He threw her a sharp, hurt look. She flashed him one of her feel-good-again-smiles and he returned it with an all-is-forgiven one of his own.

"Oh," she threw her arms around him, "let's have that Veuve finally. The thing came out last night."

"So it's the doctor," said Hirsch.

"*Sans blague*," said Uschi.

After breakfast they sat sipping champagne on her mattress in the fresh morning breeze. The sun wasn't too hot and Hirsch smoked his monogrammed Gitanes. Uschi's new face glowed in the sea air. Her skin felt fine, her arm felt fine, her rash was gone, and no one was mad at her — as far as she knew. Even Hirsch was happy — he had found a crew member to do his laundry.

"Know something?"

"The doctor?"

"Who's he?" She shrugged. "Today's the best day, oops." She spilled a little champagne on her mattress. "The best day on this ship, oops; the best day since Marseilles; and the best day since they came for us and we got kicked out. And that's the truth."

"*Sans blague?*"

"*Sans blague.*"

32

When she closed her eyes she could still see the trees. She missed the birches. They had been her friends. She'd grown up with these trees on their large estate in the Ukraine. Her heart broke when she had to leave them. Countess Olga could still hear her governess calling the children in for tea, the governess who had come to the Vatican with her, and later to Venice.

As predicted, the delicate girl had grown into a beautiful teenager, so in love with their neighbour, Count Dimitri, that she had to be sent away when he married.

She smiled behind her closed eyes. Dimitri Buzz de Uvaloff had always been a part of her life: a neighbour and playmate who brought many cherished little gifts and took the little girls for sleigh rides and dance lessons. When she grew up she would marry him, she told her governess. Then Dimitri went away to university and she only saw him on holidays. One day he came home married to a lady from the city. And Olga continued living with her aunt, her cousins and her governess. Her father came from a long line of French aristocrats, only the youngest son's wife and her children barely escaping the guillotine during the revolution. With land titled to them by the Tsar, they settled in the Ukraine. Olga's parents had died in the same train accident in which the Tsar was badly injured, and she was made her uncle's ward. He was the ambassador to the Vatican.

She seldom saw Dimitri after his marriage. She missed him terribly but her life continued in its peaceful way until that day, that terrible day in the late fall, when the mayor of the nearby village came during lunch and asked her aunt, who was in charge of the estate, to sign a document which ordered the execution of hated Russian prisoners. Her aunt twisted her hair nervously. Olga knew both that this was the sign of an impending hysterical outbreak (little did the young Countess suspect she would emulate her one day) and that her aunt would never sign the piece of paper. She was filled with her father's sense of *noblesse oblige* when she coolly told the mayor she would sign in her aunt's place. What she hadn't realized was that this obliged her to watch the hanging. She held out until they hanged a young soldier, hardly older than she was. She quickly ordered him to be cut down and revived. He came for her that night while they sat at dinner. He pointed his rifle at her. Only the pleadings of the governess saved her life.

"I should have let them finish the job," said the young Countess in a hard voice, "and if you ever come here again, I will."

She'd never forgotten. It's my destiny, she thought. From the French revolution to the Russian revolution. She was still so full of rage against anything Russian. All the years had not obliterated it. And though it was becoming harder to carry this hate inside, it was also becoming harder to forget. At times she felt her body become rigid with hatred. She drew herself up straight in her chair and squared her shoulders. Countess Olga then smiled her polished, witty smile. It no longer covered the raw pain beneath it.

33

"I'm most curious," said Hirsch, "to learn more about your Cairo adventure. I'm sorry I can only offer you a beer. My stock of Courvoisier and Veuve are being depleted and reserved for the ladies." They were sitting in Hirsch's lifeboat on the boat deck. It was late afternoon, a time good for either snoozing or conversation.

"That's all right, pal, I really am a beer man. As for the story, why do I get thinking you're picking the old brain?"

Hirsch laughed. "You may be right, Harry. But who knows, life's full of surprises and synchronicity. Many an oeuvre comes out of a good yarn. So give me your phone number, we'll stay in touch. When we were interrupted last time, the blue dragon blonde had disappeared into the café's inner sanctum and . . ." He lit a Gitane and looked at Bickersen expectantly.

"Well," said Bickersen, taking a gulp of beer and leaning back in the open lifeboat. "I linger on the threshold." He adjusted the crumpled canvas for greater comfort. "And I'm wondering what to do when a small man in a wrinkled suit steps forward, smiling a crooked smile like he has something to hide. He's got large bulging eyes and his hand is in his jacket pocket. It's enough to make me even more nervous. I know I've seen that face before. But where? Speaking in a low, breathless whisper, he asks in a faint but distinct German accent, 'Vote collar iss der sky?' It's some sort of a password and I try to remember where I've heard the tale. It must have been in this Lisbon bar, the one with the blue tiles. It looks more and more like an underground operation, dope smuggling most likely. And I'm torn between getting a great story and staying alive. I think frantically, now what colour can that damn sky be? Only a fool'd say blue. Pink, orange, purple, all those sunset colours, are also out. So what's the most unlikely? I strain the old brain, hold my breath and then blurt out, 'Yellow. The sky is yellow.' Jackpot. I hit the jackpot. Dumb luck, or maybe I had heard it in that bar. The little guy's mouth twists into a nasty leer and he takes his hand out of his jacket pocket." Bickersen narrows his eyes and looks intently at Hirsch. "Overhead, the fan turns slowly in the silence. Then somewhere nearby a latch clicks. 'Vy are you here?' the guy asks, spraying slightly. The place was real quiet, I could hear the buzzing of a fly against a window pane. The beaded curtain, beads clicking, swayed gently. His hand went back into his pocket. I swallow nervously. The little guy with the bulging eyes curled his lip contemptuously and spit out 'shurnalist.' I got the message right then and there. He didn't like my type." Bickersen shifted his position again. "Naturally, pal, I was a little worried about that bulge in his pocket." Pursing his lips and gazing at the horizon he continued: "Little bug-eyes pulls his hand slowly from his pocket and then pushes the beaded curtain aside."

"This is killing me," says Hirsch.

"Me too. Almost."

"Hi, gents," said Uschi, poking her nose into the lifeboat. "Can I join you?"

"Sure, *Liebchen*, climb in. Harry here is telling me one of his fascinating adventures. You've met, of course?"

"Sure. I'd love to hear it."

"Climb in," says Harry. "Suddenly I hear this voice saying, 'Run, Harry, run.' I turn around to determine the source of this good advice but it's too late. The little man gives me a shove and I stumble through the curtain.

"The oval room is stacked high with sacks of varying sizes in the midst of which sits this very fat man in a white suit. He sits in this white wicker chair next to a tall potted palm and is stroking a Siamese cat. He chuckles and rumbles with mirth. Needless to say, the funny part went right over my head. Smiling at his secret joke he says in a deep, throaty growl, 'Welcome Mr. Bickersen. We've been expecting you.' With an effort he manages to suppress the chuckling and rumbling. Shooing away his cat, he rises to greet me, wheezing from the struggle. I do not like his tone: it sounds 95 percent south of sincere. Before I have time to reflect any further, I feel a hard object coming into contact with my head. When I wake up my blonde friend from Baden-Baden lies dead at my feet. Her face is set in a grimace and her mouth is wide open. It's as if she had cried out to warn me. The sacks were gone."

"Have another beer," says Hirsch.

"How'd you get out of there?" asks Uschi.

"That's another story."

★ ★ ★

At first it seemed like food poisoning but rumours said it might be typhoid. Six dead, so far.

"They're talking about the six oxen. So don't believe a word of it," was the general opinion. Then more rumours about yellow fever spread through the decks and soon people were saying it was an epidemic and that the *Baleares* would be lucky to dock with a few survivors. Uschi had not seen the good doctor. No one had. He had become as invisible as the captain. He was not missed. Everyone knew there was no medicine aboard. Not enough, anyway.

Uschi took the rumours badly. They reminded her only too vividly of the old ladies in the typhoid barracks who lay desiccated and dying, gazing at you sightless out of their sunken eyes. Trying to breathe in shallowly to avoid smelling the stench they gave off — their horror reflected in her vivid hazel eyes. All day long she'd work in the barracks, quickly using up her small reservoir of compassion until by evening it had turned into blind resentment. As an assistant postmistress she carried mail, and mail was life. The barracks was death, and she hated to work with death. She'd promised herself she'd never go near a cemetery, coffin or corpse again. She wanted to live. Every night she sat brooding on her orange crate, numb but grateful to have once more escaped death. These shrivelled up women died so greedily, took so long, that Uschi begrudged them every second.

"I hate them," she said to the Prince.

Don't, my child. Every creature has a right to live, in any form, as long as possible.

"But they take my energy from me."

It's not finite, you'll find more.

"Oh, where, may I ask?"

In yourself.

Surely he was wrong. They were taking up space, from the young, the strong, the healthy; her strong handsome young friends who hadn't lived yet; who, because of these sick old people, might never live. Every morning she wanted to scream at them in the typhoid barracks: KILL YOURSELVES AND LET US LIVE!

When they finally did die, the bread truck would take them away, after making its morning deliveries. That the truck brought bread, and took away corpses, seemed horribly gratifying to Uschi. It was an unending cycle; life replaced death.

"Look," she said to Hirsch, "if there's nothing to the rumours then there's nothing to worry about. If they're true, and we'll know soon enough, it'll be easier for the rest of us."

"By us, you mean us lucky survivors, I gather?"

"Sure. Even for the captain, if he really exists. Why haven't we seen him? Remember how lovely and peaceful it was when they were all seasick?"

"You little beast."

Uschi laughed. "I know from camp. I was in the typhoid barracks. I washed them, combed their hair, fed them. They ought to start immunizing us. No one's getting any medicine and the doctor, I believe, has joined the captain. Wherever that is. But they have no drugs, no medicine, nothing aboard. When I was sick he gave me some aspirin, and a vinegar rub. Apple cider vinegar, I believe."

"The doctor?"

"No, the captain."

"Ohhhh?"

"Just kidding."

"Just like in camp. Except here it's not a non-profit enterprise. They charged us plenty and if anyone dies, of typhoid or yellow fever, we'll all rot in jail. Quarantine."

"Ooff," Uschi scratched at her sunburned nose, "they can just throw the bodies overboard and pretend they've never seen them. With 1,500 passengers, one or two won't be missed."

"*Sans blague*, you heartless wench," he smacked her cute bottom lightly but she saw that he was shocked. It pleased her in a strange way.

"My ma always says I'm made of stone. See?" She made a stone face, a close-up of Brünnhilde preparing to ride into the flames, and nestled up to him. She didn't want to shock him anymore. And she looked so inviting that Hirsch could not help kissing her. She pretended not to like it, but she could see he was beginning to understand her games.

"Well, little Miss, let's go to my lifeboat and collect my stuff. I think I'll sleep with you up on the poop deck."

When she gave him a puzzled look he continued, "Can't leave you alone during a typhoid scare, hmmm?"

Sleeping head to head, they found their own little world under a huge golden moon and the pure stars. Uschi would not let him touch her, and he didn't try.

"Ooff, my little film man," she kissed him, "I almost wish this voyage would never end."

"*Sans blague*. You sure do smell good."

* * *

Uschi and Hirsch snuck up on the burial party and saw the doctor hobbling painfully behind a board carried by two crewmen. An elongated form was strapped to it. The trio glanced through the dark of the deck as if to make sure there were no curious eyes, then stopped and put down the board with its burden.

"Why don't we jump out and cry 'Surprise, surprise?' "

"Like at a birthday party? It won't bring him back and they only get mad."

"You think it's childish?"

"Yes."

"It might make them do something, if they know we know. Cable for medicine, or something."

"How'd y'know they didn't?"

"They never do," said Uschi. "Besides, if they did, why would they let those people die?"

"You got a point, *Liebchen*. But if we show up now we won't do any good. Only delay them. They'll still throw the body overboard."

"What should we do then?"

"Talk to the captain."

"If we can find him. What's the matter with the doctor's leg?"

"Comes from chasing dames in the dark."

"With his connections, he doesn't need to chase any." Uschi smiled sweetly at Hirsch. He gave her a stern look, but said nothing. She got the feeling that he probably didn't want to know.

The doctor directed the men to carry the board toward the rail. They set it down and he bowed as if in a brief prayer. Then at a sign from him they tilted it toward the rail. The men waited a bit, till they heard a splash below, then left in the direction of the galley.

"How many's that, six?"

"Seven," said Uschi. She'd kept track.

"I hope you're writing it all down."

"For my book."

"And my film."

"My book first."

"Let's go to bed."

"No, let's follow them." She dragged Hirsch along to the open door of the galley and saw the cook's assistant laying out the board.

"I told you it was the breadboard. Always bread with the dead," Uschi said, enraged.

"I don't think they use the board. The bread's already in the oven, smell it?"

But Uschi refused to be soothed. "Why'd they have to use that board, why?"

"Know what I think?"

Uschi shrugged her shoulders, exasperated.

"It's a hatchboard."

"I don't believe it. And what's it doing in the galley?"

"They probably came in for a late snack. See?" And indeed the men were sitting with the cook's assistant.

"Where's the good doctor?"

"With his new girlfriend."

Uschi let that pass. "Tomorrow I'm gonna tell that bastard something about throwing people overboard in the dead of the night."

"Careful with the doctor, *Liebchen*. He's a slippery customer. And now let's go to sleep. I'm pooped."

So he knew! She didn't like it one bit.

"You mustn't make much out of the doctor, you know," she said soothingly, "I was sick and needed some personal attention."

"From him?"

"Are you a doctor?"

"I'm your friend."

"Oh, Alex," she said weeping, "why can't I trust anyone?"

"You've been hurt, *Liebchen*," he put his arm around her. "If it makes you feel any better, neither can I. Neither can anyone on the whole bloody ship."

"Including the doctor?"

"Him most of all."

"Has he been hurt, too, then?"

"Probably."

"The whole species?"

"Probably."

"Good, let's not trust each other, then. God, am I tired."

"What a beautiful night, we should sleep well."

"Yes, we should." Typhoid was such a stupid death, she thought, listening to his breathing. With him up here she had to will herself to stay awake, or wake up real early, if she wanted some time to think. He slept with her all the time now. She should have known. She could never get rid of people, except those she really liked. Hirsch was nice enough and good company, and at least he didn't paw her or keep after her to have sex.

"Because we're friends," Hirsch said, when she brought up the subject.

*   *   *

Lulled by the motion of the calm sea and the faint throb of the engines, Uschi watched the steady unblinking stars sweeping slowly past the masthead and breathed gently to keep pace with the sleeping Hirsch. She thought again of the camp infirmary. There only the fittest survived the fever: the others lay in a crowded little cemetery on the hill. Uschi thought of the mother of two horrible widowed spinsters who took all night to die. She was a cute little Chinadoll of a woman; "Mother still has her lovely young breasts," one of the daughters said. The mother did not die from dysentery; she lost her life to lice. Her daughters had taken the frail old lady out of the barracks to delouse her and she'd caught a nasty cold and was left to die in the infirmary.

"Her girls were greatly relieved," Uschi told the Prince.

We don't know that, little one.

"Well, I won't say they were happy, just glad it was over."

You have to learn mercy.

"Yes, sir." She had no idea what he meant. Was mercy something to acquire? She'd thought it would reside in one's breast, "Like the gentle rain from heaven."

She thought of mercy and two boys who ate bread with jam that was laced with rat poison. She trembled violently when she recalled the screams.

"Somehow, as a human being, I feel responsible for their deaths," she told the Prince. "They were so happy to have found a piece of bread and they had to die for it."

You're learning mercy.

When she thought about it, and she couldn't stop thinking about it now, she also felt responsible for the deaths of her little cousins. They were so pretty, with their blond and brown curls, their big brown eyes and long lashes. She knew they had died in a camp in the East.

Your responsibility is to survive, said the Prince. *But remember, survival alone is not enough. You have to survive whole, together, undamaged. The old world is dying. You have to work toward the new one.*

Uschi started to cry and woke Hirsch. "Please, may I sleep with you on your mattress?"

"Sure, sure, *Liebchen.*" He moved over and put his arms around her and after a while her trembling stopped.

Her mother pretended the boys had never eaten the bread, that they had died from the flu. It enraged Uschi. Her mother would never accept devastating events.

"She can't cope with the horror," her father had consoled her.

"Can't cope?" said Uschi in aggrieved tones.

She despised her mother's narrow world. "Why, she doesn't even try." Her mother was concerned, she thought, with very little outside her immediate periphery. Her principal complaints were directed at her husband who, she felt, was constantly involving himself with "things that did not concern him."

"You're not fair to her," said her father. "Give her a break, she's having a terrible time. She'll be better in the new country, you'll see."

"Oh?" said Uschi.

Sometimes she did feel sorry for her mother. Would the Prince call this mercy? Her tiny, insular world was so vulnerable, so pathetically at the mercy of every dumb person's opinion. "So what if she said that," Uschi often told her mother, "so what. It's her opinion, big deal. Are they paying your rent? Are they feeding you? No? Well then, you don't need them. You can tell them to go straight to hell. So let's have a little more independence here, Mother."

Secretly she hated the ways in which she resembled her mother. The way she did not want to face facts. Wanted them to go away. Wanted everything to be pleasant. Her sorties to Maia proved that. She also made unreasonable demands on people. This was all right with the Prince, who would merely laugh. Or with the commandant, who wanted to indulge her. Or with Hirsch and the Countess, who both treated her like a child. But deep down Uschi knew these things were not acceptable, and never would be.

More and more, Uschi avoided her mother. In camp she simply took off. Now, on the ship, she escaped to the poop deck while her mother was sick below in the holds. Uschi did not like the way her mother blamed her father for camp, the ship, the new unknown country they were going to. She believed that it was because her mother couldn't blame God that her wrath fell upon her husband. Maybe she was afraid God would strike her dead. Her husband wouldn't: he loved her.

But, thought Uschi spitefully, she had managed to prevent the family from leaving when everyone else did. A clever man, her father had seen things coming. Everyone had. Everyone except her mother. She, as usual, insisted upon clinging to her way of life. He should have made her go. As head of the household, he should have put his foot down.

34

They were heading northwest in lovely southern waters now — semi-tropical. They were moving very slow, five, six knots. The *Baleares* had been at sea for over a month. Many passengers were sunburnt again. The days were very hot and the nights cool — the moon seemed so near you could touch it. Dolphins jumped out of clear blue waters around the ship. Sunset was magical, bands of gold, mauve, silver, purple, lilac, indigo licked at the sky and turned orange. The wind had died, and the sea was hushed, waves rolled in silvery smooth, their tops breaking purple.

Tamara felt happy these long warm nights. All day long she felt passion rising inside her, ripening until it took a life of its own. It bound her into a fiery knot until she became passion itself; wide open, a chalice. Gil's blue eyes darkened, awed by the woman. A face he had only sensed was hidden under the make-up existed now, real, undeniable.

Her journey was coming to a close and she didn't want to lose a minute of him. They sat drinking beer on the boat deck and slept under the stars on a bed of canvas. She suffered with him, while he worked in the heat of the engine room, by sitting in the sun and trying to read. It was all she could do. Her mind fogged when she attempted serious thought.

"Red, white and blue is what I like to see after slaving down in a dark engine." Gil kissed her on top of her head. "Red hair, blue top, white bottom. Plus long tanned gorgeous legs. I'm a lucky guy."

"Colours on the outside, and grey on the inside."

"Aw, come on, sweetie, you're too hard on yourself. Ease up, do it for me."

"I can't. I'd like to, but I can't." She handed him a cold, sweating beer and inspected the inside of her elbow. "Ugh. These seawater showers sure don't help." Ruefully she wiped the tiny rivulets of dirt against her white shorts.

"And the stench in the toilets, men peeping into the showers, the male attendant. It's too *déjà vu*. But I don't mind since you're with me, darling."

"Is this the old Tamara?"

She laughed and lit a cigarette.

"Here, let me."

"But that's my limit, I guess. I'm not sure I could do it for too long."

"And you don't have to, my love. The trip's nearly over for you." He looked at her squarely.

"You make it sound so simple."

"Isn't it?"

She sighed, "There's Xav." She still wasn't wearing his ring.

"You're going to tell him aren't you?" He looked at her in his straightforward way and she averted her eyes.

"I . . . I don't know," she said in a low voice.

"We'll be landing in Cuba in a few days. Just make up your mind, and do it."

"I've got to talk to Xav, explain to him . . ."

"So you're not going to do it."

"I didn't say that. But I told you, Gil, that I've an obligation to him. He helped me when I needed him and he's waiting for me. And now I have to tell him, sorry, I changed my mind. I met this engineer . . ."

"Sailor."

"Seaman aboard the ship. And I'm going off with him, so thanks a lot for everything and it's been nice knowing you. He'll be hurt and think I've gone off my head."

"And haven't you? We love each other and we'll be happy."

"I have an obligation."

"Aw, come on, Tamara, he'll forgive you. I would."

"Perhaps."

"And I'll help you, you'll see."

"But where will we live?" she asked cautiously.

"Wherever you want to. In my country, or anywhere else you like."

"And you on the ships?"

"That's how I make my living, sweetie. And when I get to be chief you can come with me."

"More ocean showers."

He grinned at her grimace. "Compared to this poor little tub we'll sail luxury liners, I promise you."

But she said, "I've got a headache, I'm going to lie down." And indeed she could feel one of her sizzlers, an 18-karat gold-plated migraine coming on.

"I'll take you to your cabin," he said, throwing a protective arm round her as he walked her over. "See you later." He kissed her but she cried, "No. I need to be alone."

In her cabin she threw herself on the bunk, sobbing. She didn't want to think. Why couldn't he just leave her alone? She took three aspirins, hoping to fall asleep, but the humid air pressed in on her and she tossed restlessly.

She tried to picture herself as Gil's wife, cooking for him, meeting his family, waiting for him to come home on leave. She'd be hated by his parents and other relatives, a foreign redheaded green-eyed woman who had seduced their son. Then she was sitting at home, waiting, smoking, possibly pregnant, worrying about him.

She thought of Xav and his protectiveness, so different from Gil's, more like a father's, not sexy at all. She didn't want to sleep with Xav but that could not be avoided. Xav was a reasonable man, there would be no scenes of love and passion. She'd be a hostess in a world full of intrigue and boredom. Excitement too. But the drama would definitely lose its appeal. Such a closed little circle, the diplomatic life. Nests of gossip. You couldn't drop a pin in Havana without it being heard in Hong Kong.

The rot has eaten away at my soul, she thought disconsolately. I love Gil. But I'll crucify him. The nuns taught me to embrace saviours. J.P., Xav, Gil. All saviours. And I crucify them all. With trembling hands she lit a cigarette. She felt nauseous as she realized that her beauty had cheated her, had made her live superficially, coast on her looks. She'd denied the other parts of herself. In a way her beauty had become a weapon, because it was all she had. She had kept everyone at arm's length with her smile. It had always been complimented, even by the nuns. As if people were nothing but a smile. Behind the façade she could be reserved, in control — nothing could betray her. Her greatest fear was that people might suspect there was something behind the smile and become demanding. Might even want, God forbid, a commitment.

She thought of Gil and moaned in her sleep. Then she saw it again. As clearly as if it had been enlarged by a giant magnifying glass. It appeared in slow motion: she saw J.P., her former husband, getting up on the window ledge.

"Look, *chérie*, I can fly. Darwin's theory of evolution."

"Get down, you fool."

"This feels great. Give me a sip of Remy Martin."

"Get down," she shouted, but did not move.

"Where's my glass? Are you watching me, *chérie*?"

Still she sat motionless. It was happening again. She was perspiring despite the chill of the night air. No! I can't go through this. Not again, she thought, I just can't.

"Daedalus, my brother, here I come," called J.P. And then he spread his arms and flew into the night. One moment he was silhouetted against the inky sky and the next there was silence.

"You made a mistake, J.P.," she said softly. "You are Icarus." She got up from her chair, rushed upstairs to their bedroom and threw her things into suitcases. Her clothes, her marriage certificate, her mother's jewellery and furs. She drove in J.P.'s car to Pau, the Basses-Pyrénées capital.

She was lucky. The Spanish consul gave her a visa. She sold the car and took the train to Seville. She didn't know why. It seemed to make sense. When she thought of J.P. she saw him standing on that ledge, arms akimbo. She heard later that the verdict had been "accidental death."

Someone knocked at her door. She didn't move. It was hot in the little cabin but she had to stay away from Gil. He's too good for me, she thought. I don't deserve him.

But then Xav didn't deserve her either.

35

Uschi arched her eyebrows and wrinkled her forehead in a significant way, and Countess Olga said, "What's up, chérie? What are you trying to tell us?"

"How d'you know?"

"I've seen that expression before, chérie."

"We have," said Uschi in her best important announcer's voice, "a spy among us."

"I shouldn't wonder," said the Countess. "We have everyone else here. I hope he's MI5." A delighted, malicious smile played around her finely haired upper lip. "God knows, we have movie directors, American reporters, metal traders, rag merchants, camp supervisors, ship's company agents, delinquent doctors and invisible captains. Why not spies? Who could it be? I wonder, not *Herr* Steinheil?"

"Too stupid."

"True."

"Not *Monsieur* Hirsch?"

"Certainly not."

"We'll start with the purser's list."

"Yes, let's."

"Dimitri, oh Dimitri? Buzz, dear, we need the purser's list." Olga raised her voice to where he sat reading in the shade.

"Good," he said and turned the page.

"Dimitri, darling, you don't understand. We seem to have the MI5 aboard. Our little friend Uschi here has just informed us." Her nerves were agreeably tingling. This was intrigue, sounds and smells she'd been accustomed to since her childhood in the Ukraine and at her uncle's embassy at the Vatican.

"The list, Dimitri, dear." He liked a little intrigue, as well, but nothing so complicated and time-consuming that it might take away from his investigation into the mating habits of his dear sturgeon. The Count liked to think about himself as the innocent bystander, a scientist.

"What about the NKVD? Has she heard about them, too?"

"Dimitri, do be serious."

"*Oui, ma chère.*"

He went on reading, thought better of it and turned to speak. "Tell little Uschi about the man with the club foot."

"At the university in Budapest?"

"No, no, at UFA in Berlin."

"Hirsch's old stomping ground. Then he would know him too."

"And how," said the Count. And the two then entertained Uschi with the most hair-raising stories of their peregrinations through the capitals of Europe. They'd heard about all the skeletons, met all the corpses.

"This is better than *The 39 Steps*," said Uschi, deeply satisfied. "Too bad Hirsch isn't here."

"He knows most of it," said Countess Olga.

"Strange that he never lets on."

"Discretion is the better part of valour," said Count Dimitri.

And the *Baleares* began to alter her course to WNW.

* * *

Another harbour, another port, and still another coastguard aboard in brilliant white-and-blue-striped uniforms. This time it was a sea of no-nonsense WASP faces. They had little in common with their jolly, swarthy colleagues. A thorough search of the ship proved uneventful. No spies turned up — unless they were among the few typhoid-stricken passengers who were taken off on stretchers. A crowd gathered around the gangway to see them off and wish them a speedy recovery. Everyone was glad to see them gone.

At the pier some bored reporters loitered. "Don't look like cholera to me, Jack."

"And for this they got us out of bed."

"Yellow fever?"

"They look disgustingly healthy to me."

"Can't win them all and all that."

"Right you are, Jack, let's get a drink."

"Hey, look at that dame. Wouldn't mind examining her." He was pointing at Tamara. She stood on deck, looking down.

"How're you gonna get her off the ship? She looks even healthier than the rest."

"Jimmy can. He owes me. Hey, how about that cute plump babe." He grinned at Uschi who grinned back.

"Too young for me."

"I hear they start them off young in the camps."

Uschi waved to the two cute reporters on the pier. She liked the curly-haired one. He wasn't dark and dashing like the Spaniards, but nice-looking in a blond way. They seemed to be talking about her. She wished she could read lips.

After the ambulances drove off the reporters turned to leave. "You boys go on, I'll meet up with you later."

But the others were reluctant. "If Bland sticks around there must be something in it."

"There was something about the MI5 aboard."

"MI5's always aboard. And what about the man with the club foot?"

"Didn't notice anyone's foot sticking out under the stretchers. He wouldn't come here, he'd go to England." They laughed.

"We'll check out the hospital later. Let's go get a drink. Come on, Bland."

* * *

"They look disappointed," said Hirsch.

"I guess they figured we're all dead," said Uschi.

"Must be dull for them on the island. Nothing much happening. Lazy fellows, bloodsuckers, really, living vicariously off others' misfortunes. Used to be one myself."

"So you said. But you, lazy?"

"Too lazy to make a living," Hirsch replied. Living their lives messing into others'. Reporters, psychiatrists. Directors, too. Scratch a reporter and what do you find?"

"A director?"

"A drunk, a psychopath. A hyena who raves on at the bar and whose wife never sees him. Look at them," pointing down. "Look at Bickerson."

"But he's nice."

"An exception. I bet they're dying to get a drink so they can brag to each other about their exploits."

"Are you trying to tell me I'd better become an actress?" Uschi had been flirting with the reporter idea. "And what about the man with the club foot?"

Hirsch turned pale and pulled on his moustache. "Where d'you hear that, Miss Curious?"

"The Countess."

"Did she mention my ex-wife? Forget it, I'm tired, I'm going to get some rest in my cabin."

"But the fun's just starting," called Uschi after him.

Even if the reporters weren't happy, the island's civic committee was. A delegation came aboard to invite the children to a picnic. It was amazing how many children there were. In the daily melee they were swallowed up by the adult maelstrom. It took an army of volunteers to take them off the ship. The coastguard stood by, smiling. Uschi made herself small and left with the first launch. She threw a kiss to the Uvaloffs who called, "Enjoy yourself, *chérie.*"

Uschi discovered her brother Michael in the second boat and waved to him cheerfully. He looked happy, laughing and talking to a girl. He's growing up, she thought, suddenly feeling free under the clear blue open sky. She saw her parents at the rail and waved to them as well. With an anchor under her feet, her mother must feel better, too. A great wave of compassion welled up from within her and she loved them both again, the way she'd loved them as a child.

They landed at one of the white sandy beaches that ringed the island. When they touched ground Uschi still felt the sensation of the ship's roll. It was something like the illusion of movement she experienced when they got off the transport after a week. It wasn't disagreeable. Far from it, she felt as if the whole earth was softly rocking her, welcoming her back with a gently caressing, infinitely reassuring hello. The wonderful picnic lunch ended with gallons of strawberry ice cream. Uschi hated ice cream but ate some anyway. She hadn't had any for over two years. She remembered the transport again. During that time she'd hardly eaten anything. She just wasn't hungry and when they handed them salami and cheese at the small French railway stations she didn't want to take any with her dirty hands. The people around her had behaved like hyenas, tearing and scratching at the food. They pushed and shoved each other; everything civilized eliminated in their blind, instinctual rage to survive. Human beings didn't behave like that. Not these people, anyway, most of whom she'd known all her life. All the niceness, the polish of culture, gone. How she hated them. How she hated herself for being among them. One of them. She was not aware of it, but she made up her mind, then and there, to get away. Sooner, rather than later.

After lunch the children loafed around the pretty beach, played in the clear water, picked up shells and talked to their hostesses. The committee asked many questions and everyone was appalled by the children's stories. They later sent boxes of food and clothing aboard. The kids went swimming. Uschi was an excellent swimmer and went straight out after the sun. She got a little crazy, swimming on and on and on, until she thought she could stretch out her hand and touch the blazing disc. The water, the air and the sun intoxicated her, her strong young body gliding, pulling smoothly stroke after stroke, forward, always forward. She felt free of the whole world, free of everyone. Hirsch, the commandant, even the Prince. Someone in a boat called to her.

"Not so far out, child."

"I could've gone on forever. I could stay here on the beach," she said after her return, "it's so beautiful." The ladies kissed her.

The children returned to the ship relaxed and happy. For once even the adults were cheerful. The mood had definitely changed. Was it an absence of fear? Had it left with the sick on the stretchers?

Under the stillness of the golden moon that night, Uschi was able to take the bandages off her wounds. She licked them cautiously. And cried and cried. She rocked herself to and fro like a child. She shuddered, and in her mind gave a kick to her orange crate, the security blanket that had gotten her through camp. She no longer needed it. She let herself think of the commandant and knew she would miss him forever. He had treated her like his child bride; he had protected her and made her feel safe among the horror.

Never, she swore to herself, would she be able to love another man as she had loved him. She felt like Juliet, ready to wed her grave.

She began to cry again, but smiled through her tears. Juliet was a nut, her mother said, an eccentric teenager. Uschi was a refugee, a woman in love with a man who'd been good to her.

"Damn," she cursed at the moon. "Bet I couldn't have stayed with the old guy, anyway. We might have been shot by now. The two of us, taken out in the truck one fine Wednesday. Not even shot on my own, the final indignity." Worse still, she thought, I might have stayed with him in that rotten place another couple of years, wasted more of my life. She began to cry again, remembering the last time she'd heard his voice. It came from outside the truck that took them to the railroad. She remembered driving to freedom in the chilly dawn, huddled against her family, still warm with the heat of his big body. She couldn't see him now, could only hear his voice, calling *"Au Revoir, Uschi, au revoir, Poupée."*

Everyone she loved had been wrenched from her. Her friends at school, her little cousins, *Onkel* Fritz. Only the Prince remained. "O come to me," she cried, her arms spread toward the moon.

But it was Hirsch not her Prince who came, wearing an elegant white evening jacket. "Come, *Liebchen*, they're dancing in the cooler below."

36

Tamara and Gil sat on the boat deck in their favourite spot. Faint music from the dancing below drifted up to them.

"What's going to happen to us?" cried Tamara.

"Simple. Come back to Spain with me, darling."

She shook her head. "I can't."

"We'll pay him back his money."

"Oh, it's not the money. I made him propose to me, and I made a promise, I gave my word."

"So he's done a good deed. He was glad to help you out of a tight spot, I'm sure. Anyone would have, bread cast upon the waters and all that. But you don't have to sell your soul for the good deed."

"He's a good man, Gil. So I'm not selling my soul to the devil. I owe him a debt of honour and he's counting on me. Right now he's looking for a house, he needs a wife, a hostess."

"So the situation has changed. You met me and you're a different woman now. You're not the desperate girl in Seville anymore. Give him back his ring and we'll send him the money later."

"Stop it, Gil, you're torturing me. I can't do this to him."

"And what about me? He'll get over it, I promise you."

"So will you, darling. What do you want me to say to him, 'Sorry, but I'm going off with the ship's engineer.'"

"A poor sailor — that's it, isn't it?"

"No, no!"

"Then prove me wrong. Come with me."

"I'm afraid," she whispered. "Afraid of hurting him, afraid of hurting you. Afraid of being hurt."

"Poor Tam, my poor darling, you sound so lost. How can I help you? I love you."

But she didn't hear him. "He might turn bitter, he loves me so much."

"So do I."

"Can't we just love each other? If I hurt him he'll hurt another woman who'll hurt another man. And so we go on poisoning each other in the name of love."

"Poor darling. And you want to stop this cycle by marrying him? What kind of love is that?"

"It's the only love I know."

* * *

The *Baleares* sailed into the Cuban harbour. The coastguard came aboard again. About a quarter of the ship lined up for customs and health inspection. The others would go on to their last port.

Tamara kissed Gil and her throat was tight and sore. She tried to talk but her eyes were full of tears. He crushed her to him and said hoarsely, "*Adios, mi amor*, I'll see you soon."

She clung to him until he gave her a gentle shove toward the gangway. Mechanically, she began to walk down, her ivory case in her hand, one foot in front of the other, like a sleepwalker. Through her tears she saw the pulsating harbour below. It was very hot. Through the blur she saw Xav's tall figure.

"Everyone queue up," the man with the megaphone shouted. "Passengers from the *Baleares* over here."

"You've made the headlines, darling," called Xav, waving *El Diario* at her. "But don't fret, we'll have you out of quarantine in no time."

Tamara turned back towards the boat deck where she had so often sat drinking beer with Gil.

He was no longer there.

* * *

Life aboard became peaceful now that there was more room to breathe.

"Who would have thought it would be so nice once we got rid of them," Uschi said, her suntanned legs dangling from the rail. She was nut-brown by this time, and could balance herself like an old salt.

"I, for one. And get down from the rail, Miss," said Hirsch.

"Come, children, be charitable if not wise," said the Countess Olga.

"We are," said Uschi, hopping down.

"It's nice to have a little peace and quiet before the storm," said Olga.

"What storm?"

"You'll see."

"What d'you mean?"

"The customs officers, the reporters. Maybe quarantine."

"You can bet on it," said Bickersen, passing.

"The Big Apple," said Hirsch.

Now that they were sailing along its coast, the new land loomed large, a reality at last.

Hirsch couldn't wait, but Uschi had mixed feelings, mindful of her mother's "You'll have to work, you lazy girl." The Countess seemed stricken with a case of nerves and kept scratching herself discreetly, though her skinny arms bore telltale marks. Count Dimitri was as happy as he ever was. Bickersen, who had not been seen much recently, went around frowning and scribbling into a thick notebook.

Hirsch was giving Uschi acting lessons and suggested they put on a skit for the passengers.

"You're sure?" she asked him apprehensively.

"You stick with me, kid, and I'll make you a star."

"*Sans blague?*"

"*Sans blague.*"

The skit was a success. "A warm-up for the big time," said Hirsch.

What a full life she would live, Uschi thought. Too bad the commandant wouldn't be around to enjoy her successes. And she hoped to have a great sex life too. Although he'd predicted it, he'll miss out on that, as well, poor man. Some people just aren't lucky. Karma? She gave a huge sigh of anticipatory happiness and Hirsch asked, "What's with all the sighing, *Liebchen*?"

"That's how happy we will be," she said as she gave him a big hug. She wondered whether God would be happy, too, now that He'd gotten them out of harm's way. She hadn't forgotten. As per her contract with him, she'd have to find a great cause to devote her life to. She'd have to think about it ever so carefully.

"Is acting a noble cause, Hirsch, dear?"

"Very noble indeed, and stop addressing me as 'Hirsch, dear,' or I'll withdraw my patronage."

"OK, Alex."

Again she went over her contract with God. "Party of the first part agrees with party of the second part (God) to dedicate herself to a great cause, or causes, of the second party's choosing in a pinch, but at any rate to be submitted to the party of the second part for final approval. In return for which party of the second part (God) agrees to let party of the first part continue living on this, one of His planets."

God had kept His word and let them out of camp shortly after the contract had gone into effect. Uschi was beginning to understand that life's an exchange. You can't have everything but you can pick and choose between the best alternatives, or the least evil.

As the *Baleares* sailed toward its final destination many questions remained. Would America be healthy enough to absorb the cargo of fear about to invade it? Resilient enough to repulse the fear that, once imported, might infect others who had also fled mankind's errors? Would it become the depository of the uprooted, the persecuted, the haunted, the sick and the maimed? Could the uprooted and the scarred endure the harshness of this new land and raise strong, healthy, fearless offspring? Would they be strong enough to keep this land free so that the many, brought together from the four corners of the Earth, could melt together and find courage to seek the highest and the best in the nation's soul? And if the new land succumbed, who would rescue it, put it together again, be its saviour?

* * *

The *Baleares* steamed into its last harbour. Fear had subsided but returned quickly when the yellow flag that denoted typhoid brought a delegation of health officials. Immigration officers came with them.

As the *Baleares* passed the statue who hid her face, Countess Olga burst into tears. No sirens whistled for the tattered little freighter or it's wretched cargo. The Countess buried her aristocratic nose into her hands, Niobe grieving for the children of her longing.

"Dimitri, oh Dimitri, why ever did we decide to come here? Of all the places on the Earth, this is the most cursed."

"Olushka, darling, cheer up, we're finally *someplace*. Here, have a sip of brandy. Instead of cursed, let's say the least blessed. Strictly on a non-monetary level we'll be fine. Being someplace is better than no place at all, so we'll be OK. You'll see, the Uvaloffs always are. We adapt." The Countess took some brandy and looked comforted, suddenly composed, like a crying child lulled by a parent.

Uschi stood at the rail with Hirsch, preparing for the burial of her genuine second-hand automobile clogs. She threw them into the harbour. "Goodbye, my sweet shoes," she called fondly as she watched them sink, "rest in peace."

"There's gratitude. After all those shoes have done for you."

"To me."

"I sure hope you're not going to treat me like that." He made a show of inspecting the orange-painted toes sticking out of her new orange platforms. "Great feet, *Liebchen*, although I keep wondering about your head."

"*Sans blague.*"

"*Sans blague*, of course. And so I'm headed for Tinseltown. If you need something, anything, like me making you a starlet, or even money, comfort and friendship, just call."

Uschi gave him a quick, distracted kiss. "Will do, *Onkel* Hirsch. I have your address."

Reporters and cameramen swarmed the pier, planes droned overhead. "Here we go again." Uschi jammed her elbow into Hirsch's ribs, "And it's all for us."

"We've made the big time, kid."

"Those reporters sure do get into everything."

"And get paid for it much of the time."

"Ooff," said Uschi, scratching the new skin on her tanned nose.

"How many died?" called the reporters from down below."

"Six," bellowed Steinheil.

"It's a big story," said Hirsch, and called "sixty," magnifying things by ten.

"How many survivors?" they asked.

"That's debatable," called Hirsch.

"One thousand four hundred and fifty-one," bellowed Steinheil.

"We ate the oxen," Hirsch laughed.

Out of the corner of his eyes Steinheil was observing the photo equipment slung between the full breasts of a female journalist. *Frau* Steinheil noted the sharp divide between them and resolved to buy a new bra first thing. Squashed by the adults, the Steinheil offspring shouted trilingual obscenities at the reporters.

Pressing against the rail, the passengers laughed, shouted, cried and said cheese for the cameras. They waved at the planes overhead, and at relatives and friends who waited behind the roped-off area.

Then Uschi and Hirsch embraced for the last time. "Don't cry, *Liebchen*, I'm one friend you'll never lose."

"I'll write to you every week. Well, often. But first I have to do some serious thinking."

Uschi rejoined her parents and Michael, who had descended from the tabernacle, grinning, tanned, and a few centimetres taller than she remembered. All around people smiled and wept. This was the end of the voyage, and everyone was safe.

* * *

Uschi fell in love with the reporters. The way they elbowed their way into people's lives, and, as Hirsch said, got paid for it, too. Actresses were OK, she guessed, but they had to say the lines that others wrote for them.

"Hey, *Onkel* Hirsch," she shouted over a few dozen heads, "I think I'll forget the actress thing."

"You bet," shouted Hirsch. He hadn't heard a word and lit one of his last monogrammed cigarettes. He was saving a few to make an impression upon his final arrival. So that's that, he thought. We made it. We made it and we are ready. I wonder what the world has in store for us? More importantly, how do we tell the world what we have in store for it? He turned back and waved to Uschi who seemed to be telling him something. My little adopted niece, he thought fondly. Hirsch didn't give five cents (he'd converted from marks and pfennigs) for the rest of the ship, but my little niece, he thought, bears watching. She'll do her old *Onkel* proud. He handed out tips lavishly and stood surrounded by the crewmen who helped him ashore. Every inch showbiz, he was a VIP among the survivors and a fine addition to the native culture.

They queued up for the last time. Those with a normal temperature could go, while the others had to be quarantined. Passing through immigration was their last act as refugees. Hereafter, like other citizens, they were free to queue for whatever they chose: the movies, theatre, opera, and concert tickets (if they had the money); at banks, at bus stops; to check out in supermarkets; at train and airplane ticket counters; for the cleaner's and at telephone booths and hairdressers and fortune tellers.

They smiled, but beneath those smiles were only half-concealed grimaces which, like strontium-90, would in the end fall out and poison people. Their experience would poison the denizens of this new land. Their broken bodies and spirits were far more virulent and contagious than yellow fever.

The light slanted through the high, dirty windows of the pier and dust motes floated in the air. Little clumps of obscure officials with papers and lists gathered for brief conferences. Here, thought Uschi, life is different. The important people walk fast while workers walk slowly. Small electric trucks, empty or with one or two small packages, glided about like toys.

As Uschi looked at the new land, the sun transformed the shoving, cursing crowd into poor frail men and women whose souls were trying to break free. It was uncanny how closely they resembled those at the pier in Seville, and perhaps at all the piers the world over. The sun dispersed the clouds that covered the harbour, and the fog lifted before Uschi's eyes. Maia receded, maybe for the last time, and the new land came clearly into focus. It beckoned, welcoming her despite the Countess's tears, and Uschi saw that it wanted to love her.

She said goodbye to her Prince. Uschi could see now that she'd be far too busy for him. For a moment she felt empty, aborted. Then love rushed in and pushed out the fear which had dominated her life for so long. Why are we so afraid, she wondered, why is the whole damn planet so afraid? Afraid of being unloved. Afraid to be loved.

She realized that fear had made her submit to the doctor, the male nurse, the old man and the commandant. She was afraid she was unloved. No, no. Not the commandant.

"My sweet Prince, how dumb I was."

But the Prince had gone.

As the new land reached out to her she no longer regretted leaving Spain. Spain was everywhere. Uschi stood grinning. Tanned, plump, and hazel-eyed, she squinted at the reporters and the planes overhead. Her family started down the gangway and she rushed past them, after the reporters and cameramen: "Hey, you," she yelled, "hey, wait for me!"

* * *

On her return voyage the *Baleares* was torpedoed. Most of her crew was lost.

Tamara did not know if Gil survived. She thought of him often, and of the crowded little ship and the frightened passengers whom she no longer despised. For in the midst of fear, greed, and stupidity she had found love. Hers, she had decided, would be a busy, useful life. She married Xav in a quiet ceremony.

* * *

A ship dies, a human is born. And on still nights, fear her chief cargo, the ghost of the *Baleares* sails silently along the shores of the new land, waiting for love to redeem her.